I0594824

STARLIT SKIES

Suzanne Cass

SC
STORM CLOUD
PRESS

Starlit Skies

Storm Cloud Press, Perth Australia

Copyright © 2021 by Suzanne Cass

Edits by Tanya Saari

Cover by Vikncharlie

All rights reserved.

All rights reserved. No part of this publication may be reproduced, stored in a retrieval system, or transmitted in any form, or by any means, electronic, mechanical, photocopying, recording or otherwise, without permission in writing from the publisher.

This is a work of fiction. Names, characters, places and incidents are products of the authors imagination or are used fictitiously. Any resemblance to actual events, locales, organisations, or persons, living or dead, is entirely coincidental.

To strong women all over the world.

CHAPTER ONE

Skylar Williams straightened, arching her back to ease her stiff muscles. The weeds were going crazy; it was a never-ending task to keep up with them. But her kitchen garden was going from strength to strength, and it made her heart lighter to see how well everything was growing. Her good friend, Daisy, was doing a great job helping her design some large, raised beds in which to grow the native bush tucker foods Skylar used to create her gourmet meals. Together, she and Daisy had slowly added more and more varieties of native foods. They'd even started a small orchard down the hill, where Daisy was cultivating finger limes and Kakadu plum trees. Skylar would have to remember to tell Daisy about the weeds before they completely overran the rest of the garden.

She'd only meant to come out and pick a handful of warrigal greens for the meal tonight and head straight back inside. The bitter greens, much like English spinach, would be perfect with her lamb kofta and beetroot salad. But she couldn't help herself, and had pulled some weeds. Just a few to start with, because she really needed to get back to her cooking. Then a few more, and before she knew it, ten minutes had passed.

Lifting her head, she let her gaze linger on the purple sky. The sun had already set over the escarpment that towered over the lodge and its raft of luxury cabins, and the bright oranges were fading to a dull, bruised gray. The billabong at the bottom of the hill reflected the last of the dying rays of light, shimmering as the first stars appeared in the sky. Hundreds of birds twittered in the eucalyptus trees at the edge of the billabong, trilling their nighttime orchestra.

She really did live in paradise. This was one of the most beautiful places on Earth, and she'd do well to take more time to appreciate it. What better place to locate a luxury, eco-resort, than on the edge of a perfect billabong, in the middle of far North Queensland? Stormcloud Station was full to capacity tonight, with over twenty guests. And she was partly responsible for their continuing success, enticing more patrons with her award-winning food.

Breathing in, she filled her lungs, letting the balmy night air permeate her with peace. She needed to get back to the kitchen; she didn't have time to be standing around just breathing.

There was a noise; a squeak like that of a frightened animal, that was out of place with the evening sounds. A small noise, but one that made her heart jump with fright. Skylar froze, willing the birds to stop their singing so she might hear better. What was it?

She strained her ears, but there was nothing more.

It must've been her imagination. She bent down to retrieve her basket of warrigal greens, but stopped halfway.

There it was again.

This time it was accompanied by an indistinct thump.

Skylar turned her attention toward the nearest cabin, partially hidden farther down the hill by her burgeoning new orchard.

There were ten luxury cabins strung out around the edge

of the billabong, like pearls on a necklace. Set well apart, each one was secluded, with their own private balconies off the back, so guests could sit and enjoy the beauty of the bush. Solar lights twinkled in the growing dark, lighting the pathways for anyone who needed to walk between the lodge and their nighttime accommodation.

Originally, there'd been eight cabins, but demand had been so high that Steve and Daniella had built two more in the past few months. Skylar had been against the new buildings, as they encroached on the area she'd earmarked for more orchard space. But arguing with Daniella had been pointless; her mother merely declared there was plenty of land farther up the hill to grow her trees, and Skylar would have to walk a little, that was all.

Cabin number ten at the end of the row was dark, except for one light in what she knew would be the bedroom. Three of the cabins had two bedrooms, and the rest had only one. The lodge catered for adults only; no children allowed. Sometimes they might get a mother and her grown daughter, or father and adult son, or even a group of friends, but the majority of the guests were couples.

Skylar stared at the building. Nothing moved inside, and there were no more noises.

She must've imagined it.

Her chef's assistant, Bindi, would be wondering where she was. Service was up in half an hour, and the guests would begin drifting into the large, open plan dining area any moment now. So, she turned toward the lodge.

There it was again. Unmistakeable, this time.

She knew that noise. Knew it from past experience. It was the sound of a muffled scream. Muffled by a hand over a mouth.

Shit.

What should she do? Her gaze travelled to the lodge, and

then back to the cabin. Should she go and find Dale and get him to investigate? What if she was wrong? What if the couple in cabin ten were just enjoying some conjugal activities—the extra loud variety—or something else completely innocent?

There was another muted thump.

Shit.

She threw down the basket and stomped down the hill, ducking under the branches of the plum trees and weaving between the spiky leaves of the limes.

This was the last thing she needed, to be wasting time investigating noises that were probably completely normal. If only the little hairs on the back of her neck would stop prickling, then she'd turn around and walk away.

It wouldn't be the first time they'd had a case of domestic violence at the station. Just last year, Daniella had quietly asked a couple to leave, after the wife came to the breakfast table with a black eye. The husband had blustered that it was all a mistake, and his wife had merely walked into a low-hanging branch. Daniella hadn't believed him, and neither had anyone else who'd witnessed the wife's cowering obedience when he'd shouted at her to get up and go and pack her bags. And there'd been other instances, loud arguments in the middle of the night; one man had even banged on the door of the lodge early one morning in a panic, with his wife in hot pursuit, threatening to cut off his cock if he ever came near her again. And it all imprinted on Skylar even further, that married life was never meant to be blissful.

Skylar had never confronted anyone on their property before, however.

As she skirted the edge of the cabin, she searched the windows for any sign of what was going on inside. Nobody moved, and there were no more noises. She had to push her way between an overgrown acacia shrub and the side of the building, but she finally made it around to the front of the small structure. It was dark now; the sunset draining the last dregs of light from the sky, and she stumbled over a small rock, nearly colliding with the first step of the little front porch.

Collecting herself, she drew in a deep breath.

Was she really going to do this? Her heart was going a million miles an hour. Was there even anyone inside? They might've already left to walk up to the lodge for dinner. Perhaps she should have a story ready, for when someone opened the door.

She should leave. Turn around and walk away. This was none of her business.

Her hand went involuntarily to encircle her wrist, and she remembered the terrible cracking sound it made as Craig's foot came down upon it, like a twig snapping. Remembered the pain, excruciating, surprising her with how much it incapacitated her. It was fine now, no one could even tell it'd ever been broken. And that's the way she liked to keep it. Not even her brother, Dale, knew.

Nope, she didn't need to get involved in whatever was going on in there.

The barest hint of a noise came from inside. A whimper of pain. All of Skylar's pretend excuses for leaving that front porch evaporated. There was another woman in there in need of help. Perhaps if Skylar had had someone prepared to stand up for her, things might've ended differently.

Skylar raised her fist and knocked on the door.

There was no answer. It was as if the cabin were holding its breath.

She knocked again, louder this time.

There was a murmur, and a male voice swore softly, then a light came on inside, followed almost immediately by the porch light flicking on, nearly blinding her.

The door rattled and swung open. A man stood there, bare-chested, with trousers on, but no shirt or shoes.

"What do you want?" he asked, not hiding the brittle tone in his voice. Or the slight slur in his words. The man was drunk. She knew this couple; this was their third night at the station. Dan Sanders and his wife, Patty. They were in their late fifties. Had seemed like any normal couple—albeit rich—up from Sydney to spend a few nights soaking in the amazing Queensland countryside. He was fit and tanned, sporting a muscled chest with a sprinkling of gray hair. He kept his large body firmly wedged in the door, blocking her view.

Skylar squared her shoulders. "I heard noises. Where's Patty? I'd like to see her, please." There was no point in trying to be tactful. If she needed to, she'd apologize later. Her mother would probably kill her if she got this wrong. The guests were always right in Daniella's eyes.

He narrowed his eyes, his mouth going tight and hard. Without shifting his steely gaze from her face, Dan called out, "Patty, get out here. The cook wants to talk to you."

At least he knew who she was, hopefully recognized that she had some authority here.

There was the sound of bare feet on the wooden floorboards, and Patty's frightened face peered around the side of her husband's impressive bicep. The look in her eyes, one of wary confusion and fear, made Skylar's blood start to boil. She knew that look; recognized it from her own face staring back at her from the mirror after a night when Craig's temper had got the better of him.

Right at that second, Skylar hated all men. They were all driven by their big, fat egos. All of them thought they were the Lord's gift to humankind, and had every right to treat women with disdain and contempt. And she should know. Skylar had lived with just such a man. One who thought he could dominate her. But she'd escaped, and so could this woman.

Skylar spoke to the woman, ignoring the big, hairy man right in front of her. "Hi, Patty, I'm Skylar. The head chef up at the lodge."

Patty merely nodded in acknowledgment. Her short auburn hair was normally sleek and stylish. Tonight, it was ruffled and unkempt. Skylar could only see the woman's head, the rest of her body was hidden behind Dan.

"I was in the kitchen garden, and I heard noises. I wanted to make sure you were okay?"

Patty's eyes, which were already large, went wider still at Skylar's words. Her hand flew to her throat in what Skylar knew to be an unconscious reflex. To cover the bruises that were now just starting to appear. Her lips moved, but no answer was forthcoming. Dan simply stood there, smirking, watching Skylar like a hawk, seemingly untroubled, as if he knew Patty would never betray him.

Skylar asked again, "Patty, are you okay? I want to make sure you're not hurt."

Tears shone in the other woman's eyes, even as she shook her head in the negative. But Skylar could clearly see the bruises now, finger-marks on Patty's neck where her disgusting excuse for a husband had obviously tried to strangle her.

"I think you've got this all wrong," Dan intoned; a magnanimous teacher talking to a naughty child. "As you can see, Patty's fine. We're both fine. I'm not sure what you heard, but maybe you've blown it out of proportion. Who knows, perhaps the problem is in your own head." His smirk got wider, and Skylar wanted to spit in his face.

She'd had enough of this lying fuck and his subterfuge and innuendo. Patty was obviously being abused, and if she wouldn't stand up for herself, then Skylar damn well would.

"Say what you like, but I know what I heard. I'm calling the police. They can sort this out." Skylar went to turn on her heel and walk back up to the lodge.

There was a roar of rage from behind her, and before she knew it, Skylar had been jerked backward, losing her balance, and falling against the husband's chest. A hand covered her mouth as she was dragged over the hearth, the door slamming in front of her.

"You won't dare call the cops on me, you little whore."

Sheer surprise made her go limp. She was trapped inside, being held against Dan's chest like a rag doll. No one else knew where she was. The hand covering her mouth was large and sweaty, and she struggled to call out. Struggled to breathe. Adrenaline coursed through her body, but it was as if she were paralyzed. Frozen with fear.

Memories steamrolled over her. Memories of being held by Craig in exactly the same way. Memories of helplessness and self-loathing.

No.

She wouldn't let this happen to her again.

Gathering her energy, she drew back her foot—glad that she was wearing her good old Blundstones—and drove a boot down onto the man's bare toes.

He howled in pain, but didn't let go as she'd been expecting. "You fucking bitch." He threw her to the ground with such force that her head cracked against the floorboards and for many seconds, all she could see was bright lights. This man was strong. And determined.

When her vision finally cleared, Skylar could see Patty huddled in the corner like a frightened rabbit. Skylar knew she wouldn't do anything to help herself, but maybe she might act if it were to help someone else.

"Do something," she yelled at the woman. "Go and get help. Get—"

A foot landed squarely in her stomach, knocking all the air out of her lungs. She tried to scream, but no sound came out. Instead, she made small, pathetic, gasping noises.

"Patty knows better than to do anything she's not supposed to," Dan yelled, spittle flying from his lips. "And you're going to learn how to behave, as well. You won't be calling the cops, have you got that?"

Skylar didn't know how to answer; couldn't, in fact, answer because she was still struggling to breathe. The man was clearly deluded if he thought he could coerce Skylar into submission. She wouldn't let him do that to her. She tried to tell herself not to be afraid. This man was a coward, who beat up women to make himself feel big. But as he advanced toward her, fear clawed like a wild animal inside her belly. Was he going to hurt her again?

His knee landed on her stomach, pinning her to the floor. He picked up her arm, easily trapped her wrist in his large paw of a hand. Her broken wrist. She struggled against him, tried to wrench herself free, but he bent her hand backward at such an angle that pain sliced through her. She gasped. No, not again. Surely, he wouldn't be so stupid. Wouldn't do something so insane as to injure her? Not while she was on her own property. In her own home.

Keeping the pressure on her wrist, Dan smiled down at her. "Now, I want you to say after me, *'I won't go to the cops, Dan. In fact, I won't tell anyone what happened here tonight. I'll keep it to myself.'* Got it? That way, I won't have to hurt you."

The pain got worse as Dan increased the pressure, and she let out a whimper. Maybe the smart thing to do would be to agree with him. Pretend to acquiesce. Then call the police as soon as he let her go.

"Now, now. I can see it in your eyes. You're one of those feisty girls who think they're above their own station. One of those non-believers." He raised his head and smiled at his wife, who was still cowering in the corner. "Patty used to be a non-believer, too. But she's a good girl now. Aren't you?" Patty nodded emphatically. "She learned early on, that nobody says no to Dan Sanders. A lesson you're about to learn too, little missy. Because if you don't do as I say, I'll have to come back and make you pay." Dan's eyes were slivers of blue ice. Skylar's fear ratcheted up a few notches. He truly believed what he was saying. There was a clarity in this man's eyes. A conviction that he had every right to do whatever he liked. To maintain dominance.

Unlike Craig, whose eyes had always clouded over whenever he lost his temper. As if he wasn't truly in control. Almost as if he'd been two different people.

This man knew exactly what he was doing. Took pleasure in his supremacy. Took pleasure in other people's pain.

He was staring at her with those ice-blue eyes, waiting for her answer.

"I won't tell," she said, her voice coming out in a frightened squeak. And in that exact instant, she doubted if she would tell. All she wanted was to be let free. To go back to her safe life and forget this ever happened. Leave Patty to her own torment. Perhaps live with the guilt of turning a blind eye, but if that's what it took to stay out of harm's way, sheltered behind the walls of Stormcloud lodge, then so be it.

"I promise, I won't tell." She made herself relax. Made herself take a few deep breaths. Dan had to believe she was telling the truth. How could she convince him? "I swear on my grandmother's gr—"

The front door burst open, and Dale leaped into the room. "Get off my sister," he growled, then grabbed Dan in a headlock and dragged him to the floor.

CHAPTER TWO

Senior Constable Nash King clenched his jaw in an effort not to say the words that wanted to spill from his lips. *What on earth possessed you? Why did you put yourself in such danger?* Skylar sat at the small table opposite him, her hands wrapped around a hot mug of tea. But she couldn't hide the slight tremble in her fingers. She was suffering from shock. Daniella hovered protectively behind her daughter's chair. He should remember to tell Daniella and Steve to keep an eye on her.

Nash had to resist the urge to lean across the table and take her hands in his. For the life of him, he couldn't figure out why she thought she should go dashing into a cabin to confront a man twice her size.

Skylar Williams was a determined woman, that was for sure. Determined and beautiful.

"Hey fuckface, when do I get to see my lawyer?" Nash lowered his eyebrows and turned to look at the man he'd handcuffed to the table leg of the large dining table on the other side of the room.

Dale Williams stood at the end of that same table, glowering at the man, ready to pounce if the other guy even twitched a finger the wrong way. Dale's girlfriend, Daisy, stood a little way off, watching him like a hawk, ready to stop

Dale from doing anything stupid. Nash silently thanked the wisdom of women when it came to heated scenarios. At least Daisy understood that if Dale assaulted Dan again—without reasonable cause this time—Nash might have to charge him.

Dan's wife—Patty was her name—sat straight-faced and calm in a chair a few removed from her husband. She didn't even look at him as he spoke. The bruises on her neck were covered by a large, silk scarf.

Luckily, Nash had been at the station doing overtime that evening, filling out paperwork, when Daniella's call had come in. Daniella had calmly relayed that they had a man on the station who'd assaulted Skylar, and could he please come and take him to jail? Dimbulah police station was a one-man affair, and his sector covered a large area, so he wasn't always in close proximity when a crime occurred. It was nearly a forty-five-minute drive out to Stormcloud.

The scene confronting Nash at the cabin when he'd first arrived had been highly charged and volatile. Dale was being forcibly held back by his stepfather, Steve, ranting that he wanted to kill the fucker. Dan Sanders was on the floor, cowering, a black eye, and bruises on his face testament to the justice Dale had already meted out. Daniella had been holding onto Skylar's arm, both women glaring at the man on the ground, almost as if they wanted to egg Dale on. They were a formidable family, and he wouldn't want to get on the wrong side of them.

Nash had quickly removed Dan from the scene—handcuffing him and marching him up to the lodge, cautioning him to make sure he understood his rights and the reason for his arrest—leaving Steve to calm Dale down and telling Dan's wife to get dressed and bring Dan a shirt.

Daisy had arrived in a flurry of questions, at the same time Nash had marched Dan Sanders into the lodge. Daisy lived in an outstation on an adjoining property, but Nash knew she spent most nights here with Dale. This must've been one of the few times she'd actually gone home for the night.

The rest of the Stormcloud staff had been gathered in the dining room, looking more like a lynch mob than anything else. Wazza, the station's big, burly stock hand spearheaded the group and made a beeline for Dan Sanders. The others, Alek, Bindi and the new girl, Sasha, all hovered behind him, ready to back him up.

Nash was used to working on his own most of the time, and he'd handled plenty of situations where the friends and family wanted to exact their own revenge on the perpetrator. Wazza and the rest of the staff were protective of their own, and if they thought this scumbag had hurt Skylar, then he didn't blame them for getting angry. When police were thin on the ground, like they were here, country people often dispensed their own form of justice, but he couldn't let that happen this time.

"I want to hurt you so bad, right now," Wazza growled.

"And I'm right behind you," Alek had added, although Alek's threat seemed less menacing. The Polish man, with his slicked-back hair tied up in a man bun, and his perfectly manicured hands, wasn't nearly as scary as the gruff station hand.

"Now, guys, back off. I have this under control." Nash held up a hand and added with calm authority, "This guy is on his way to jail. But I don't need to be taking more of you in on assault charges, now do I?"

Right at that second, as Nash squared off with Wazza and Alek, hoping they didn't do anything stupid and force his hand, Julie stalked into the room. "Jesus wept, what the hell do you think you clowns are up to?" Nash liked Julie; she didn't pull any punches. You knew where you stood with her. She was Steve's daughter, a stepsister to Dale and Skylar, and had been working at the lodge for nearly a year now.

Nash sent her a grateful glance. He wasn't worried that he couldn't handle the situation, but it was always better when it didn't escalate in the first place.

Julie clapped her hands, shooing the staff like a gaggle of geese, but they stood around as if unsure whether to obey her.

Then Daniella arrived with Steve, Dale and Skylar in tow, and took in the scene in an instant. "We have guests to serve. Get into the kitchen, right now. They'll be eating their dinner in their cabins tonight, which means I need all hands on deck to ferry the meals down." Daniella flicked a quick, worried glance in Dan Sanders' direction, the only hint that she wasn't completely in control. "Julie and Bindi, are you up to finishing the meal? Skylar's a little indisposed at the moment."

"Yes, ma'am," both women answered simultaneously as they drifted through the door and disappeared into the kitchen.

"Wazza, and Sasha, go and help them deliver the food," Daniella commanded. "And Alek, can you please come up with an after-dinner activity that the guests can do outside? We need to keep them away from the lodge tonight." The other three staff jumped at Daniella's authoritative tone and they, too, had disappeared through the door. Nash had drawn a big sigh of relief.

Now Nash returned his concentration to the woman sitting opposite him. Daniella still hovered, laying a comforting hand on Skylar's shoulder, but Skylar merely stared, unseeing, out the window into the dark bushland. Nash wanted to talk to her alone.

"I'd kill for a cup of coffee," he said gently, while looking directly at Daniella.

The older woman seemed ready to argue, but then nodded and took the hint, giving her daughter one more swift touch on the shoulder before she left. But right before she turned to go, her gaze met Nash's. *Take care of her,* her eyes seemed to say. He lifted his eyebrow in reply. Skylar was safe in his hands.

He needed to record her initial statement, but he'd take it slow, not wanting to stress her even more than she already was. Nash took out his notebook and pen and laid them on the table.

"How are you? Are you up to answering a few questions?" he asked gently.

Her blue eyes darted around the room, but wouldn't meet his gaze. "Sure, I'm fine. What is it you want to know?"

That was a lie, if ever he'd heard one. She was anything but fine. If she didn't want to admit it, then there wasn't a lot he could do to persuade her. She kept touching her wrist, almost as if it were an unconscious habit, and Nash again felt the urge to take her hands in his.

"Can you tell me, in your own words, what happened tonight?" he asked, keeping his tone light.

"Yeah, this bastard was hitting his wife, that's what happened." She glared over at Dan, her jaw working as she ground her teeth together. "But that wasn't enough. He had to attack me as well, because I stood up to him." Venom dripped from her words. She was angry. Really angry. But there was something else behind that anger. Something Nash couldn't quite put his finger on. It was more than plain fear or panic. Almost as if she were reliving some other deep horror. As if she'd seen this kind of thing before.

"I have rights, you know," Dan snarled across the room when he saw them looking at him. "Let's get this shit over with. Get me out of here." Dan Sanders was a rich, arrogant man, who thought he could buy his way out of any situation. Well, he might just find that country people didn't take kindly to being bullied. He could wait until Nash was damn well good and ready to take him back to the station. Nash wanted to make sure Skylar was all right, first. It was going to be a long night, with lots more paperwork; five more minutes at Stormcloud wouldn't hurt.

"We'll be leaving shortly," he replied, tone clipped and formal. He was nothing, if not professional and calm. Even if he did want to take a turn where Dale had left off, smacking that smug smile off the abuser's face, he'd never actually do it.

This family had it rough over the past year. Nash had been involved in the murder investigation almost a year ago, when one of their station hands had been killed. The whole sordid affair had ended with another of their staff, Sally Tsun, along with her boyfriend, being arrested for the murder. But the reputation of the luxury eco-resort didn't seem to have been tarnished. In fact, the whole torturous situation seemed to have brought them more guests and more accolades. You couldn't argue with a tasty morsel of gossip to bring the vultures crowding around. Human beings were strange creatures.

Skylar had seemingly taken the whole thing in her stride. As she liked to say, it was Dale and his girlfriend, Daisy, who'd been at the heart of the trouble last year. But as Nash watched her now, he could see the way she scanned the room, almost as if looking for an escape. This situation seemed to be affecting her differently than the one last year.

He turned back toward Skylar, ignoring any further comments from his prisoner. Her long, blonde hair had escaped from its ponytail, probably during the attack, and she was trying to wrestle it into some form of submission. With a sigh, she gave up and let it hang in loose tangles around her shoulders.

Skylar was a stunner, but she seemed not to notice most of the time. He'd noticed it, however. Right from the very first day he'd moved to Dimbulah to take charge of the run-down police station. He'd come across her in the street as she was standing next to her four-wheel-drive, peering under the hood. It was the blue of her eyes that he found irresistible. So blue, like a lake in the middle of summer, or a brilliant-cut topaz, sparkling in the sun. He'd helped her jump-start her vehicle—it was merely a dead battery—and then watched her drive away. A stunner, certainly, but also one with mental guards firmly in place. She'd been friendly, but cool. Polite, but detached.

She was looking at him now with that same reserve. "Will he be charged?"

He talked quietly enough so the man couldn't hear him. "Yes, he assaulted you. That's enough to put him before a judge, at the very least."

"So, he won't...you won't let him go?"

"No. As long as you're prepared to lay charges." He looked at her for confirmation, and she nodded. "Then he'll be transferred to Cairns, and a judge will decide if he warrants bail."

"He could get out on bail?"

"Yes." What was she getting at? Then it struck him. Skylar was afraid that this excuse for a man was going to come back and try and hurt her. What had he said to her?

"These monsters often act first and think later. They're so arrogant and full of themselves, they think they're untouchable. But they're not. He'll end up in jail, just like anyone else who's broken the law. His privilege won't stop that. You have witnesses to this assault. And if we can get his wife to testify...well, he might be going away for a very long time."

"I don't think she will," Skylar said flatly, her gaze seeking out the wife. "Women like that...who've been beaten and coerced, so they don't even know who they are anymore, it's hard for them to break free of that overwhelming fear."

It almost seemed as if Skylar was speaking from experience. But that was crazy. She wasn't the type of woman who'd put up with domestic abuse. Was she? She was much too strong and ballsy to let any guy dominate her. Look at how she'd marched into that cabin and confronted this dick. She was brave enough to want to help a woman who wouldn't help herself.

"Whatever he said to you, he's wrong. If he thought he could keep you quiet by intimidating you, he's wrong," Nash repeated the words, hoping Skylar would believe them.

Skylar stared at Nash for many long seconds, her gaze drifting over to the man handcuffed to the table. "Yeah, I guess you're right." But the conviction behind Skylar's words was missing.

Nash spent five more minutes getting Skylar's statement. By the time he'd finished, Sanders' demands to *get on with it, because he was an important man with better places to be'* were beginning to grate on Nash's nerves.

He decided to get the rest of the statements from Dale— who'd broken into the cabin and saved Skylar—Steve, and Daniella, later. He could drive back out tomorrow. So, he put the husband in the back of his police four-wheel-drive behind the barricade. Sanders demanded that Patty come with him, and Nash told the wife to follow behind in her car. The woman fixed her gaze on Nash for a second—she was certainly a cool customer, obviously very used to hiding her husband's abuse behind a façade of controlled composure— then agreed. He felt sorry for her. Sorry that she'd lived with such a brute for so long. Would this be the straw that broke the camel's back? Would she finally be able to move away from her overbearing husband? As he watched her calmly step into their black Mercedes SUV, he somehow doubted it.

Nash hid a yawn. It was only dinner time, but he'd been

up since dawn. This job was tiring. But it was also the most rewarding thing he'd ever done. The position had come up two years ago; the Dimbulah station had been unmanned for three years, but they finally had enough money to reopen it. The job was a promotion and after seven years spent working in a variety of stations in Brisbane, Nash decided he wanted a change.

Moving to the bush had been life changing, in so many ways. The isolation took a lot of getting used to. As did the laid-back lifestyle, and the way the locals were a hell of a lot more independent. He'd got used to driving long distances; everything was far away out here.

He wasn't lonely. There was always so much to do. So much so, that he hadn't had a girlfriend since he'd moved out here. Not that there weren't plenty of women who weren't eager for him to look their way. But their subtle desperation didn't entice him. In the back recesses of his brain, he knew he was attractive to women. They always cooed about his beautiful blue eyes and gorgeous blond hair. But he wasn't one of those guys who played on his looks. He liked to earn everything he was entitled to. And there was no one who'd really caught his eye out here. Except Skylar.

After seeing her a few times in town, having short, polite, and vaguely unsatisfying conversations, he'd been surprised to see her arrive at a local charity ball one night in Mareeba. She'd taken his breath away, dressed in a simple red dress, with her hair down and her eyes dark with eyeliner, she'd left him gasping for air when she looked his way. A lot of the other men were equally affected, too. There was a live band—albeit playing country music—and people waltzing, and so he'd pushed his way through the gaggle of attending men to ask her for a dance. After they'd danced, and with a few beers for courage under his belt, he'd asked her out on a date. Her refusal had taken him by surprise. She'd been courteous and polite, saying that she didn't have time to date anyone at the moment. Her work kept her too busy. But the rejection stung for a long time afterwards.

He shook his head and turned his concentration back to the road. The sun had set a few hours ago, and this was the time that native wildlife came out to feed at the edges of the road; he needed to keep his wits about him. It was September, and they were nearing the end of the dry season, so there were fewer cane toads on the roads. Once the rains started again, they'd sometimes be so thick on the ground he'd lose count of how many he ran over with his police car. He checked that the wife was still following behind him, her headlights flickering in his rear-view mirror.

Pushing the button on his police radio, he called the arrest in to the Mareeba Station. Letting them know he'd keep Sanders in Dimbulah lockup for the night, and asking for someone from Cairns to pick the prisoner up in the morning, so he could be arraigned. Senior Sergeant Robinson was in charge at Mareeba, and was technically Nash's boss. He'd worked with Robinson a few times recently, especially during the case of the Stormcloud murder. He respected Robinson, he was a good cop and a good man. But too overqualified to be running this small section of North Queensland. There were rumors that Robinson would be moving onwards and upwards soon; to oversee the much larger Townsville Station. There were also rumors that Nash might be getting a constable to come and work at the Dimbulah station with him. But he wasn't holding his breath.

He finished his report and turned off the radio.

The silence was broken by Sanders making a loud grunting noise from behind the barricade in the rear seat.

"These handcuffs are too tight, they're hurting my wrists," he growled.

Nash didn't respond.

"But you don't give a crap, do you?"

Again, Nash knew better than to engage with the prisoner. He could rant all he liked; he wasn't going to get a rise out of this senior constable.

"Well, you'd better give a crap," Sanders snarled. "You say you don't care who I am, that everyone who commits a crime is treated the same. Well, I know your name. I know who you are. You'd better watch your back, boy, and sleep with one eye open from now on."

What the hell? Was this doofus actually threatening him? What an idiot. Nash didn't deign to even flick a glance in the other man's direction.

CHAPTER THREE

"King is here," Dale called, as he strode through the kitchen on his way out the back door.

Skylar looked up from where she and Daisy were prepping the salad for lunch. "Oh, right." Her stomach did a vague somersault, and she immediately felt foolish. She didn't care if she never saw the senior constable again. She just wished her stomach understood that. Now that she thought about it, he had mentioned he'd be back today to take everybody else's statements, so she guessed she should've been expecting him.

Dale stopped to sweep Daisy up in his arms for a quick kiss. "Hello, gorgeous. Have you become Stormcloud's newest kitchen helper?" he joked.

"No, just giving Skylar a hand, that's all." Daisy shot a beaming smile at her brother.

More like become her self-appointed babysitter, Skylar thought grumpily. Daisy hadn't left Skylar's side all morning. Fussing over Skylar, making sure she wasn't left alone. She and Daisy had become very close over the past six months, she'd almost go as far as saying they were best friends, but this morning Daisy was silently driving Skylar insane.

Skylar liked to process things on her own. She hated it

when people fussed over her.

Julie hadn't been much better, checking in on Skylar more often than usual during the morning. At least Julie would be helping Steve and Dale take the guests out trekking on the horses this afternoon, which'd get her out of Skylar's hair for a while. She loved Julie, they got on well, probably better than a lot of stepsisters. Julie was a bit of a joker, liked to be the bright, positive person in the room. She'd certainly lifted up Stormcloud lodge with her presence ever since she'd agreed to come and replace their staff member, Karri, who'd been brutally murdered by Sally Tsun. Most of the time, Skylar enjoyed Julie's company. Just not today.

"I'll go and show King through to the business suite," Dale said. "It might be better if he uses that room, away from the prying eyes of the guests. Can you bring us through some coffee, please?" Dale let go of Daisy and turned to look at his sister. "You didn't happen to bake any of your delicious pumpkin and wattleseed scones today?"

"No, sorry. You'll have to make do with the chocolate-chip cookies I made yesterday."

Dale frowned at her. Then he walked around the large island bench and draped an arm over her shoulders. Skylar didn't really like to be touched. Dale was the only person she allowed this sort of liberty. And perhaps Julie, and now Daisy. Everyone else knew to keep their distance. "You okay, sis? That whole thing last night was pretty fucked up. Maybe you should take the day off."

"I don't need to take the day off," she countered, lifting her knife and waving it in his face. "And I don't need my little brother telling me what to do."

Daisy knew better than to interfere, but Skylar could tell she was judging her with her eyes.

"I'm just worried about you," he said, raising both hands in surrender.

"I know." She screwed up her mouth and looked at the ceiling. "I'm sorry. But I'm fine, really. Now, go let Nash… Senior Constable King in. I'll bring the coffee soon."

She was fine. If she kept telling herself that, then it'd become true, sooner or later. At least the tell-tale tremble in her fingers this morning when she'd first picked up the frying pan to cook breakfast had subsided. She could do this. She could conquer this thing. She'd done it once; she could do it again.

"I can take the coffee, if you like," Daisy said.

Skylar had to clamp her mouth shut to physically hold back the words, *stop treating me like an invalid. I'm fine.* Everyone was only trying to help. But why couldn't they see that she just needed to get on with life? Last night was a distant memory. Well, it would be, if the bloody senior constable wouldn't keep making her rehash the events.

Skylar gritted her teeth, and answered as calmly as she could, "No, it's fine, I'll take it."

Five minutes later, she pushed the door to the business suite open with her toe and placed her tray of coffee and cookies carefully down on the large meeting table in the center of the room. Dale and Nash were seated at one corner of the table.

"Morning, Skylar." Nash's voice was deep and mellow. She steeled herself before she turned around.

"Morning, Senior Constable."

He raised an eyebrow at her official greeting. "How are you feeling today?"

She should probably tell him the truth. Something told her that if she didn't, he wouldn't drop the subject until she did. "My ribs are a little sore from where he kicked me. And I've got an impressive lump on the back of my head."

Dale half-stood. "You didn't tell me that. I'll—"

"Sit down, you big oaf. I'm fine." She cast her brother a

quelling glance. "I talked to a nurse over the health hotline last night, and she agreed that nothing was broken." At Daniella's urging, Skylar had rung the hotline. It was a godsend for people who couldn't get to a doctor quickly.

She almost told Daniella that she knew her ribs weren't broken, because she was familiar with what that felt like, and this was nothing in comparison.

"She also said I should watch out for concussion, but Daniella sat up with me for half the night to make sure I was okay. So, all in all, I'm in pretty good shape, considering."

"Yeah, considering I burst in when I did," Dale said darkly. "Things might've been a lot worse for you, if I hadn't."

"Yes," Skylar sighed. "And I'm eternally grateful, little brother." She didn't mean to sound sarcastic, because she was a little afraid of what Dan Sanders might've done to her if Dale hadn't appeared. Dale told her later that Bindi was fretting over dinner, not sure what to do next, and so she'd asked Dale to call his sister in from the garden. When he couldn't immediately see her amongst the raised vegetable beds, he'd gone down to the orchard, where he'd heard the commotion in the Sanders' cabin. Peering through the window, he'd seen Skylar on the floor and rushed to her aid.

Before Skylar could say any more, the door opened behind her, and Daniella and Steve filed in.

"Daisy told me you were here," Daniella said, in a clipped tone. "If you give me a list of people you want to talk to, I'll organize the staff to come in one by one."

"That would be great," Nash replied.

Daniella hesitated, but her mother was hardly ever subtle. "Ah…any news on this guy? Is his wife going to lay charges?" she blurted. "I'm sorry, I know you probably can't tell us anything, it's just that…"

Nash's face softened, and he smiled sympathetically at Daniella. Skylar was almost jealous, wishing she could be the recipient of such a smile. His lips curled enticingly up at the corners, his blue gaze direct and unwavering. What was such a good-looking man doing out here, working as a cop in this tinpot town of Dimbulah?

"It's okay, I can tell you quite a few things, actually."

Steve and her mother took a seat opposite Nash, but she remained standing. Belatedly, she thought of the coffee. Moving the plate of cookies onto the table between them, she handed them each a mug. As Nash reached for his mug, an appreciative smile playing on his lips, the short sleeves of his dark-blue uniform rode up, and she noticed scarring on his upper arms. It was subtle; they were clearly old scars. Burns, by the looks of them. Most of the time, the scars would be hidden by the sleeves of his uniform. She'd noticed them last night, as well, but hadn't been in the right headspace to pay them much heed. Where had they come from? Had he got them on the job, rescuing someone from a burning building, perhaps? In her imagination, she could see Nash rushing into a collapsing house, broad shoulders barging through the doorway, blue eyes fierce and determined.

"Mm, good coffee," Nash murmured, after taking a sip. "I needed that."

Skylar returned her mind to the present and shook away those stupid flights of fancy, hoping she wasn't blushing. She watched Nash take another big gulp of coffee and wondered how much sleep he'd managed to get last night. Now that she was looking, she could see gray smudges beneath his eyes, his tanned face slightly pale beneath his surfer good-looks.

"I learned a few interesting things about Dan Sanders. He is a part-owner of the Crown Casino down in Melbourne, and has a reputation for being a savvy businessman. He's a multi, multi-millionaire. So at least we know his ravings about being uber-rich are correct." Nash gave a wry smile. "Not that it gives him the right to go around beating up women, as he seems to think it does. He also has a reputation for having a foul temper."

"All that makes perfect sense. I still can't believe there are men like him out there," Daniella said into the silence.

Skylar flinched, then crossed her arms over her chest, sweat suddenly beading on her forehead. Her fingers itched to encircle her wrist, stroke away the remembered pain. If only her mother knew how prevalent these types of men really were. Daniella would be so disappointed to find out her own daughter had been a victim of one of those *men like him*, as she put it. Which was one of the reasons she'd never told her. None of her family knew how she'd suffered at the hands of Craig. They all believed her relationship with the talented chef was one-hundred-percent perfect. And because she'd been living and working in Cairns, they never guessed otherwise.

"I hate to think we need to vet our guests from now on. But how else are we going to stop monsters like him from coming to our lodge?" Daniella asked.

"You're not," Steve said, speaking up for the first time, and Daniella looked up, surprised. "How were you supposed to know?" Steve softened his tone, but his eyes remained steely. "How were any of us supposed to know? And his wife was obviously complicit in hiding whatever was going on."

"That's true," Daniela sighed.

"Of course, it's true, Mum," Dale said with a frown. "We never really know what's going on behind closed doors in any marriage. We might think we do, but that's why domestic violence is so insidious. It's this big, dark secret."

Skylar stared at Dale, wondering how he'd suddenly become so insightful. Perhaps she had Daisy to thank for opening his eyes to life outside their little Stormcloud bubble. Daisy's indigenous heritage, along with her connection to her culture, was a good thing for Dale to be involved in, because now he got to see some of the day-to-day hardships she had to endure; including both the subtle and the blatant racism she encountered nearly every day. And perhaps Dale had also learned a few valuable lessons during his time spent on their uncle's ranch in Montana. He, along with the rest of the staff at the ranch, had been unwitting victims in an arson attempt by a disgruntled employee. Thankfully, that sordid tale had turned out okay; no one had been hurt. But Dale was beginning to see that life in the real world wasn't always rosy.

Nash nodded his agreement. "The best part about my whole night, is that I think I may have convinced Patty to press charges against him." Nash sat back and let his words soak in.

"Oh, wow, that's great," Skylar said, uncrossing her arms and leaning forward.

"Yes, it is." Nash speared her with his hypnotizing gaze. "And I think it's all because of you."

"Really?"

"Yep. She told me, it was when she saw you on the floor, with Dan yelling at you and kicking you in the stomach, that she suddenly knew what she had to do. It was like a switch had flicked inside her. Up until then, she'd been blocking out what was happening to her, telling herself that it wasn't really that bad, and Dan was doing it because he loved her and wanted the best for her. But when she looked at you, she finally saw herself lying on the floor. Saw herself as a victim of that violence."

"So, my interference was a good thing, after all?"

"I wouldn't say that you putting yourself in danger and getting beaten up by that pig was a good thing," Dale growled.

She gave him a look of exasperation. "You know what I mean," she said. "If Patty is finally ready to see this man for what he really is, and to make him pay for his bad deeds, then it was all worth it." And it was. She'd take more bruised ribs any day, if it meant she could free even one woman from a man's tyranny. If only she'd been that lucky, to have someone willing to help her.

"I'll still need to get all of your statements from last night, to help with the case of assault against Skyler," Nash continued. "I'm assuming you're going ahead with that?" he asked, a sudden frown marring his handsome face.

"Yes, of course." She wasn't letting this scumbag get away with it. She'd let Craig get away with it, because she wanted her freedom more than she wanted him to pay for his crimes. All she wanted was to never see Craig again. But this guy needed to rot in a jail cell. Perhaps, in a twisted sort of way, she was using Dan Sanders to get her revenge on Craig. On all men. Perhaps a psychologist might say she needed help, needed to purge herself of all this hurt and bitterness, by talking it through. But she didn't care, this was her form of therapy. Better than any talking.

"Good. That'll definitely help to convince the judge that Patty is also telling the truth. This guy might have some powerful lawyers, but no one is above the law," Nash said, a relieved look on his face. "He's already been transported to Cairns, where he'll be arraigned. I've requested he not be granted bail, because of his history of violence, and also because of his threats toward you."

A chill ran down Skylar's spine as she remembered Dan's words. *"If you don't do as I say, I will have to come back and make you pay."* At the time, she'd believed him. She'd even been willing to make him any promise he demanded, just to secure her freedom. Now, however, she was embarrassed to think she'd paid heed to his words. He was merely a simpering coward, who used his words as weapons. She wasn't going to be intimidated by him.

Nash continued, "A court date will be set. I'm not sure yet

if the charges will be heard together, or if they'll require two separate trials. The judge will have to decide. It might be a few weeks before we know exactly. But this…guy will end up in jail. I'm sure of it."

Skylar wondered at his slight hesitation. What had Nash been about to call Dan Sanders?

Daniella raised her eyebrows, but the tilt of her mouth told Skylar she was happy with the outcome. As was Skylar. This would all work out perfectly. She reached over to grab Dale and Nash's empty mugs, ready to take them back to the kitchen and get on with her meal prep. Her day was looking much better with this new information.

Then Nash speared her with his gaze. "You'll be required to go on the witness stand, Skylar. I'm assuming you're happy to do that?"

"What?" Skylar stilled, her heart rate suddenly becoming erratic, the mugs rattling together on the tray.

"Yes, it'll mean going to Cairns for a day or two," Nash continued, clearly unaware of her sudden panic. "But I'm sure Dale can organize a helicopter for you, so you don't have to drive up."

Oh, wow, she hadn't thought of that. Leaving the safety of Stormcloud. The last time she'd been to Cairns had been a few years ago. Recently, she'd used the excuse that she was too busy to leave the station, except to take quick trips into Dimbulah. And sometimes she'd drive over to Daisy's place for dinner and a glass of wine. All her supplies and any food she needed that she couldn't grow on the station were ordered online and delivered straight to her back door.

No one seemed to have noticed that she hardly left the station anymore.

Well, almost no one. Dale had asked if she wanted to join him on a trip to Townsville a few weeks ago, said it'd be good for her to get a little R and R, and regaled her with facts about the amazing hotel he'd be staying at while he was there. But even though he'd frowned when she'd refused, he hadn't pushed the point. It wasn't that she couldn't leave the station, she didn't really need to. She certainly wasn't agoraphobic, or anything like that.

Could she do that? Go to Cairns to take the stand in front of lots of people, then recount what that monster had done to her? Recount what she'd seen him doing to his wife? With all those people staring at her. Judging her.

Skylar shook her head and backed away.

CHAPTER FOUR

Nash pulled into the lot behind the lodge and parked beside a row of other cars, most of them dusty, white, four-wheel-drives belonging to the station. Sprinkled in between were a couple of luxury SUVs, belonging to the guests. Most people chose to fly into the isolated lodge via helicopter; it was much quicker and more efficient. But some people liked to drive or combine it with a longer trip around the top end.

Nash leaped out of his car and ran around to the tailgate to retrieve his overnight bag. He was running late. It was only eight-thirty in the morning, but he already felt like he'd worked a full day. The helicopter that was to take him to Cairns was already waiting on the Stormcloud landing pad, rotors spinning lazily. He liked to make a point of being punctual, but out here, it was sometimes impossible. This morning had been spent showing Constable Willow around his station. Robinson had sent the young constable down to fill in while Nash was in Cairns for the next two days, attending Dan Sanders' court case. Willow was young and eager to learn, clean-cut and astute, but perhaps a little too arrogant, and overly confident. Nash sincerely hoped that nothing major happened in the next two days.

He'd spent more time than he bargained, bringing Willow

up to speed as to where everything was stored in the station, as well as pointing out a few of the idiosyncrasies of the police vehicle. The four-wheel-drive was an older version—it badly needed an upgrade—with a manual gearshift, and the young constable needed a quick refresher on how to drive such a vehicle. Nash had run home to get changed, and then then added his uniform and locked gun case containing his Glock into his bag with a spare change of clothes, as well as all the documents he might need in court—which he'd thankfully packed the night before—and dumped it into his personal car to drive to Stormcloud.

Dale sauntered out of the back door and came to meet him halfway.

"Sorry I'm late," Nash apologized.

"No hurry, mate." Dale smiled, flashing a matching set of dimples. "The helicopter only touched down ten minutes ago. Daniella took the pilot a cup of coffee and one of Skylar's chocolate brownies, and is plying him for all the gossip from the big city." Dale glanced down the hill to where the bright-red helicopter glinted through the trees. "Actually, now I think about it, perhaps we should go and rescue Paul from my mother." He laughed, his eyes crinkling at the corners. It was good to see the easy, relaxed Dale was back. Unlike the angry-as-a-bull, ready-to-charge man he'd seen the night he arrested Dan Sanders. It was only two weeks ago, but it felt like a year.

A door banged behind them, and they both turned to watch Skylar walking toward them, carrying a small, overnight bag in one hand. She looked different, and it took Nash a few moments to figure out why. Instead of her normal jeans and loose-fitting, linen shirt, she was wearing a simple, figure hugging, black knit dress. It draped to her knees, showing shapely calves, made to look longer by the high-heeled, black pumps on her feet. Today, her hair was still tied back in a ponytail, but it was a loose version sitting low on her neck, not the sleek, high ponytail she usually sported. It was a softer look, more relaxed, and ultimately more feminine.

Something in his gut tightened way down low. She was stunning, and certain parts of his body appreciated how good she looked. He glanced away, filling his vision with the billabong instead, anything to distract him.

"Morning," she said, once she was within earshot. Her gaze flicked over him quickly and he got the distinct impression she might be appreciating him as well. "Why are you…? Oh, sorry." She waved a hand in the air. "You caught me by surprise. I was expecting you to be wearing your uniform."

Nash glanced down at his outfit. Long, black trousers, shiny, black shoes, and a white, long-sleeved shirt, rolled up to the elbows. "I'm in civvies this morning," he explained. "I'm off duty until I get into court."

"Oh, right." She frowned. "Won't you be hot in those?"

"Nope, I'm used to it." His civilian clothes were almost a uniform in themselves. He wore the same thing all the time. Trousers looked neat and practical, projected an air of professionalism. But there was another reason for the long pants. To cover the scars on his lower legs. The long shirt sleeves were for the same reason, to hide the burns on his upper arms. He wasn't ashamed of the scars, not exactly, just unwilling to talk about how he got them. If people never saw them, he never had to answer their questions.

"Sorry, I just imagined you'd be a shorts-and-Hawaiian-shirt sort of guy, that's all," she joked. "But I guess it's no different to what we wear on the station most of the time." She glanced toward Dale in his blue jeans, cowboy boots, and button-up shirt, also rolled up to the elbow.

"That's true." He hadn't really thought about it before, but their clothes were worn as much for safety as anything else.

"I'll walk you down, if you're ready?" Dale tilted his chin in the direction of the helicopter. "Let's go and rescue Paul from my mother." He reached for Skylar's bag, and after a second's hesitation, she handed it over.

Then she turned toward the lodge, reluctance in her gaze.

"Julie and Bindi will be fine while you're away, sis. We've got this all under control, don't worry."

Skylar chewed her bottom lip. "I know." But her feet remained resolutely pointing at the lodge as if she might change her mind about coming to Cairns and sprint back through the door.

"You've practically pre-cooked everything for them, all they have to do is heat and serve it," Dale prompted. But his tone was gentle, as if he knew how hard this was for his sister to leave her kitchen in someone else's hands. "It's only two days," he prompted. "You'll be back in time to help with dinner tomorrow night. Nothing calamitous can happen in that time, surely."

Nash thought back to Skylar's seeming reluctance two weeks ago when he announced she would need to take the witness stand. Perhaps this was part of the reason for her hesitation. She'd built a reputation as an amazing chef at Stormcloud, and she didn't want anything to tarnish it.

Right that second, Julie burst through the rear door and jogged over to Skylar. Her short caramel hair was spiked up, as if she'd run a harried hand through it recently. But her face lit up in a huge smile, meant for Skylar alone. Julie was slightly curvier than Skylar, and a tad taller. She was also a good-looking woman in her own right, and Nash took a second to appreciate Skylar's stepsister. She had a way of walking that spoke of optimism and fun, and she fixed her bright, tawny eyes on Skylar.

"Stop shilly-shallying, woman," she scalded. "Get on the

helicopter. Go on, shoo." She enfolded Skylar in a hug, which Skylar belatedly returned, and then Julie pushed her toward the path.

"Yes, yes," Skylar grumbled. "I'm going. God, it's almost like you're all desperate to get rid of me," she groused. As Skylar turned away, Julie rolled her eyes in Dale's direction, and they shared a look of communication. Nash decided that Skylar might be right, and they did have a conspiracy going to make sure she got on that helicopter.

Nash didn't have time to wonder why, however, as Dale led the way down a gravel pathway and Nash indicated for Skylar to precede him. Even though he'd only ever seen her wearing high heels once before, at the charity ball in Mareeba, she seemed to be right at home wearing them today, walking along the gravel pathway as if it were no problem at all. Nash admired the way her hips swayed hypnotically before him, letting his gaze drift up her backside to savor her narrow waist, and how her blonde hair curled over her shoulders.

"Hi, Paul," Dale called out as they approached. "I've got your passengers here, ready to board."

The look on the pilot's face was sheer relief as he handed Daniella his empty mug and plate. Nash wondered what information Daniella had been after. She was a formidable woman, and you wouldn't want to get on the wrong side of her.

Paul extended his hand. "I'm Paul Dorper, I'll be your pilot today."

Nash shook it and replied, "Senior Constable King. Nice to meet you. Call me Nash."

"Dale told me all about you. It's a pleasure to be escorting one of Queensland's finest."

Paul turned to greet Skylar—they were obviously acquainted—and then he was showing them to their seats. It was a small, Bell 505, five-seater helicopter, with two seats up front and three in the back. The pilot offered one of them to sit up next to him, but Skyler shook her head, agitation clear on her face. Was she a nervous flyer? Nash chose to sit with her in the back row. Perhaps she might need moral support. Paul began to run through the safety protocols of flying in the small chopper, and Dale waved goodbye, tugging his reluctant mother by the sleeve to get her to follow him. Paul handed him a set of headphones and showed him how to put them on. Then he did the same with Skylar.

Before Nash knew it, they were in the air, hovering over the lodge and its surrounding cabins. Nash had never travelled by helicopter before. What an amazing view. He craned his neck to get a better look at the countryside spread out below them, looking dry and sparse from this vantage point. September was near the end of the dry season, and he could see how thirsty the country looked. The Jimbu River ran like a ribbon of green away on the horizon. And the billabong and its surrounding lush vegetation was an oasis in the low foothills of Mount Mulligan. Soon, the small township of Dimbulah appeared, rows of small, white boxes and straight roads, the only true sign of human habitation for hundreds of miles. It really put it all into perspective, how tiny and remote they were. He tried to locate his own small cottage on the outskirts of town, but they were flying too fast, and he missed it.

It took him a few moments to notice that Skylar didn't seem to be enjoying the view as much as he was. Her gaze was fixed forward, her hands clenched tightly in her lap.

He spoke a little hesitantly into the microphone by his chin. "Are you an anxious flyer?" he asked, not unkindly, ready to offer her a comforting pat on the shoulder, or a sick bag, whatever she needed.

"No, I've done this plenty of times before." Her disembodied voice came back through the headphones, her tone so low and tense, he struggled to hear it over the noise of the rotor blades.

"Okay," he acknowledged. So, if that wasn't her problem, what was it?

Just when he thought she wasn't going to give him more of an answer, she blurted, "I don't like to leave the station. I'm not good with crowds. And I'm not looking forward to this whole court case thing."

"Right." That was a lot of surprising information. It was a side of Skylar he'd never imagined, she'd always seemed so together, so independent, and undaunted. Just look at how she handled that wife beater the other night. He wasn't sure he could help her with the nervousness around crowds, or the fact that she saw the station as some kind of safe haven. But he could definitely help make the courtroom seem a little less scary. "That's completely understandable. I can talk to you through it, if it'd help. What'll be expected of you, who'll be there, all that kind of thing. Your lawyer will also do that, but I've got first-hand experience of what it feels like to stand in a witness box."

"Thank you," she replied simply. But her eyes seemed to clear a little.

The rest of the twenty-minute flight was spent with Nash interrogating Paul on the finer points of being a helicopter pilot. This chopper was relatively new to the fleet. The company Paul worked for owned six helicopters, and he was one of nine pilots they used in rotation. Nash was fascinated with how simple the controls seemed to be. Paul told him these newer choppers were becoming easier and easier to fly; almost as easy as driving a car. Nash doubted that. Stormcloud used Paul's company to ferry guests to and from the station, as well as take family or staff in and out when needed. Not for the first time, Nash wondered why Stormcloud didn't have its own helicopter; a lot of the large, outback stations had more than one. But then he guessed that would then require someone to pilot the craft. Perhaps it was easier this way.

Paul pointed out a few things of interest on the way, and Nash saw the vegetation below slowly turn greener as they neared the coast. In some places, the tangle of foliage was so thick it covered everything in an impenetrable blanket of jade, and it went on and on for miles. It looked cool and inviting down there under the canopy, but Nash wasn't fooled. He knew from experience that it'd be hot, humid, and sticky, and he was glad he was sailing through the air well above it all. The dichotomy of the landscape in far North Queensland was made more obvious from his vantage point up in the sky. The dry, flat floodplains, verging on desolate, were now replaced with soaring mountains, covered in waterfalls and lush foliage. Australia certainly was a place of contrasts as well as wonder, and he wouldn't want to live anywhere else.

Sooner than he expected, they were flying over the outskirts of Cairns. With a population of around one-hundred-and-seventy-thousand people, it was a popular tourist destination, the gateway to the Great Barrier Reef, as well as Daintree National Park, and many other tropical delights. Nash had been to the town many times, but never lived here, and he'd never seen it from the air.

Paul touched the chopper down lightly at the airfield, and they disembarked. Nash watched Skylar's back as she walked across the tarmac to the hangar, bag in one hand, heels clicking on the blacktop. If anything, she seemed more tense now than she had been in the helicopter. As if she were bracing herself for what was to come.

They'd head straight to the courthouse. Dan Sanders' trial was due to start at nine am. But neither he nor Skylar would be needed until after lunch. Both the charges, of domestic violence toward his wife Patty, and of causing grievous bodily harm to Skylar, would be heard together, as the judge deemed them to be related; Skylar's testimony would be key to proving that Dan assaulted his wife. Which was a good thing for Skylar, as it meant she'd only have to endure sitting through one trial. The morning would be filled with opening statements from the lawyers. It'd give the prosecution team time to go over Skylar's testimony with her. Hopefully, he'd have time to sit down and talk her through it, as well.

It was a matter of protocol that the arresting officer always attended the trial. At best, his testimony would help put a criminal in jail. But some cases dragged on and on, and at worst it was annoying, often a waste of his time, hours spent pacing up and down corridors, or watching from the back docks, when Nash could be doing other more important things. He'd spent every spare minute over the last few days checking his records from his little notebook from the arrest, as well as reading all witness statements, to make sure he remembered everything clearly.

Nash hurried to catch up with Skylar. "I'll call us a taxi," he said.

She merely inclined her head by way of answer, her back so stiff he wondered if she might shatter if he touched her. It looked as if her words about not being comfortable in a crowd might be correct.

Once they were safely ensconced in the back of the taxi, he asked her, "Which hotel are you staying at? I haven't booked one yet. We may as well stay close together."

Skylar was staying overnight, just in case they needed to call her in tomorrow to clarify any points. Nash was required to attend most days. So, today being Thursday, he'd spend the night, then fly home with Skylar tomorrow after the court finished for the day. He was rostered on to work on Saturday, and then would look forward to his day off on Sunday. The trial would resume on Monday—these things usually took at least a week to play out—but Nash would drive back on Monday morning. The helicopter ride was gratis because Stormcloud was bringing in guests, but there was no way police management would pay for him to do it again.

Skylar blew out a breath between pursed lips and then gave him an unreadable glance. "I'm at the Shangri La."

"Great, I'll see if I can get a booking." Nash tapped away on his phone for the next few minutes and secured himself a room, wincing when he saw the price. It wasn't his normal type of accommodation, but if Skylar was staying there, so was he. He wasn't quite sure why, but a small thrill went through him at the thought he'd be at the same hotel. Even though Skylar had made it painfully obvious she wasn't in the right space for dating, he couldn't help but dream.

They arrived at the courthouse, and Nash paid the driver, then jumped out, grabbing both of their bags from the trunk. But when he came around on to the sidewalk, Skylar was still sitting in the back of the taxi, staring out the window at the impressive building.

From the look on her face, he understood exactly how hard this was for her. What'd happened to make her so wary? There must be something in her history to cause such anxiety.

Nash's thoughts traveled back to the night Dan Sanders had attacked her. Some of the things she'd said had caused him to wonder if she hadn't experienced something similar already. He remembered thinking that surely Skylar couldn't possibly be the victim of domestic violence. But now, looking at the naked fear on her face as she tried to force herself out of the car, he began to wonder.

Opening the door, he bent his knees and looked in. "Take my hand, if it helps," he said, stretching out his fingers.

She shook her head, as if trying to deny her own feelings. But then her crystal-blue eyes fixed on his face. "I should be able to do this on my own," she said, in a small voice.

"You are doing this on your own," he urged. "I'm just here to help you out of the car, that's all. Come on, let me do my chivalrous deed for the day." But he knew if she needed to use him as a crutch to get through the day, then he'd be a more than a willing volunteer.

Skylar drew in a deep breath, still glaring at his hand as if it might bite her. Hesitantly, she reached out and slipped her fingers into his.

"Thank you," she said.

She stepped out of the taxi, long legs elegant in her high heels, shoulders so straight, she looked regal. Her fingers dug into the back of his hand, she was hanging on so tight, like a drowning woman gasping for her last breath. But no one looking on would guess she was fighting internal demons merely to get out of the car. Would she even be able to take the stand, if she could barely walk through the door of the courthouse? They'd have to cross that bridge when they came to it, he decided.

Standing on the sidewalk, she craned her neck to stare up at the building towering above them. The Cairns Courthouse was of modern, concrete construction, with lots of glass windows, and wide, concrete pillars. She hadn't let go of his hand, and so he tugged her gently toward the main door. Her fingers were slim and cool inside his own. Juggling both of their bags on one arm, he coaxed her through the door, and into the cool interior.

CHAPTER FIVE

Skylar sank into the rear seat of the taxi. Lying her head against the backrest, she closed her eyes for a second and pinched the bridge of her nose. Thank God that was over. The whole day had been a blur. But one thing she did remember clearly was Nash. He'd stayed by her side for most of the day, when he wasn't giving evidence. He'd been her rock. She hadn't realized how bad her anxiety had become until she tried to step out of the taxi in front of the courthouse this morning. Her heart had been racing a million miles an hour; it felt as if the taxi was closing around her, like she was in a tin can being crushed by the weight of expectation.

"Bet you're glad that's over," Nash said in his convivial way, lips tweaking upward in that cute, crooked smile. Nash had changed back into his civilian clothes. "You did an amazing job, by the way. I'm sure your testimony will put that bastard away for a long time."

"Thank you. I couldn't have done it without you."

"Of course, you could." He raised one eyebrow.

She liked that he was so humble. That he didn't feel the need to rub her face in her failings. Unlike Craig. Toward the end of their relationship, Craig seemed to be hellbent on dragging her self-confidence down at every opportunity he got.

It'd taken all of Skylar's self-control to force herself to step up onto the witness stand this afternoon. But the lovely junior lawyer, Samantha, who'd helped to prepare her for the questions, was staring at her expectantly. Everyone was staring at her expectantly. Nash was there, sitting in the second row back. Wearing his smart dress uniform, he looked good enough to eat, the dark-blue of his jacket bringing out his cobalt eyes. He'd already given his testimony, and his gaze was urging her on, giving her the confidence that she could do this. The wife, Patty, was nowhere to be seen. But Samantha told her that was standard. She'd be watching the trial through closed-circuit TV, because she didn't want to face her husband. Skylar sympathized with the other woman. Dan Sanders was there, or course, giving her that know-it-all smirk. It was that smirk that finally got her feet moving. She'd taken one step, then two steps, and then she was sitting in the chair.

Once in the chair, Skylar concentrated on Camden, the lead prosecution lawyer, who asked her questions in a cool, unwavering voice, soothing away her fears. Soon, the rest of the court faded into the background. It was only her and Camden. Her reverie was broken slightly when the defense lawyer began to cross-examine her. But Samantha had warned her this guy would try to rattle her, try to discredit her testimony, make it seem like she didn't remember things properly. By that stage, all Skylar wanted was to make sure Dan Sanders didn't get away with any more of his bullshit. She used her rage against him—and her bottled-up rage against Craig—to fight away the waves of anxiety if they threatened to overwhelm her.

In the end, it was all over quicker than she expected, and the judge was asking her to step down. Perhaps it'd been the relief flooding her veins because she'd made it through the ordeal, that was the reason Dan Sanders' menacing remark had caught her so off guard.

"You're still a non-believer, I see," he'd said, in a low voice as she passed by the front bench to return to her seat. She'd turned to look at him, startled by his audacity. And his threat. "Just you remember what I said about making you pay for your lack of obedience." His dark eyes had glittered with intimidation, even as his lawyer tugged at his sleeve. She'd stumbled and almost fallen, just managing to save herself by grabbing the edge of the desk before she hit the ground. Nash stood up in his seat, but she waved for him to sit back down.

"The defendant will not speak to the witness," the judge had barked, but it was too late by then. Dan leaned back with a supreme smirk on his face, as if he hadn't a care in the world. A chill had run down Skylar's spine.

The memory of that moment sent a shiver down Skylar's spine, the rear taxi seat somehow suddenly feeling cold and confined. Perhaps it was the way her smile changed, from triumphant to worried, but Nash narrowed his eyes.

"What did Sanders say to you as you left the dock?" he asked, as if reading her mind.

Should she tell him? Would it matter? Make a difference to the outcome of the trial? Probably not. "He was just being a pig," Skylar said. "But why would we expect anything else from an ignorant man like that?"

Nash looked like he was about to say something more, when his gaze went out the window behind her and his eyes got bigger and bigger. "Whoa..." he said, staring, open-mouthed at the hotel as they pulled into the driveway. She and the rest of her family always stayed at The Shangri La when they came to Cairns. Owning a luxury eco-resort made them all more aware that you got what you paid for. And the Shangri-La was worth it. She never thought about the price, because she didn't need to. Overlooking the main marina, with a gorgeous view toward the Great Barrier Reef, there was no better place to stay in Cairns. But looking at Nash's face, she began to see things in a different light. Could he even afford a night in this five-star hotel? She very much doubted that any overnight subsidy he was getting from the police force would cover the cost of this hotel. But then again, he was the one who suggested they stayed at the same place. She shrugged and climbed out of the taxi.

A doorman came to collect the luggage. Walking through the automatic doors, into the cool lobby of the hotel, she felt most of her tension drain away. The composed Skylar was returning. She'd come to terms with her anxiety. If she could take the stand in front of Dan Sanders, all those jurors, the judge, and all the spectators, then checking into a hotel would be a breeze.

"Are you here together?" The receptionist asked in a saccharine voice.

"Yes," Nash answered, at the same time as she said, "No."

"We're not staying in the same room," Skylar qualified hurriedly. "But if you could give us rooms close by, that would be nice." She wasn't sure why she said that. This wasn't supposed to be a holiday spent flirting with the handsome policeman. Actually, she'd been more than a little surprised when Dale had announced yesterday that Nash would be joining her in the helicopter. Dale told her that when he'd found out the senior constable would be attending the court case as well, it was just naturally polite to offer him a lift and save him the long drive. And she guessed she agreed with him. But she was here to do one thing only, and that was to make sure that monster ended up in jail.

The girl behind reception flicked her long, dark hair over her shoulder with the barest hint of irritation. "Certainly, madam. I've got two ocean-view rooms right next to each other up on the third floor. Would that be okay?"

"Yes, thank you," she replied. Rooms right next to each other, she hadn't been expecting that. A tingle of unwanted awareness slid down her spine.

"Shall we have dinner together tonight?" Nash's casual question caught her off guard. "We don't have to eat in the restaurant, if you don't think you're up to it," he amended, when he caught her hesitation.

She'd been looking forward to a long soak in the tub, to help her unwind, and then perhaps some champagne and canapés on her balcony. Did she really want to have dinner with Nash?

Part of her *definitely* wanted to have dinner with Nash. The illogical, indulgent side of her. The side that, whenever he looked at her, sent heat licking through all her womanly parts that'd been sorely ignored over the past four years. The same part who'd almost agreed to date him when he'd asked her out at the ball. She'd been able to turn him down then. But now… Fraternization with the cute cop hadn't been part of the plan.

He stood, waiting patiently for her answer.

"Why don't you come to my room at around seven o'clock? I'll order in room service." Her answer surprised her. She could just as easily have said no. But they were both here now, and it'd be nice to share a few relaxing drinks and the amazing view with somebody, rather than spending her time alone. Again. As long as he didn't get the wrong idea, of course. She'd already turned him down once. Surely, he'd got the hint? Surely, he wasn't a sucker for punishment? And if he was, Skylar wouldn't have a problem rejecting him a second time. She had no place in her life for a man. She didn't need a man, or want a man. They only caused trouble and heartache.

"Great." A tiny flash of surprise flickered over his face, as if he'd been expecting her to turn him down. "I'm going to check out the pool, first. And perhaps take a look at the gym. See you tonight." He picked up his bag and followed the sign pointing toward the pool, leaving her to find the elevator and take it up to the third floor. As she turned inside the lift, she caught sight of Nash disappearing around the corner. He had a happy grin on his face, like he was looking forward to an adventure, and, for some stupid reason, it lifted her mood as well. She allowed her gaze to rove up over his backside, enjoying the sight of the black trousers hugging his buttocks and thighs. The white shirt seemed almost tailor-made, and she admired those lovely, broad shoulders, tapering down to masculine hips. For a second, Skylar wondered what he'd look like minus the shirt and pants. Perhaps she could nip down to the pool a little later to catch a glimpse of him swimming, bare chested and… She roped in her galloping imagination. *Not here to socialize*, she reminded herself. Why then, did she suddenly feel so hot?

* * *

Two hours later, right on the dot of seven, there was a knock at Skylar's door. Of course, he would be strictly punctual. She hurried to open the door, fighting the urge to readjust her black knit dress. It looked fine. Besides, it was all she had. She'd packed shorts and a T-shirt for the trip home in the helicopter tomorrow, and a pair of pyjamas, but that was the extent of her clothing. This wasn't a date, she reminded herself, for the tenth time.

Pausing for a second, her hand resting on the doorknob, she took a moment to compose herself. Then she swung the door open and there he was, still dressed in the same black pants and white shirt, she noted. Good, it meant he hadn't planned this, either.

"Evening," he drawled.

"Come in," she replied, gesturing for him to precede her into her hotel room. "How was your swim? Did you make it to the gym? I had a lovely long bath, and I feel much better now." She was rambling. He wouldn't want to hear about her sitting in her room all afternoon, but she couldn't seem to stop herself.

"The pool was fantastic, thanks. Too many people for my liking, however."

"Oh." Why had she suddenly seemed to run out of conversation?

"I hope you don't mind, but I brought a six-pack." He held up a collection of beer from a boutique brewery she'd never heard of.

"Great. That's perfect. I wasn't sure what you liked to drink." She hovered near the kitchenette, unsure whether to offer him a glass, or let him drink straight out of the bottle. Why was she being so dithery? Normally, she was completely in control, especially when it came to matters of food or drink.

He made the decision for her by cracking a bottle out of the packaging. "Would you like to join me?"

"Yes, please." She didn't drink a lot of alcohol, usually it was only to taste a wine to ensure it'd go with the meal she intended to cook. But in her younger days, back when she'd been an apprentice, she'd been known to enjoy a beer or two. She found the bottle opener, while Nash found a space in the small refrigerator to stash the rest of the beers.

"Cheers." Nash held up his bottle, and she touched the neck of her beer to his. "To a successful day in court. May the bastard rot in jail."

"Amen to that." Skylar actively pushed the look of intimidation in Dan's eyes as he'd glowered at her in court to the back of her mind. He was going to jail. End of story. She took a swig, enjoying the malty, bitter taste on her tongue. Nash did the same, then looked at her expectantly over the rim of the bottle. Now what were they going to do? She hadn't planned this night at all. Why had she agreed to this? She suddenly couldn't think of a single thing to say, and she took another swig of her beer to cover the awkward silence. He was standing so close. Too close. His presence was muddling her brain. There was no other explanation for it. She shuffled her feet and looked out the window. God, he must think she was a moron.

"Beautiful view." Nash walked out onto the balcony, and she gave a silent sigh of relief as he took his aura of maleness —there was no other word for it—outside with him.

Taking another fortifying swig of beer, she followed him, making sure to position herself at the other end of the balcony, as far away from his confusing charisma as she could get. He cocked an eyebrow in her direction, but then nonchalantly leaned his elbows against the railing. If he noticed the distance she'd put between them, he didn't say anything.

"Yes, it is," she agreed, mirroring his position by resting her own elbows against the wooden barrier. She'd left her feet bare, and the wooden floorboards were still warm beneath her toes. The marina nestled directly below them in the mouth of Chinaman's Creek. On the other side of the creek, a row of dark headlands marched into the distance. The sun had just dropped below the top of those forested hills, painting the clouds on the horizon with a gorgeous, subtle pink. It was something she didn't get to see often; the sun setting over the ocean. Of course, they got glorious sunsets at Stormcloud. But it was nice for a change of view sometimes.

"It makes me miss the sunsets we used to get when I lived in Brisbane," Nash said wistfully. "But that's all I miss about living in Brisbane," he added.

"So, you like being a cop in a small, inland town, then?" All she knew about Nash was that he'd arrived in Dimbulah over two years ago, to the great delight of the locals. The station had been unmanned for the previous three years, due to funding cuts. But an uptick in rural spending meant that instead of bulldozing the old building, they could once again have a police presence nearby. Skylar had heard through the grapevine, that Nash had been handpicked for the job, coming directly from Brisbane. But a lot of locals worried that he was a city boy and wouldn't understand how things worked out here.

She was suddenly abashed that she hadn't bothered to find out any more about him. This was her chance, she guessed.

"Yes, I do." He turned to face her, leaning his hip against the wood. "Believe it or not, that answer actually surprises me." He gave a wry grin, his sumptuous lips curling up at the corners. "Because when I was first offered the position, I saw it as a way to gain a promotion, and not much more. But now that I've lived there, and worked closely with the community, there's something really different about living in the country."

"Watch out, when the far north gets its claws into you, there's no going back." She was joking, but there was also an ounce of truth to her words. She'd heard it time and time again, where people stayed on, even after hardships and tough times. The Atherton Tablelands had a special kind of allure. She'd heard many of their guests wonder quietly at the beauty of the place, and then return over and over again, as if addicted to a certain type of natural drug.

"Yeah, I've heard that." He took another sip of his beer. "My contract is up in a few months. When I first signed on, I was going to use this as a steppingstone. I was determined I'd be going back to the city after two years. Maybe not Brisbane, but perhaps Melbourne, or maybe even Canberra. Perhaps request to join a specialty group, like homicide, something like that."

"But now?" Skylar was intrigued. "Are you thinking of staying?"

"I don't know." His gaze floated out over the marina, and she could see the confusion in his eyes. "It seems like there's a lot to keep me in Dimbulah. I'm making friends. Getting to know people. Putting down roots, or something stupid like that."

She didn't know how to reply to that, wasn't sure what he was inferring. They both watched a small yacht meander into the marina, perhaps returning after a sunset cruise in the bay.

Skylar wondered about Nash's statement. Surely, he couldn't be including her in that list of people, could he? Nash had asked her out on a date, and she'd turned him down. End of story.

She searched his eyes, wondering if her rejection had caused any lasting scars. Did he resent her? Feel awkward around her, knowing she'd spurned him? Did he perhaps harbor a secret hatred of all women and was privately plotting his revenge? No, that was stupid. It was only Craig who had those sick tendencies. She shouldn't keep comparing all men to Craig.

He looked up and smiled, that warm, lilting smile that made her feel all safe and gooey inside.

It didn't seem like he held any grudge against her. In fact… that look in his eyes seemed to hint at the exact opposite.

He upended his beer, and Skylar was surprised to see his bottle was empty, as was hers. That'd gone down way too easily.

"Can I get you another one?" he asked.

"Yes, please." She handed over her bottle, careful not to come in contact with his fingers as she did so. "I'll find the menu. I don't know about you, but I'm hungry, and the food is good here."

Skylar followed Nash inside and went around the bed to retrieve the room service menu, which she'd been perusing right before Nash arrived. She already had an idea of what she wanted to order, a selection of their delicious tapas; the chefs in this restaurant were well known for producing modern and exquisite food, and she'd been hoping to taste it for a while. She flicked on the bedside lamp so she could read the menu.

A hand landed on her shoulder, and instinctively she flinched and ducked, raising her palms to ward him off. The fight-or-flight instinct taking hold.

"Sorry," Nash apologized, stepping backward, a look of confusion clouding his face. "I just wanted to give you a beer."

It took a second for Skylar to work out that it wasn't Craig reaching for her. That Nash was a friend, and she'd reacted badly.

"It's not your fault. It's…nothing. Sorry," she mumbled.

Shit, now she'd done it.

CHAPTER SIX

Nash wasn't sure what to do or how to respond to her over-the-top reaction. He was holding two bottles by the neck in one hand, his other hand up in the air as if in surrender. "Are you sure you're okay?" he asked gently, because she obviously wasn't.

"Sorry," she apologized again.

That look of pure horror that'd passed over her face before she could mask it was still flashing behind her eyes. All he'd done was touch her shoulder. He'd noticed that she'd been overly careful to avoid coming in contact with him all day. The only exception she'd made was when she let him help her out of the taxi. But even then, she'd been the one to initiate the contact.

"It's just that… I don't like to be touched."

That was a major understatement. This woman was full of surprises. And not all good ones. There was definitely something going on here. He had half a mind to ask her what'd happened to make her so twitchy. The way she found it hard to leave Stormcloud, as if it was a sanctuary for her. Her anxiety around groups of people she didn't know, and her reticence to visit the city. And now she revealed that she hated to be touched. Everything was adding up to the fact that Skylar had suffered from some form of trauma.

But the look on her face, one of contrite mortification, stopped his questions before they left his mouth.

"All good. Now I know, I'll try to make sure we don't come into contact again." Did that sound a little spiteful? He hadn't meant it that way. "What were you going to order?" Time to get this conversation back on track. He handed her one of the beers and she passed him the menu. "The food looks good," he added.

Skylar took the bottle and sidled around the bed until she was standing in the doorway to the balcony. Putting space between them. Now, he had an inkling as to why she'd gone to the other end of the balcony when they'd first gone out to look at the sunset. She touched her wrist as she stared out toward the ocean. He was coming to recognize it was an unconscious habit whenever she was in a stressful situation. Why her wrist, though? Did it have something to do with her not liking to be touched?

He perused the menu as if nothing was amiss. "A crocodile burger, now that sounds interesting. What do you recommend?" He finally looked up and met her gaze. She'd stopped fidgeting with her wrist, and was now fidgeting with the label on the bottle instead, tugging at a loose corner with her fingernail.

"All the food here is good. I haven't had the crocodile burger, myself, but I dare say it's probably delicious." The shadow of shame still lingered behind her eyes, but he could see she was trying to hide it, trying to pretend nothing had happened. "I'm going to order a selection of tapas. They have some interesting choices, using different ingredients, and I've wanted to taste them for a while, to see if I can incorporate some ideas into my own cooking."

So, she had an ulterior motive for choosing this hotel. As he was beginning to find out, Skylar was all about work, and not much about pleasure. She was a strong woman who didn't like to be viewed as anything less. The image she projected, one of strict professionalism, especially when it came to her cooking, was what everyone always saw first. Perhaps some people also saw it as her being a little aloof; she certainly isolated herself away, even when she was at Stormcloud, using her need to be in the kitchen as an excuse not to mingle often.

Tonight, however, Nash had been given a glimpse into the real world behind Skylar's polished exterior. She wasn't as all-together as she made out. Some men might shy away from that. A woman with baggage and battling internal demons was something most men wouldn't put up with. But it made her all that more intriguing to him.

She was watching him over the rim of the bottle, blue eyes wary and shuttered. Leaning her hip against the doorway, she took another sip of beer. That same black dress she had on earlier hugged her body, showing her hips and breasts off in the soft light from the bedside lamp. Tonight, she'd allowed her long, blonde hair to fall loose over her shoulders, the flaxen locks contrasting against the black dress nicely. There were still hints of the makeup she'd applied this morning before she attended court. The dark eyeliner made her eyes smolder. Nash couldn't ever remember Skylar wearing makeup during her workday.

She was a damn fine-looking woman. Cool and classy. Sexy as hell. And God help him, he wanted to know more about her. Wanted to delve into the depths of the oceans where the true Skylar resided.

* * *

Nash's arms were so full of bags, he almost couldn't see where he was going. The tarmac shimmered with heat haze as he followed Skylar out to the waiting helicopter. It was late afternoon, and Skylar had spent the whole morning shopping, while Nash had returned to court to continue to watch over proceedings. Neither the prosecution, nor the defense, had required more information from Skylar, so she'd been free to pick up a few things she said she needed to take home.

Paul met them halfway across the tarmac, offering to take some of the bags from Skylar, who was also laden down with more baggage than she could manage.

Arms full, Paul dropped back to walk beside Nash. "What the hell have you got in here?" he murmured.

"I don't actually know," Nash confided. "I think she was stocking up on things the family wanted. You know, when you live remotely it's all the little luxuries that you miss. I think her brother, Dale, asked for a stash of Bounty Bars. Supposedly you can't buy them in the Dimbulah grocery store."

Paul snorted in reply, seemingly not impressed.

"Sorry, we're late," Nash added, hoping to placate the man. Paul was due out at Stormcloud to ferry another couple back to Cairns this afternoon, and with all of Skylar's shopping exploits, they were fifteen minutes late getting to the airport.

"Yeah, well, let's get a hurry on. I'm not even sure where this is all going to fit," Paul added darkly, and hurried toward his chopper.

Nash shuffled his armload higher and watched Skylar reorganize her own load of bags in front of him. His gaze drifted down to stare at her slim, toned legs. This morning, when she'd emerged from her hotel room, his jaw had nearly hit the ground. While he was wearing his long trousers and a second clean, white shirt, she'd come out in a pair of cut-offs that showed off her glorious legs to their full magnitude, and a tank top that barely covered her midriff. This wasn't the subdued, earnest Skylar he'd been expecting. She was dressed like one of the tourists who flocked to The Esplanade to shop and buy trinkets. And she looked sexy as hell. Nash had to put his wandering thoughts on a tight leash, before they took him down the path of wondering what it would feel like to run a palm down the whole length of those silken thighs.

"What's wrong?" she'd asked testily, when she'd noticed Nash staring.

"Nothing. Nothing at all," he'd replied, trying to regain his professional equilibrium. Which was going to be hard to do if she kept staring at him with her hands on her hips, baring a small strip of creamy skin above her waistband.

"I used to live in Cairns, remember? I wore this sort of thing every day."

She might well have worn that sort of attire once upon a time, but it was the first time Nash had seen in her in anything but jeans and a shirt, or the occasional classy dress like last night.

"Well, this look suits you. You should wear it more often," he replied. What else could he say? It was the truth, but he might regret his words, because if she did start wearing this down the main street of Dimbulah, he might find himself chasing off every male over the age of twelve. The idea stirred something dark low down in his gut. He didn't like the idea of other men drooling over her.

Skylar stumbled and nearly lost one of her packages, and Nash rushed to her side to lend a hand. He tried to banish all further thoughts of Skylar's long, elegant legs and firm ass rolling along in front of him. And he almost succeeded.

Ten minutes later, some of the shopping bags had been stashed in the small luggage compartment of the helicopter along with their overnight bags, and the rest were crammed on the spare seat, or around their legs on the floor.

Skylar said into her microphone, "I'm so sorry, Paul. I think I got a little carried away. Can you ever forgive me for stuffing your beautiful helicopter full of my brother's candy bars?" She gave the pilot a contrite smile, and touched his arm by way of apology.

Paul turned and winked at Skylar. "No probs. The tourists who fly in my chopper are much worse. You should see some of the luggage they try and squeeze in here. I have to remind them about the weight restrictions. You're lucky, if there were any more passengers today, you'd have to leave half this stuff behind." The annoyed frown left the pilot's face, but Nash wasn't surprised. Skylar was relaxed and happy this afternoon. The most relaxed he'd seen her for the past two days; the thought of going home was clearly putting her at ease. And what man wouldn't react when she smiled at them like that?

His thoughts flashed back to their dinner in the hotel room last night. After that brief glimpse of the true Skylar when she'd flinched away from his touch, she'd returned to the well-guarded Skylar he knew so well.

Well, almost.

Now he knew what to look for, he was starting to view her aloofness as more of an insecurity. And he could see between the cracks of her veneer, to the softer, more vulnerable layer beneath.

In an attempt to get the night back on track, Nash had phoned through their room service order, and then set up the little table and chairs outside on the balcony, so they could look at the view while they ate. When the food arrived, Skylar had fussed over the placement of all the plates on the table, and he'd covertly watched as she uncovered each of the meals with the same delight as a child unwrapping a present on Christmas morning. It was fascinating to see how she lit up as she revealed each of the tasty morsels.

The burger was mouth-watering, as she'd predicted. But he found more pleasure in watching her experience her food than he did in eating his own. Skylar would close her eyes and roll each mouthful around and around, chewing it thoughtfully, before finally swallowing. While her eyes were closed, he observed her face, and he could see the stress drain from her muscles as she concentrated on the flavors and textures of the food.

Her barriers had come down a little more as they chatted and drank another beer. At one stage, she even offered him a taste of food from her fork. He'd leaned in and they'd locked gazes, sharing a few intimate seconds, before he sat back, and the moment vanished. He felt as if he'd learned something important about her right then, but he couldn't put his finger on exactly what.

He'd enjoyed his time with her so much, he'd had to force himself to get out of his chair at the end of the night, each step toward the door a little harder to take. Even though he knew he was kidding himself; there was nothing between them. And never would be.

"All right, here we go." Paul's voice brought Nash back to the present. The whine of the rotors increased and then they were off the ground, lifting as light as a feather in the breeze. Nash decided that if he ever quit policing, he might like to become a helicopter pilot instead. What a life of freedom it'd be, with just the hint of danger to add some spice.

Nash was hoping the pilot might give them a quick trip out over the beach—he could see the strip of sand edging the ocean of blue off to their right—but no such luck. Paul must be in a hurry to collect his next passengers. The chopper zoomed into the air, heading directly inland, straight toward Stormcloud Station. They soon cleared the outskirts of Cairns, and houses and roads were replaced by never-ending lush jungle vegetation. Nash was happy to sit in companionable silence with Skylar as they both watched the ground speed past below them.

They'd been in the air for a little over five minutes when Paul made a noise of disgust.

"What's up?" Nash asked through the headphones.

"Some idiot who doesn't know what they're doing." Paul indicated out the side window to the left. "They're flying way too close."

Both Nash and Skylar craned their necks. Nash was sitting on the left and so had a better view. He was shocked to see another helicopter flying alongside. What the hell were they doing? Paul was right, they were extremely close. Paul talked into his comms, asking the aircraft to identify themselves.

"It must be a privately owned helicopter," Skylar said. She was right, the other helicopter had no markings to identify it, unlike Paul's, which had the aviation company logo splattered all over it. It was a smaller aircraft, a little two-seater. More of a flying glass bubble, than a proper chopper. Nash had seen something similar being used to round up cattle out on the stations. He could make out the features of the two men inside clearly now. What were they up to?

Paul was still calmly speaking into his microphone, warning the helicopter to move away.

But the chopper came closer still. It was flying parallel, keeping pace.

"Are they going to crash into us?" Skylar suddenly asked.

Nash was still staring at the two men and so he saw the exact moment when the one in the passenger seat slid open a small side window and raised a gun to point directly at them. Nash recognized a semi-automatic rifle when he saw one. It was the sort of weapon a sniper might use for long range as well as precision, but these guns were illegal in Australia. Which only meant one thing.

"Get down," he yelled. "They have a gun." He threw himself on top of Skylar, covering her body with his own.

"What?" Paul didn't seem to comprehend Nash's words.

Then the glass shattered right where Nash's head had been a split second ago. Skylar screamed and struggled beneath him.

"They're shooting at us," he yelled again. "Get us out of here."

Fuck, he needed his gun. But it was inside the special lockbox, in his overnight bag, which was tucked away in the luggage compartment. There was no way to reach it from here.

Another slug slammed into the side of the large windshield, barely missing Paul's head. Nash felt, rather than saw, the chopper nosedive to the right, away from the men with the gun, taking evasive action. At least Paul had finally got the message.

"Mayday! Mayday, this is Victor-Hotel-Yankee-Whiskey," Paul shouted into his headset. "Someone is shooting at us. I repeat, someone is shooting at us. Mayday. Mayday."

Skylar squirmed underneath Nash, but there was no way he was letting her up. "Stay down," he growled. His instinct was to get as low as possible. Should they unstrap themselves and lay on the floor? But what if the chopper was damaged, and they had to make a forced landing? Or worse; what if they crashed? They'd fare better if they remained strapped in.

He needed to call this in, get them some help. With one hand holding onto Skylar, he fumbled his phone out of his back pocket and dialed 0-0-0.

"What is your emergency?" a voice on the other end of the phone said.

As Nash put the phone to his ear, more bullets rang out, but this time, they pinged off the fuselage above them, instead of crashing through the windows. It seemed the men had a change of plan. Instead of firing to kill the pilot, they were aiming at the rotor.

These guys meant business. Nash counted at least five

more bullets hit the helicopter. Who the hell were they, and what did they want?

"Fuck, fuck, fuck," Paul swore. "What the hell…?"

Nash felt the chopper shudder, and then it dropped, bucking like a bronco as Paul fought to control it. Nash's phone tumbled from his hand. Skylar squealed from somewhere under his chest. The rotor blades whined and began to make a clunking noise that sounded a hell of a lot like a death rattle.

Nash peeked from beneath his elbow. His phone was on the floor, a disembodied voice still asking about his emergency, but he couldn't reach it. Shit. Nash tried yelling instructions at his phone, but he had no way of knowing if the dispatcher could hear him.

Paul was struggling mightily with the controls. He gripped the stick with both hands and was hauling back on it, while desperately punching buttons on the dashboard. Whatever Paul was doing wasn't stopping their downward trajectory, and they hurtled toward the ground.

"Brace, brace, brace," Paul called, never taking his eyes off the trees below. "We're going in for a heavy landing."

More like a crash landing. Nash clung even tighter to Skylar, who'd stopped struggling beneath him.

"I'm aiming for that clearing down there," Paul yelled.

Nash glanced quickly at the ground, then decided that was a bad idea, it made him sick to his stomach to see everything lurching sideways. But he needed to know what Paul was saying, any small piece of information might help them come out of this alive. His police training kicked in, and he forced himself to continue searching the oncoming terrain, even though his stomach threatened to empty its contents all over the floor.

Paul seemed to have managed to stop the helicopter's headlong dash toward the ground, and while they were still dropping lower, the trees were skimming beneath the skids, rather than coming straight at them. Nash twisted his neck, scanning the surrounding skies. He caught a glimpse of the other helicopter flying well above them, watching and waiting.

"Mayday, Mayday, this is Victor-Hotel-Yankee-Whiskey. We are in a forced landing. Coming down over Lamb Range. Mayday, Mayday, I repeat, coming down hard, fifty kilometers west of Cairns." Paul's voice was loud, but calm, now, as if all his energy was being poured into one emotion. Intense concentration. He wanted to get this helicopter down in one piece.

"I see it," Nash said. "The clearing, I can see it up ahead." There was a granite knoll, devoid of trees, lying along a ridgeback of low hills.

But then, the helicopter began to spiral, slowly at first, then increasing in speed, like a macabre carnival ride.

Paul wrestled valiantly with the controls, his feet working the pedals up and down. Their mid-air spin slowed, and eventually stopped.

They were skating along the tops of the trees now, the clearing still a few hundred meters ahead. The skids broke through the branches of a tall tree, leaves and branches flying everywhere.

"Come on, baby, just a few more feet," Paul said, his voice low and urgent. The clearing was maybe one hundred meters away now. The belly of the helicopter scraped along the crowns of even more trees. Shit, if they got snagged in a branch, they'd never make it to the clearing, the helicopter would be dragged down into the foliage, perhaps even turned upside down.

All of a sudden, the vegetation disappeared. They were over the clearing. It was now or never.

"Land it, land it," Nash screamed. The trees on the other

side of the clearing careened toward them. Paul needed to cut some of their forward speed.

"I'm trying."

A skid touched down onto rock and then bounced up. But it was too late, they were running out of room, their forward momentum still too fast. The trees on the other side of the clearing raced toward them, and the small helicopter buried itself into the dark rainforest, smashing a path through the underbrush. Nash clung to Skylar and prayed.

CHATPER SEVEN

Skylar groaned. What was that heavy weight on top of her? She pushed, but the weight was unyielding. She was cramped in a fetal position, lying at an obscure angle, head downward. Something was wrapped painfully across her abdomen, biting into her shoulders and chest.

It felt like an impossible task, but she finally opened her eyes. Where was she?

Then, in an instant, it all came flooding back. Their helicopter had crashed.

No, wait. Their helicopter had been shot down. Who would do such a thing? And why? She took in what was left of the chopper. What she could see of it, anyway, from beneath this heavy thing lying on top of her, blocking her view. It wasn't good. It was like she was in some massive beer can that'd been stomped on by a giant foot.

But she hadn't been in the chopper alone.

Nash. Was Nash okay?

Finally, her brain began firing on all cylinders, and she worked out that he was the weight confining her to the seat. A dead weight. Oh, shit. Was he dead? She couldn't see his face because she was trapped beneath his chest.

"Nash," she called, reaching a hand up until she found his

head, slumped against the seat above her. She patted his face. "Nash," she called again. "Wake up."

There was no answer.

"Please, wake up." This time, her plea was more of a sob.

There was a soft groan from above, and she patted his cheek harder, almost a slap.

"Hey," he accused groggily. "Stop that."

Then abruptly, his weight lifted as he sat up, and she gasped in relief.

"Fuck. Are you okay?" Big hands cradled her face, turning it so he could look at her.

"I don't know," she answered truthfully. "What about you?"

"I'm not sure, either," he admitted.

"Your face," she said, her gaze roaming over his features, cataloging the many small cuts and abrasions covering his face and the large gash running down his cheek, dripping blood onto the floor. "Oh, shit."

He reached up a hand and tentatively dabbed at the blood. "Is it bad?"

"That's the worst one," she said, "But I think it looks worse than it really is. The rest are small, like you've been hit by tiny bits of flying glass." Which he probably had been.

"What about me?" She could feel a burning sensation on her forehead.

"There's a large bruise on the top of your head, but that's about it."

"At least we're both alive."

"Yes, Paul did an amazing job, getting us down in one piece," he replied.

Even though that wasn't really the truth. Now that she was sitting, she could see the helicopter was practically destroyed. The only part that remained fully intact was the compartment they were sitting in. The chopper had been ripped in two, and

Skylar could see that the front of the aircraft was settled five meters away, a gaping hole separating them, the wreckage was filled with broken branches and dirt gouged out of the forest. If she leaned forward, Skylar could make out the edge of the tree line about fifty meters back, up a slight incline. The chopper had plowed a path through the underbrush, breaking into smaller pieces as it went.

They'd finally come to rest against the trunk of a large fig tree. Paul's section was farther down the hill, his headlong rush stopped by a jumble of limestone boulders.

"Paul. We need to check on Paul." She struggled with her harness, but couldn't get it undone.

"I'm on it," Nash said. "You stay here." He grappled with his own harness and shrugged his way out of it.

Not likely. She wasn't about to stay in this wreck for a second longer than she had to. Nash didn't get to tell her what to do. At last, she shrugged out of her harness, wincing as pain sliced through her chest and shoulders where the webbing had cut into her. But she'd rather have bruising from the harness than the alternative, because it'd probably helped save her life.

Nash got to his feet, careful to stay low to avoid the smashed-in roof. "Ow." His loud exclamation made her turn her head sharply.

"What?" She followed his gaze down to see a piece of metal protruding out of his thigh.

"Oh, shit." Her head began to spin. She wasn't good with gory stuff.

"That's not good," Nash said, glaring at the offending object.

"What should we do?" she asked faintly. Her mother had made sure all of them working at Stormcloud were efficient when it came to first aid. It was a must when you were dealing with guests in an isolated landscape. Help was often a long way away. But all that first aid training completely deserted her at the sight of that object sticking out of Nash's thigh muscle.

Nash sat back down and tore the fabric of his pants away from the wound, examining it closely. She had to grit her teeth and look away before she threw up.

"It's not bleeding too bad; it doesn't look like it's hit an artery." His voice was clinical, as if he were scrutinizing a picture in a book, rather than his own flesh and blood.

Then she remembered he was a police officer. Of course, he'd know what to do.

It seemed that Nash had come out of the crash worse off than she had. He'd been using himself as a human shield, and it'd worked. But now he was injured.

"I'm going to pull it out," he said suddenly.

"Wait." She held up a hand. "Shouldn't you just leave it?" She couldn't believe he would do such a thing. "People will be here to rescue us, soon." Someone back at Cairns airport must have heard Paul's Mayday call. Surely, they'd be scrambling to get search and rescue in the air.

Nash shot her an unreadable glance, and began to shake his head. Then, as if someone had heard her thoughts, the sound of a helicopter hovering overhead made them look up.

Was that someone come to rescue them already? That was damn quick.

"See, I told you," she said, patting his knee. "You wait here. I'll go outside and see if I can attract their attention."

"No." Nash's harsh command as well as his hand on her arm stopped her from rising from the seat. The sound of the chopper got louder, and the branches above them began to rattle in the downdraft from the rotor. It was close. Possibly hovering dead overhead.

"What? Why not? I'm quite capable of waving down a helicopter," she snapped.

"I don't think it's a rescue chopper." He almost had to yell over the sound of the aircraft above them.

Then it dawned on her. This might be the men who'd shot them out of the sky. Come to see if anyone had survived; come to finish the job.

"Stay really still. Don't move a muscle," he commended.

She could see flashes of silver through the holes in the fuselage above, as the chopper circled them. How much was visible from the air? From down here, it felt like they were buried beneath the canopy. The chopper had careened a fair way into the forest before it finally came to a halt. Leaves dangled in through the holes, branches, and twigs from broken vegetation, making it hard to see what was going on above.

The chopper hovered for what felt like hours over the top of the crash site, while she and Nash cowered inside, not daring to move, hardly daring to breathe. Skylar covered her face to stop the debris flying around getting in her eyes. What if they landed? What if they decided to come looking for them, to make sure the job was really done? They wouldn't stand a chance against the man and his rifle. They'd be sitting ducks. Skylar came up with a million and one different scenarios, escape routes. Then she remembered that Nash had a piece of metal sticking out of his leg.

But, unbelievably, the sound of the chopper finally receded, leaving a deathly silence in its wake. The leaves and dust settled, and the metal of the wrecked aircraft stopped shaking around them.

"Why did they leave?" Skylar asked when they could finally hear to talk.

"I don't know." Nash shrugged. "Maybe, they were just looking for signs of life. Maybe they decided no one could have survived this. It might look even worse from above."

"Or maybe, they'll be back with reinforcements," Skylar

added darkly.

He lifted his head to stare at her, not hiding his unease. Oh, shit, that might in fact be a distinct possibility. His face was pale as he tried, but failed, to hide the grimace of pain.

"We should get moving, then." She certainly didn't want to be a sitting duck if they did come back. But a more likely scenario was that they also needed to be ready for when search and rescue found them. They needed to get back to the clearing so they could signal for help.

"I'm going to check on Paul, first." Nash half-stood, and then winced, grabbing for a loose wire hanging from the ceiling to steady himself.

She glared at him. He still had a piece of metal poking out of his leg. He was in no fit state to climb through the twisted wreck.

"You stay here. I'll do it." She pushed him back down onto the seat.

He began to argue with her. "I'm the cop. I have a duty to see that you and Paul are kept safe. It's my jo—"

"Oh, shush. I'm not injured, and I'm the better choice. You see if you can find a first aid kit or something we can use to bandage your leg, while I'm gone. I won't be long."

He stared at her for so long she was sure he was going to ignore her and jump out of the helicopter, wounded leg, and all. But he finally said, "Are you sure?"

No, she wasn't sure, but this was a life-and-death situation, and she wasn't going to be one of those women who went all to pieces when things got bad. Daniella had brought her up to be strong and resourceful. If she couldn't bring those traits into play now, when would she ever be able to?

"I'll be back with Paul in tow soon, and then we can all get out of here," she replied.

"Be careful," he warned as she moved to the front of the wreckage.

It was harder than she expected to get out of the cocoon of metal. The ripped fuselage was sharp, and it was covered in trailing wires as well as broken plastic from the interior. She finally found a hole large enough to crawl through—scraping her bare knee on the way—and lowered herself gingerly onto the ground. The front half of the chopper was five or six meters away, and she craned her neck to see if she could locate Paul amongst the debris. She could make out the rear of the two front seats. They seemed to have been pushed forward, into what was left of the front windshield. As she scrambled through the broken underbrush, climbing over smashed branches, and skirting around large pieces of metal, she discovered that perhaps it was the other way around, and the windshield had been forced onto the seats. When she finally got close enough, she edged around to the side where Paul had been sitting.

Skylar covered her mouth with her hand, and her stomach roiled dangerously.

Oh, no!

A large boulder had caved in the whole front of the chopper and was now sitting where the controls had once been, the windshield shattered into millions of shards of glass. Paul's chair was wedged up against limestone.

She didn't want to look.

But she had to.

"Paul," she called out tentatively, even though she knew he wasn't going to answer. As she edged around farther, she could see a leg and a foot protruding from the side of the seat. Blood trickled down, running over the mangled floor and pooling in a bright-red puddle in the dirt below.

Skylar gagged again. *No, no, no.* She couldn't look.

But she had to do this. She had to make sure. For Paul's sake.

Closing her eyes for a second, she steeled herself and then

crept a few more feet around the side until she could look into Paul's chair.

She gasped and drew back in horror. Then promptly threw up, retching over and over again into the uncaring greenery. There was hardly anything left of Paul, besides a mangled mess of crushed bones and flesh.

She'd never seen anything like it before. And hoped to never see anything like it again.

Despair overtook her, and she sank down onto the ground, her legs unable to hold her weight any longer. Paul was dead. Had died a horrible death. Because some strangers had shot him out of the sky. For what reason?

Now, bugs were beginning to swarm, attracted by the warm, sticky pool of blood forming beneath the chopper. Their annoying buzzing was enough to finally drive her to her feet.

She and Nash were still alive, she needed to remember that. She had to get back to him. There was no way she was going to search the front of the cockpit for a first aid kit, she couldn't bear to go any closer to Paul's body. Instead, she struggled back up the hill, but instead of returning to the where Nash sat waiting inside, she worked her way through the encroaching vegetation to see if she could locate the luggage compartment, situated behind their seats. But when she got around the back, she was surprised to see the whole tail section missing, sheared off by the force of the crash. Her gaze followed the trail of destruction back toward the edge of the clearing, and there it was, bent and twisted almost beyond recognition, around twenty meters away, with their luggage strewn all over the ground in between.

A white T-shirt dangled from a branch a few feet away. She reached for it almost on instinct. Did it belong to Nash? Or Paul? She had no idea, but it might make a good bandage. A blue backpack lay on the ground a little farther up the hill. It might've belonged to Paul, there was a book and a pair of shorts still left inside. She slung that over her shoulder and went to retrieve a ripped, dark-blue shirt from the ground a few feet away. Part of Nash's police uniform.

Wait. She suddenly remembered her phone. How stupid of her. She'd heard Nash try and call in the emergency while they'd been in the air, but then he must've lost his phone in the crash. And Paul had issued a Mayday call. But she should call emergency and let people know where she was. Quickly, she dragged it out of her back pocket and held it in front of her face. A large crack split the screen, but it still lit up when she pushed the button. No reception. Shit. There might be reception higher up the hill. Holding it aloft, she walked forward, keeping her eyes on the little bars that'd tell her she had reception. Still nothing. She twirled around on the spot, hoping, praying for one bar that would connect her to the outside world. Her foot caught on a trailing vine as she spun around. Because she was still looking upward, she stumbled, off balance. She grabbed a small shrub beside her, but it didn't save her downward plunge, and she landed heavily on her backside, knocking the air out of her lungs. Instinct made her put her palms out to save her from tumbling over backward completely. Her phone was knocked from her hand, landing facedown on an outcrop of limestone a few feet away.

"Oh, no. Please, no," she said softly. But when she scrambled to her feet and picked up the phone, her worst fears were realized. It was smashed. No longer working. What had she done?

"Skylar, are you there?" Nash's worried voice filtered through the underbrush. She tucked the useless phone into her pocket once more.

Hanging her head, she returned with her meagre provisions back to their broken chopper, clambering through the same hole she'd left by.

Nash stretched out a hand to help her in. "Paul?" he asked. But the hopeful light in his eyes died as her face crumpled.

"It was horrible, Nash. I can't even begin to describe it."

"I'm so sorry. I shouldn't have let you go. I should've been the one to find him. It's my job." He dragged her down to sit next to him, cradling her in his arms and soothing her like a lost kitten. She made sure not to look directly at his wounded leg, not wanting to start retching again. Her body began to shake, a reaction to what she'd just seen set in. But her eyes remained dry. There would be time to cry for Paul later. First, they had to survive.

She sat up. "I broke my phone," she said. "Where's yours? Did you find it yet?" she asked. "We need to phone the police. Get someone up here to—"

Why was Nash shaking his head?

"I've searched through the debris, but it could be anywhere. I'm sorry."

"So, neither of us has a working phone?" Skylar felt the weight of disappointment settle over her. "Great. Just great."

"Did you find a first aid kit?" Nash asked hopefully.

"No sorry, but I found some stuff we can probably use as bandages." She held up her meagre finds to show him.

"My shirt," Nash said, looking up, an eager gleam in his eyes. "Did you find my bag, then?"

"No, sorry, everything is scattered around everywhere. It's like a bomb went off in the luggage compartment."

"Oh. Shit." His face fell. "My gun was in a lockbox in my bag. I need to find it."

"We can have another look once we get your leg sorted," she replied.

"I gathered a few things together, while you were away," Nash said quickly. Skylar looked down to see a pile of stuff at his feet. It must've come from the scattered shopping bags full of her haul from Cairns this morning. Three large, plastic bottles of water, two packets of chicken chips—they'd been for Bindi, she loved the savory snacks—a bottle of Jack Daniels whiskey, that'd been for Alek, a new boning knife she'd bought for herself because her other was too small, along with a set of bamboo serving spoons she'd liked the look of, and roughly ten of Dale's Bounty Bars. That made her smile, thinking of her brother. But the smile quickly faded when the thought of never seeing him again flashed thorough her mind.

"The whiskey is to clean the wound," Nash said.

"What?" She hadn't been concentrating.

"I'm going to pull the metal out, and we'll need to disinfect it," he reiterated calmly.

How could he be so calm about something like that? "Are you sure?" She still thought that perhaps they should wait. She'd heard of people who'd died from massive blood loss once a penetrating object was removed, because the object had been blocking a severed artery.

"Yes, I am." Without any further warning, Nash grasped the twisted metal and pulled, letting out a shout of pain at the same time.

"Oh, Jesus," she cried. "You really did it."

They both gaped at his thigh, where a slow trickle of blood seeped from the wound through the hole in his pants. But there was no gushing geyser, as she'd feared. Skylar covered her mouth at the sight. Oh, lord, she might be about to faint.

"Fuck, that hurt," he ground out between gritted teeth. "Better to do it quick."

Averting her gaze from the wound, Skylar scrabbled around to find the white T-shirt she'd dragged off the branch and folded it into the semblance of a pad. "Here, put this over the wound, and put pressure on it." She waved it at him from a distance, not wanting to touch his leg.

He shook his head, teeth locked tightly together in a grimace. "Disinfect it first."

That was probably a good idea. She unscrewed the whiskey and, without thinking, tipped half the bottle over his leg. He sucked in a breath and clamped his lips tightly shut.

"Sorry. Better to do it quick," she parroted his words.

"Mmm," he grunted, as if not trusting himself to speak. He took the T-shirt and placed the makeshift pad over the wound, putting pressure on it. At least the blood was mostly covered up now.

Skylar began ripping Nash's uniform into ribbons. She could use the strips to tie around his leg. But when she went to tie the first one, she found his trousers got in the way.

"Do you mind if I tear the bottom off these?" she asked. "It'll make it easier to access your wound."

"Sure, do whatever you need to do," he replied through gritted teeth.

Skylar looked around. She needed a pair of scissors, or a… knife. Like the one in Nash's pile of goodies.

"Stay still," she warned. Boning knives were long and thin and very, very sharp. The last thing they needed was for her to slip and slash his calf open, as well. With a couple of expert flicks of her wrist, she turned his long pants into a pair of shorts, exposing Nash's lower leg up to the knee.

Skylar stilled as she caught sight of his calf. The lower part of his leg was covered with scars. Burn scars, if she wasn't mistaken. The same types of scars that rippled over his upper arms.

"I've got them on both legs," he said quietly.

"I'm sorry, I didn't mean to stare." But some things were starting to make sense. She'd often wondered vaguely why he insisted on wearing long pants, when he would've been much more comfortable wearing shorts in North Queensland's famous humidity. Now, she had her answer.

The hole Nash had ripped, when he first exposed the wound, gaped open, the two edges flapping down to drape over the sides of his thigh. Now she had complete access to his injury. She decided she could also use the sections she cut off his slacks as extra bandages, if need be.

"You may as well make them even, while you're at it," Nash commented. "It's as hot as Hades in here, and I'd rather be cool than make a fashion statement."

Skylar hacked at his other pants leg, and soon, Nash was wearing a pair of raggedy shorts. She tried not to stare this time as she exposed his other leg. But it was hard not to see the raised edges of the scars, the texture of the skin slightly lighter in color, and then completely smooth in some places. Skylar had never been up close and personal to a burn injury before.

"They don't hurt," he said, as if reading her mind. "I got them years ago, in a car crash, before I became a policeman." Something dark flittered through his eyes, an emotion Skylar couldn't decipher. There was a story there, and maybe one day he would tell her. But not today.

Skylar busied herself tying strips of cloth around Nash's thigh. He watched her without comment, blue eyes cool and unreadable.

Just as she finished tying off the last strip, a low rumble sounded in the air above. They both stopped and listened.

"Is that...?" She could hardly bring herself to say the words. "Could that be a rescue helicopter, come to look for us?" She stood up so quickly she nearly banged her head on the broken fuselage above. "Quick, we need to get up to the clearing, to make sure they see us."

"It might be." Nash's wary tone stalled her enthusiasm. "I'm sure they're looking for us by now. But we need to be careful, just in case." Nash began shoving all the goodies he'd gathered into the pile, into the blue backpack Skylar had found outside, including the boning knife, which he wrapped in a strip of fabric.

"What are you doing?"

"Preparing for any occurrence," he replied.

What did that even mean? She had no time to argue. "Come on," she urged impatiently. "We don't want them to fly right past us."

Nash got to his feet, slung the backpack over his shoulders, and hobbled to the gap that Skylar had used earlier. She wanted to rush ahead of him, run up to the clearing and wave her arms in the air. The sound of the helicopter was getting closer. Rescue. She wanted to be rescued. She didn't want to have to spend even one night out here. Not with the image of Paul's body haunting her. But Nash was injured, and she couldn't leave him. He lowered himself through the hole.

"How is it?" she asked, once they were both out of the ruined chopper.

Nash tested his leg, taking a few steps. "I can walk," he said. "It hurts like hell, but I can walk."

"Good. That's good," she said impatiently. They both looked up at the sound of the helicopter buzzing overhead. She caught flashes of it high above, through the waving branches. It was late afternoon; the sun would set in less than half an hour. If she didn't signal them now, they might lose the opportunity to be rescued.

She glanced behind, watching Nash's slow progress up the incline. He would make it, but they might miss the chopper. What if she offered to help him? Even if she did, it'd be slow going. It was too much to bear. "I'll see you up there," she said and took off, running where the terrain allowed, pushing aside large branches, with long grasses and small shrubs scratching at her bare legs.

"Skylar, wait. We need to be careful..." The rest of his

words became indistinct as she drew away from him, replaced by the sound of her crashing through the undergrowth,

She broke through the edge of the tree line in time to see the tail of helicopter disappear over the ridge. Too late. She was too late.

Despair settled over her and she sat down heavily on the rough, limestone rocks, head in her hands. This day had started off with such promise. Her trip had been a success; it looked like Dan Sanders would be sent to jail for a long time. She'd overcome her anxiety about being in town long enough to get a whole heap of shopping done. And she was so looking forward to gifting everyone with their presents when she got back to the lodge. But then some asshole had shot them out of the sky. What was going on with that? Now Paul was dead, and the day was going from bad to worse. If they had to spend the night out here…

"Skylar, are you okay?" She looked up to see Nash's concerned face peering from out from the scar of broken vegetation where the chopper had veered down the slope. He was panting hard, as if he'd run up the last section, to try and keep up with her.

Now she felt bad for making him run.

There was a sound, and Skylar looked up just as a sleek, black helicopter popped up over the top of the ridge.

They'd come back. They were going to be rescued, after all.

Skylar stood and waved her arms frantically in the air.

Nash called to her, "Skylar, wait, it's not a rescue—"

Gunfire erupted all around her, the sound deafening. Sharp pieces of rock flew in all directions as the bullets struck the limestone nearby, and Skylar ran for her life.

CHAPTER EIGHT

Nash watched in horror as bullets from the semiautomatic rained down from the helicopter. He could do nothing to help Skylar, he was too far away, all he could do was pray that she made it to the safety beneath the tree canopy.

If only he had his gun, he might be able to return fire, draw the attention of the attackers away.

She was almost to him now, ducking and weaving, blonde hair flying out behind her, beautiful mouth drawn back in a rictus of fear.

A cry of pain left her lips, and she clutched at her shoulder, but kept running. Good girl, only a few more steps. And she was underneath the tree canopy. He grabbed her hand and dragged her deeper into the underbrush, ignoring the pain lancing through his leg. The hail of ammunition followed them, but without a clear objective, the bullets went wide of the mark. He made her keep running, pushing her in front of him, down the hill and away from the crash site. Their progress was slow, more because of his leg than he'd like to admit, but once they were well into the forest, Nash found a fallen tree and they hunkered down behind it to catch their breath.

It was no use telling Skylar that she should've listened to

him; that it was her fault they were now being targeted. The damage was done, and all they could do was hope the criminals didn't take it into their heads to land the helicopter and come after them. He was thankful for his premonition that'd warned him to bring the backpack. If they needed to go on the run, at least they had a little food and water.

"Oh, God, Nash, I'm sorry—" He put his hand over her mouth and shook his head. They needed to listen. There'd be time for apologies later. Her eyes said that she understood. One hand was still holding onto her shoulder. Had she been shot? He needed to know that she wasn't going to bleed to death, so without speaking, he motioned for her to turn around, gently pulling down her tank top, and then he sighed with relief. It was only a graze. A bullet must've clipped her, or perhaps a flying shard of rock. Either way, it wasn't bad. He took her hand and squeezed it, letting her know without words that she'd be okay.

He could still hear the chopper circling above, perhaps trying to spot them through the trees. If they stayed still, maybe the criminals would leave again. They had to be taking a risk flying around like this, because the air would be full of rescue aircraft soon enough. They wouldn't want to take the chance of drawing too much attention to themselves. Why had they come back? Nash pondered the question but could come up with no real answer. Perhaps they'd had to leave to avoid attracting the attention of a nearby rescue aircraft. Perhaps they'd been ordered back by whoever was running the outfit to make one-hundred-percent sure the targets were dead. Who knew?

The sound of the rotor blades changed slightly, and hope sparked through Nash. They were leaving.

But no, the tops of the trees began to shake in the down-draught, and as Nash peered up through the trees, he could make out the black shape of the helicopter touching down on the bare rock face in the clearing above. Then a figure slipped out of the aircraft, running fast and low toward the tree line.

"Fuck. We need to get out of here," he said in a low voice.

She didn't argue, but got to her feet, tugging him up by his hand. Which way should they go? He had no idea where they were, or any notion of what this country was like. Right before they'd crashed, Paul had said they were flying over Lamb Range. They did seem to be at the top of some sort of ridgeline. Should they head downhill? That seemed to be the most logical path. Most people would flee directly away from the danger. But the last thing they should be was predictable. So, instead, he led Skylar on a bearing running parallel with the tree line above. Away from the crash site, but around the mountainside instead of down it.

They walked in silence, only the sound of their labored breathing to keep them company. Nash fought the urge to run. His leg wasn't up to it, and a slow, steady pace would also allow them to hear if anyone was following.

This whole thing was one big clusterfuck. He wanted his gun, and he wanted his leg to be free of injury.

The light was fading fast. What were they going to do when it got dark? They couldn't blunder around in the bush all night; it'd be madness. Especially with a gunman on their tail. The rescue search would be called off until first light, which would leave them to fend for themselves. He could no longer hear the black helicopter, which probably meant they'd walked farther than he thought. Or the chopper had gone, leaving the lone gunman to track them on foot.

"Where are we going?" Skylar whispered from behind.

"I don't really know," he admitted in a similarly hushed voice.

"Well, we can't keep walking around here all night."

"I realize that. But until we know whether that gunman is following us or not, my gut tells me we need to keep moving." A line of shrubs reared up in front of them, and he had to force his way through. The thick branches resisted, almost pushing him backward. Anger at his impotence with the whole situation boiled over and he threw his whole body weight against the hedge-like shrubbery in frustration, until they gave way with a loud crack.

"Nash, wait…" Skylar grabbed for the back of his shirt, but she was too late. He tried to steady himself, but his injured leg wouldn't take his weight, and he found himself sliding down a steep slope, covered in small gravel that acted like a bed of marbles. The drop was around twenty feet, and he landed heavily on his backside, jarring his wounded thigh. He let out a grunt of pain. What an idiot. He shouldn't have let his temper get the better of him.

He could hear Skylar calling his name from up above. She needed to be quiet; they couldn't afford to attract any attention. He was about to risk calling up to her, when he heard a scrabbling noise as Skylar descended, taking more care than he had, managing to stay on her feet, using her hands to steady herself when needed. She landed next to him; her face streaked with dirt and worry emanating from every pore.

"Oh, shit, are you hurt?"

"You mean, apart from my ego?" he asked with a grunt. "A few scratches maybe, but otherwise I'm fine." He examined his hands, which had copped the worst of it, as he'd tried to slow his downward slide. They were dirty and scuffed, but didn't seem to be too bad. He checked to make sure the backpack was over his shoulders.

Nash lifted his head to survey their surroundings. They were in some sort of narrow ravine. Perhaps a dry creek bed. The sides rose to around double his height, getting steeper, until they were almost a mini cliff as the ravine ran down the hill. He'd been lucky not to push through the shrubs farther downhill, the fall might have broken a bone or two.

The sound of a distant aircraft had them both craning their necks up.

"Is that…?" Skylar didn't finish her sentence, because they heard another helicopter lifting off from their hillside above. That must be the guys with the semiautomatic. Perhaps search and rescue had come close enough to scare them off. It was a catch twenty-two. They needed to get back to the top of the ridge to wave down a chopper. But they dare not be spotted by the wrong one. Nash glimpsed the black chopper skimming over the treetops above them, navigation lights glinting in the encroaching darkness.

But Skylar's eyes lit up as she watched the helicopter fly away. "Shall we head back to the clearing? They're gone. Now's our chance to try and signal."

"No." Nash shook his head. How did he put this, so he didn't scare her? Her beautiful eyes widened at his refusal and in the end, there was no other way to say it. "What if the pilot took off and left the gunman behind? What if he's lying in wait for us? Luring us into a trap?"

Skylar's cheeks turned pale. "Do you really think they'd do that?"

"They seemed pretty keen to see us dead," he replied flatly. "Not only did they try to shoot down a helicopter containing a Queensland police officer, but for them to take the risk of coming back to the crash site…" That took some balls. And that kind of arrogance spoke of organized crime.

"Do you think it was you they were targeting, then?"

"It's the most likely scenario," he said with a grunt. Although, who would want him dead, Nash had no clue. Of course, he had enemies. What cop didn't? But no one with this sort of ruthlessness, this kind of reckless abandon for the law. This was someone with connections. And money. Most of the two-bit criminals he'd helped put behind bars wouldn't have the resources or the contacts to carry out something like this.

They should get moving before they lost all the light. Nash attempted to get to his feet, but pain so sharp it took his breath away speared through his leg, and he landed on his backside with a thump.

"Oh, no." Skylar's soft cry of fear made his stomach contract. All he wanted was to get them out of here; to get Skylar to safety. But his body was letting him down. He wasn't sure how much farther he could go.

If they were going to have to stay in this godforsaken wilderness overnight, maybe they should stay here. It was as good a place as any. Easy to defend if need be. He should take another look at his leg, check on the bleeding. And at Skylar's wound, as well.

"We're camping here for the night," he said with an edge of finality.

"What? But I thought… I don't know what I thought." Skylar stared at him as his words sank in. He could see her internal struggle, her desperate need to get out of here, balanced against the practicalities of their position. Logic won in the end, and she merely nodded. Once more, this woman surprised him with her steely resolve. There were no tears and no tantrums. Just prosaic acceptance of their situation.

"I agree," she said finally. "It'd be stupid to keep going in the dark. They'll call off the search soon, anyway. We may as well stay put. Keep hidden if there is someone out there hunting us, and make a fresh start in the morning."

Staring at her in the fading light, he noticed how vulnerable she looked. Her face was so pale it made her blue eyes seem huge. There were lines of dirt around her mouth and leaves in her hair. He wanted to brush his thumb over her cheekbone, wipe away the smudge of dust, straighten the wisps of blonde hair falling across her face. Right at that moment, sitting here in the dust at the bottom of a ravine, he thought she was possibly the most beautiful woman he'd ever seen.

"How about I take a look at your shoulder?" he said gently.

"Oh, right, I'd almost forgotten about that in all the chaos. You won't be able to see much, it's nearly dark."

"Aha, but I was a Boy Scout back in the days." He rummaged around in his pocket and was pleased to find the warm weight of his little Swiss Army knife. He pulled it out and flourished it like it was their saving grace. He'd bought this one specifically because it had a little LED light in one end. Possibly the smallest flashlight in the world, but it was better than nothing.

"Why don't we find somewhere a little more comfortable and sheltered, first?" he suggested.

"Great idea." Skylar stood and offered him her hand. Trying not to give away exactly how much pain he was in, he used her arm to lever himself off the ground. Then he slowly hobbled down the ravine. It was flat along the bottom, mostly dry dust, which was easier for him to negotiate than having to climb over logs or dodge around boulders.

A hundred meters down the gulley, they came to a spot where the cliffs soared almost straight up, and a rock ledge formed a slight overhang right above a cleft in the rock face. Not quite a cave, but not bad. It'd be nice to have something at their backs. One less direction for them to have to watch. They were lucky it was the dry season. This gorge might well flood in times of rain. But it was as dry as a bone right now.

Using the tiny flashlight, he found a nice flat spot and dropped the backpack, then lowered himself gingerly onto the dirt and leaned back with a sigh of relief. Skylar settled in beside him.

"There was water in there, right?" She pointed to the bag.

"Yep." He was once again glad he'd taken those few

precious seconds to shove all the stuff into the bag. It was a survival kit of sorts. "You may as well take out the whiskey and the rags, as well. We're going to need them," he added, watching her rummage through the bag.

"Oh, yummy, dinner," she said, brandishing a couple of Bounty Bars and the two packets of chips.

It was a tad ironic; he'd been trying to get Skyler to go on a date with him forever. And now they were finally alone, but instead of being able to offer her candlelight and wine, they were stuck in the middle of the bush with only water and candy bars.

"Let me see your shoulder," he said. "Before we settle down to our gourmet meal." He indicated that she turn around, so he could inspect the damage. "Can you pour a bit of that whiskey on one of the rags, please," he requested, pointing the flashlight in the direction of her shoulder.

As he reached to pull aside the tattered tank top, a sudden memory came back to him, of Skylar flinching away from his hand in the hotel room last night. Her aversion seemed to have disappeared ever since the crash, as he'd touched her numerous times without complaint, but he thought he'd better check, anyway. "Is it okay if I touch you?"

"What?" She half turned, and he could see her eyes glowing in the weak beam of light. "Oh, yes, that phobia went out the window the second the helicopter crashed." He could tell she was trying to make light of it, but these kinds of phobias didn't just go away. Perhaps what she meant was that she no longer had a problem with *him* touching her. That thought sent a spike of heat through his chest. Did it mean she was finally starting to trust him? He liked that idea. Liked the idea he could lay his hands on her silky skin.

The bullet had left a clean rip in the fabric of her top. Prying the hole open with two fingers, he studied the wound. "Yep, it looks like you've been kissed by a bullet."

"What?" She tried to turn around to look at him, but his hand on her shoulder stopped her.

"It means the bullet grazed your skin but didn't penetrate into the flesh. It's like when you graze your knee if you fall off your bike, it's taken some skin off, but it's not deep and not even bleeding much."

"I suppose that's a good thing." She sounded relieved.

"Of course, it's a good thing. But this is still going to sting like buggery when I douse it in whiskey. Are you ready?"

"Yep." She pulled her knees up in front and wrapped her arms around them, hugging them in tight.

"Here goes." He dabbed gently at her shoulder blade and heard the hiss of air over her teeth as she sucked in a deep breath. There wasn't much more he could do for her. The wound could probably do with a sticky bandage to keep it clean, but there weren't any of those available.

"All done," he said.

"Now it's your turn," she said. She was putting on a brave face, but he could hear the trepidation in her voice. She was squeamish around blood; she'd admitted that much back in the helicopter. But he was going to need her help, even if it was just to hold the flashlight for him.

He'd been avoiding looking at his leg, and as they both looked down simultaneously, he understood why. Blood had soaked completely through the makeshift pad and bandages. It was a mess. All that walking and exertion had kept the blood flowing. Perhaps if he'd been able to sit still, it wouldn't look so bad.

She gave a little whimper and averted her gaze. But then she forced her eyes back to his leg, and he applauded her self-control. He'd become used to all kinds of grisly injuries during his time in the force, and so sometimes he forgot that most people found this sort of thing disgusting. "I can help. What do you want me to do?" she said.

"Can you hold the flashlight, please? You need to keep that little button depressed." He showed her how to keep the light on. Then he undid the hastily tied knots and unwrapped the lengths of fabric. He dropped the bloody bandages in a pile in the dust. Then steeled himself for what was to come and lifted what was left of his white T-shirt. Clenching his teeth, he forced himself to study the wound with a clinical eye, as if his leg belonged to someone else.

"How is it?" Skylar asked. Her gaze was focused on the ground near his thigh, but at least she was there helping and not fainting on the ground like some women might've done.

"It's actually not too bad," he admitted. "It's deep, but a clean cut, almost like a stab wound. And it's in the meat of the muscle. I think it's just bleeding a lot because of all the exercise."

"Thank God for small mercies," Skylar whispered faintly. "Right," she said, rallying and reaching over to grab the whiskey. Her knuckles were white around the neck of the bottle. "You should pour more of this on it."

"Wait," he called as she began to tip it over his thigh. "I need a swig of that before we do this." Nash held out his hand for the bottle.

"I might join you," she said, taking a large slug before handing the bottle over, then smothering a coughing fit as the burning liquid slid down her throat.

Nash took two large hits of whiskey and then, before he had too much time to think, poured a large splash over the wound.

"Holy mother of…" he ground out between teeth locked together so tight he thought he might shatter a molar. But he dare not cry out. They still had no idea if there was someone out here in the bush with them.

"Oh, that's horrible," Skylar said, her mouth pulling back in a grimace of distaste. He wasn't sure if she was referring to the whiskey or his leg. "Here quick, put this on." She handed him a folded piece of clothing and he pressed it onto the wound. This rag looked like it might have been a pair of socks she'd put together. His blue police socks, no less.

"You need to get that properly tended," she said. "It needs stitches. And antibiotics. And…you need a hospital."

"I know." He kept his tone calm, he could tell by the rising timbre of her voice, she was starting to freak out. "And we'll get there soon enough. We just have to stay put until morning." He didn't add that morning might not bring them anymore relief. Daylight would make them visible to search and rescue. But it'd also make them visible to unfriendly eyes, as well. He wondered about the logistics of their situation. If they couldn't rely on search and rescue, would they be able to get themselves to safety?

"Do you have any idea where we are?" he asked, reaching out his hand for the whiskey bottle. He wasn't aiming to get drunk, but anything that might take the edge of the pain would help.

"Not really." She handed over the whiskey with a lift of her eyebrow, but then began to tear what was left of the bottom of his pants into long strips. "Paul said something about Lamb Range before we went down. If that's where we are, then we're about sixty kilometers away from Cairns."

"That's not so far," Nash mused.

She didn't say anything, merely looked from his leg up to his face and back again. Her message was clear. It was too far for someone with a damaged leg to walk out. But that might be their only option.

CHATPER NINE

Skylar shivered. Now that the sun had disappeared, the air in the ravine was cooling. Her little shorts, tank top, and white sneakers might have seemed the perfect choice for a hot and steamy tropical afternoon in Cairns. It was a break from her normal work attire of jeans and a button-up shirt, a nod to the fact she was away from the station, and perhaps even feeling a little in a holiday mood. And the way Nash had stared at her when he first saw her this morning had definitely made it worthwhile. Even though she hadn't been aiming for that reaction when she'd shoved the outfit in her bag, she had been woman enough to enjoy that look of hunger in Nash's eyes. But now she was regretting letting silly fancies get away from her. Jeans, a work shirt, and boots would've been much more appropriate for surviving a crash and a night spent in the wilderness.

"Are you cold?" Nash's disembodied whisper came out of the dark. After they'd dressed his wound and she'd tended to the other smaller injuries, especially the gash on the side of his face, which was probably going to leave a scar, they'd eaten their meal of chips and candy bars washed down with half a bottle of water. Then he'd made her turn the little flashlight off. To save batteries, he said. But she also knew it was an unspoken worry that it'd attract the gunman. If he was actually out there.

Her eyes had slowly adjusted to the dark, but there was no moon tonight, and down here, she could barely make out the edge of the ravine against the night sky, let alone see her hand in front of her face. Stars twinkled high above, but their cold light hardly reached them in their hideout beneath the overhanging rock.

Skylar was unconvinced that the man was still out there somewhere. Nash seemed pretty sure, however, and perhaps she should listen to him. He was a cop, after all, using his cop knowledge and instincts to make the deduction. But she was finding it hard to believe someone had been brazen enough to shoot a helicopter out of the sky; let alone be prowling around in the darkness like some sort of vigilante commando straight out of a bad TV show. It was all too much for Skylar to compute.

"A little," she whispered back.

"Come over here." Nash was a dark, amorphous shape, against an equally dark background, and she sensed his movement, more than saw it: he'd opened an arm wide, inviting her to come and lie next to him. She hesitated.

"I could do with a little warming up, myself," he added. Nash was injured, he needed to be looked after. It wouldn't do if he got cold tonight.

"Okay." She shuffled across the few feet separating them, reaching out a hand to feel her way. He was using the backpack as a pillow to prop himself against the cliff face. He tucked her beneath his armpit, wrapping his arm around her waist, and she steeled herself against the feelings of apprehension that always came upon her whenever someone who wasn't part of her close family touched her. That automatic, instinctive reaction to flinch away, to protect herself. She'd sometimes even break out in a cold sweat at the mere thought of it. It was one of the reasons she never entertained the idea of dating again. She'd been afraid those feelings would stop her from forming any sort of attachment. From having a normal relationship again. But those feelings never came. Being in close contact with Nash over the past few hours, all that they'd been through together, seemed to have cured her. Perhaps, subconsciously, her brain accepted him, understood that he meant her no harm.

As she relaxed, the tension oozing from her muscles, her legs stretched out along the length of his, and she actually snuggled into his chest. He made a noise of contentment and shuffled his arm, so it was a pillow for her head. But she began to doubt his assertion that he was cold. Because as soon as she settled in beside him, heat emanated from his body. And a very male body it was, too. Even if she was never to date again, she could still appreciate a nice-looking man from a distance. And Nash was nice looking. She remembered once that Daisy had referred to Nash as that golden God surfer dude. It was a fairly accurate description.

"The stars are so much clearer out here," Nash said, interrupting her train of thought. "I noticed that the very first night I moved to Dimbulah. When you live in the city, you don't tend to pay much attention to the night sky. It's a bit immaterial. But out in the bush, it becomes more a part of you, don't you think?"

Skylar welcomed the distraction of conversation. It took her mind off all those hardened muscles lying right next to her.

"Yeah, I guess. I've never been much of a stargazer," she said. Maybe it was because her whole world revolved around food. She was interested in how things grew, interested in the soil that supported the plants that she loved. Dale and Daisy might've agreed with Nash, they were constantly gushing about how bright the stars were at night. But she was a tad ambivalent.

"I thought with a name like Skylar, you'd love staring up at the stars. Or at the sky, at least," Nash said, and she could hear the slight confusion in his voice.

She gave a loud snort. "My name has nothing to do with the sky. It's derived from a Dutch surname, and it means *scholar*. Daniella loved the name for some reason. But don't read any connotations into it." She laughed softly.

"Oh. Right." There was a prolonged silence, and she wondered what sort of hidden meanings he might have been reading into her name. It was just a name, nothing more. Her hand absently began playing with the corner of Nash's shirt. Slowly, she disentangled her fingers. This wouldn't do. They might be huddling together to stay warm, but she didn't need to get carried away with the moment.

By way of diversion, she asked the first thing that popped into her mind. "What about you? Where does the name Nash come from?"

It was his turn to give a gentle snort of contempt. "My story is much the same as yours. My mother thought it was a good idea. It's short for Ignatius, but I hate that name. So, if you ever tell anyone, I'll have to kill you."

She laughed out loud, then quickly covered her mouth, belatedly remembering they were supposed to be staying quiet.

"Well, Nash is a nice name. Very manly. It suits you. And I promise I'll never let your secret out."

She felt rather than heard the deep rumble of mirth pass through his chest. Then he went still, and Skylar wondered what'd happened to his good mood.

"I'm sorry about all this."

"Sorry? About what?" Where had that come from?

"If those thugs were after me, and I put you in danger..." she felt him tense beside her. "And if Paul died, because of me. Well, I'll never forgive myself."

Poor Nash, she hadn't realized he was beating himself up over something that might not even be true. She lay a hand on his chest as a comfort. "Perhaps it was Paul they wanted. Or…" She'd meant the words to appease his guilty conscience, but now that she thought about it, the possibility was more than a little real. "What if it was me who was the target?"

"I can't see why—"

"No, listen." She broke through his protestation. "Hear me out for a second." Her mind was racing as she considered this new angle. "What if this is something to do with Dan Sanders? He threatened me on the night you arrested him. I ignored the threats at the time, because I thought he was just a crazy wife beater." She hesitated for a beat, then sucked in a fortifying breath. "And I should've told you this earlier…but when Dan spoke to me in court yesterday…"

"Yes," Nash said softly, but she could hear the quiet censure in his tone.

"He said I would pay for my lack of obedience."

"Hmm." Nash looked down, and she caught the glimmer of starlight reflected in his eyes. "Yes, you should have told me yesterday," he growled. "It does cast more of an ominous light on this whole thing." Nash paused as if considering his next words. "Sanders would certainly have the money to fund this sort of operation. But what would he stand to gain from it? He's already going to prison, that's pretty much assured."

Without thinking, her fingers began to trace small circles on his shirt again. "Revenge perhaps? He struck me as the sort of man who doesn't let any perceived wrong done against him to go unchecked." The more Skylar turned the idea over in her head, the more certain she became. And if it were the case, maybe it was both of them the gunman had been aiming for. Dan would see them both as equally guilty in putting him away. That'd mean poor Paul was merely collateral damage.

"It's possible," he conceded. "But I think it's more likely something to do with an arrest I've made, or someone I've pissed off during my career."

"Hm." Skylar still wasn't sure. Suddenly, she realized what her hand was doing. She was stroking Nash's chest, enjoying the feel of the ridges of firm muscle beneath her fingers. Had Nash noticed?

She slowly withdrew her hand, and they sat in silence, both contemplating who their enemies might be. The silence stretched on, and Skylar decided they had a long night ahead of them, and they may as well fill it up with something. Even though Skylar knew it was a dangerous path to go down, because the more she found out about this man, the more she liked him, she asked, anyway. "What made you want to become a police officer?"

His hesitation was slight, but she felt it, anyway. "It's a bit of a pathetic story, are you sure you want to hear it?"

Skylar doubted that anything Nash did was pathetic. She nodded and then tipped her head back, using Nash's arm as a rest so she could stare at the sky as he talked. "Yes, please."

"You might not believe this, but I was a bit of a rebel in my youth."

"No." She made a mocking sound with her tongue. But it didn't surprise her, he had that air of being a risk-taker around him. It was tempered by his police uniform and his professional personality, at least when he was on the job. But there was an underlying aura of Nash being a little untamed.

"Yes. I was into fixing up old cars, tricking up the engines, and giving them a new paint job. Turning them into street machines."

"Nice," Skylar mumbled. She could see it now, Nash as a

young hothead, hanging out the window of some hot rod as he did burnouts in the street. Pissing off all the neighbors. She laughed to herself. Good on him. It was nice to know he hadn't always been Mister Perfect.

"My father taught me everything I know, he loved tinkering in the back shed. He was always doing up some old car out there. My mum hated it, said her backyard looked like a spare parts shop."

"Your poor mum." It was the standard cry of women all over the world, having to deal with the messes their men produced.

"Yeah, I think she probably would've eaten her words after dad died, though. She told me once that she would've put up with a hundred cars in her backyard, if only dad was still alive."

"Oh, that's terribly sad. I'm so sorry for your loss." His dad was dead? That was a surprise twist.

"I was only fifteen. He died of a heart attack at work. They said it was so quick, he didn't stand a chance. He was such a fit bloke, didn't drink, didn't smoke. Makes you wonder, doesn't it?"

Skylar couldn't help it; her hand began to stroke his chest again. She could feel Nash's anguish emanating from him, and now regretted asking the seemingly simple question.

What would she do if she ever lost one of her parents? Not her biological father, because she'd barely seen him since she was seven years old. But what if she lost Steve, who was like a father to her? Or heaven forbid, Daniella? She and her mother had a volatile relationship, but she also understood that Daniella's tough love had helped shape Skylar into the woman she was today.

"I went off the rails after dad died. My poor mother, she had three young daughters to look after, and a teenage son who was spiralling out of control. I couldn't see it then, because I was too caught up in my grief. But I can't apologize enough to my mother now."

"I'm sure she understands." And it was probably true. Mothers had such a capacity for forgiveness. She tried to imagine what Nash's mother looked like. And he had three sisters, too. She was finding out more about Nash in this last five minutes than she'd known about him in the past two years.

"I'm sure she does, but that didn't help at the time. Anyway, you asked how I became a policeman. I was driving my friend's car, a hot rod I helped him build. He was in the passenger seat. We were racing another car, out on the back roads of Brisbane, and I was winning. Then I lost control and crashed into a tree."

"Holy Jesus," Skylar murmured. This story was going from bad to worse. Her heart was beating like a drum, and she wanted to take him in her arms. First his father died, then suffering from grief he didn't know how to control, he'd taken up with the wrong crowd. She moved in closer, hoping to offer him comfort with her presence. She wrapped her arm across his waist and lay her head on his shoulder.

"The car burst into flames. That's how I got the scars on my legs." Nash's voice took on a faraway edge. "But I got out. And then I tried to get my friend out of the passenger seat. I wrapped my hands in my T-shirt to drag him out of the burning car. But he was stuck. Right then, a police cruiser pulled up, and this constable grabbed the shirt from my hands and pulled Mic out. He saved his life when I couldn't help him. That was the moment I decided I wanted to be like that constable. I didn't want to keep going in my downward spiral and end up dead."

Skylar had no words. She hadn't been expecting such a heart-rending story. Nash had survived the crash, but what a terrible thing to happen. He'd been through hell. But it'd made him a stronger person. Had her own personal hell made her a stronger person, as well?

"That's quite an amazing story." Skylar didn't know where to start first. Nash had suffered so much trauma at such a young age. But he'd pulled through, and at least on the surface, he seemed fine. Those kinds of mental scars often ran deep. She knew that from experience. Nash had clearly coped with most of the emotional damage by channelling it into becoming the best cop he could possibly be.

"I'm sorry you had to go through all that." She tilted her head up so she could see his eyes, and he stared down at her. In the dark, it was hard to make out his expression, but his face was close to hers now. A trickle of heat ran through her belly.

He gave a slight shrug underneath her ear. "It was bad at the time. And I was pretty messed up for a few months. You know, wracked with guilt over Mic's injuries." Nash's hand came up to stroke her cheek. It felt so natural, so nice. She had no inclination to flinch away from him. Nash would never hurt her. In fact, she wanted more, and so she leaned into his touch. "But when Mic eventually got out of hospital, and I knew he was going to be okay, that's when I applied to join the police force," Nash continued, his fingers finding their way to the side of her face, tugging on a strand of her hair. "And it was the right choice for me. I love being a cop. And just think, I wouldn't be here with you right now, if I'd followed a different path." His thumb moved to her chin, slowly caressing it. What had he meant about being here with her? Could he feel this thing…this electricity…zinging between them? Was he going to kiss her? He was staring into her eyes, and she could see the stars reflected in his.

It was almost as if he was asking a question, not wanting to scare her, merely waiting for her to make a choice. She could pull away if she wanted to. He was so close, the heat of his breath touched her lips. He smelled good, too. All musky and manly.

She was attracted to Nash, there was no doubt about it. It was one of the reasons she'd turned down his offer of a date, because she knew if she'd gone out with him even once that he'd be dangerous to her state of mind. He might've convinced her to go on a second date, and perhaps a third. He was hot. Just ask any woman in the area. Those crystal-blue eyes, that curly, blond hair, and killer smile, he was a hard package to resist. But she had to ask herself, was her body reacting like this because she was feeling sorry for him? Wanting to help ease his heartache?

She couldn't take that chance.

Withdrawing her face a smidgen, she said, "So, out of tragedy, you managed to find your true calling."

It was enough to break the spell. He tipped his head, so it was leaning against the rock face, and gazed up at the sky. "Yes, I did." he agreed.

If he was disappointed in her rejection, he didn't show it. He certainly didn't push her away. Almost the opposite. Instead, he settled his arm around her shoulder and tucked her head against his chest. If only she could tell him why she was like this. Why she trusted no one, especially not men. But she'd made a vow to bury that piece of her past. It was the only way she knew how to cope. If she told anyone now about how Craig had abused her—had raped her when she tried to leave him—they'd want her to tell the police. Nash most certainly would advocate that. But she couldn't do it. She couldn't go through the whole burden of a trial. Rehashing all the terrible things Craig had done to her. Dredging up memories she just wanted to forget. No one would truly understand her motives. In some way, seeing Dan Sanders go to jail was almost a form of therapy for Skylar.

"Try and get some sleep," he suggested. "I'll keep a lookout." She snuggled in closer, deciding to enjoy the luxury of lying next to Nash. To soak in his presence, absorb the benefit from having a warm, human body next to hers, rather than a cold, empty bed for once, and not second-guess herself for this one night only.

CHAPTER TEN

Nash wasn't sure what had woken him. To anyone watching, he might've looked like he was still asleep. He never moved a muscle, but he was suddenly very aware of his surroundings. He opened his eyes just a slit. The earth was cold and hard beneath him, but Skylar was warm and soft, draped over his left side. His neck ached from sleeping half-propped up, and there was a dull throb coming from his injured thigh. He'd slept fitfully, keeping one ear open for any unusual sounds.

And that was perhaps what'd woken him now. Dawn couldn't be too far away; a pink glow lit the sky above the ravine.

There it was again. A faint sound that didn't belong to the early-morning bush. The snap of a twig coming from somewhere above.

Very gently, he shook Skylar awake, placing a finger against her lips to make sure she remained quiet. She looked up at him, confusion and growing concern in her sleepy gaze. He shook his head, and then slowly drew his legs up, pointing at Skylar to do the same. His leg spasmed with every movement, but he ignored it.

If someone was looking down from directly above, the overhanging rock overhead might just give them enough cover so as not to be seen. Nash thought about the boning knife in the backpack. But he dared not move to retrieve it.

They sat like that for many minutes, arms entwined, staying as still as possible, barely daring to breathe. If there was someone up there, it was highly unlikely they'd even found the ravine. Nash had only stumbled upon it by sheer luck. The thick shrubbery running along the top edge acted as camouflage. If someone had broken through those bushes, surely they would've heard it.

Just as Nash was about to release Skylar, another sound reached their ears. Someone was definitely stalking stealthily through the bush above them. There was so much dry leaf litter, and so many small twigs on the forest floor, it'd be impossible to move noiselessly. This guy was taking care, but they could still hear the occasional crunch of a booted foot in the undergrowth. Nash listened intently, but it seemed that the person was heading uphill, away from them. The noises grew fainter and fainter, and Nash finally let out a gusting breath of relief.

Skylar's eyes were wide. Last night, she almost scoffed at the idea they were still being hunted. Given her choice, she would've returned to the top of the hill. At least she now believed him. They had proof the gunman was still in the area and posed an immediate threat. It meant they had to keep moving. They couldn't stay here any longer. If only one of their phones had survived the crash. His cell phone was probably lying in the tangle of debris below the copter, but it was impossible to go back and retrieve it. They had only one option; to try and walk out.

Without a word, he stood, using the rock face to help him up. His body protested, all the little cuts and bruises making themselves known in that instant. His muscles were stiff from sleeping on the ground. But he shouldered the backpack and extended his hand to Skylar. She hesitated for a second, then nodded in consent, taking his help to stand up.

They may as well follow the ravine. It was heading downhill, in the opposite direction to which their hunter had just disappeared. They walked in silence, Nash hobbling along as best he could.

As the light grew, they began to hear activity in the sky above. The buzzing of a helicopter, or the drone of a fixed-wing aircraft flying overhead. It was so frustrating. Rescue was so close, yet so far away. The canopy above was too dense, they'd never be spotted down here. If they could only find their way to a cleared area, then they could perhaps signal for rescue. But the ravine offered them protection from unfriendly eyes. He couldn't take the chance that the gunman was still around. The guy might just be desperate enough to take a shot at them, even with search and rescue flying above. Nash kept alert, constantly stopping to check behind them, and listening for any sound that might give away that someone was following them.

Once their crashed helicopter was discovered, this place would be crawling with police and the local SES volunteer rescue services. But that could take hours, or possibly days; time they didn't have.

At one stage, Skylar tapped him on the shoulder, and when he turned around, she offered him a broken branch. She mimed for him to use it as a walking stick. Clever girl, why hadn't he thought of that?

After another half an hour of slow progress, the sides of the ravine became shallower. They could now see over the top to the thick underbrush growing on each side. The vegetation had changed slightly, becoming greener and lusher. The gorge was still heading downhill and had turned to the left. They must be almost to the bottom of this valley, their crashed helicopter well above them on top of the ridgeline now.

"Can we stop for a drink?" Skylar whispered.

Nash halted, his sharp gaze searching the surrounding bushland. Then he nodded; it looked safe enough. He'd be glad to rest his leg for a while, although Skylar didn't need to know that. He'd checked his leg surreptitiously as they walked, and while the strenuous exercise this morning had caused blood to seep through the makeshift bandages again, it wasn't as bad as it'd been last night.

"Over here." He pointed to the base of a large fig tree perched atop a small rise to the right of the shallow dip of the ravine. He dropped to the ground between the sizable buttress roots, using the trunk as a backrest. It'd hide them from anyone coming from behind, if there was still someone following them. They'd heard the stranger working his way back up the hill, likely still hoping to trap him and Skylar if they came up to signal to the rescue helicopters now buzzing around the area. The tree gave them a good vantage point to survey the surrounding terrain. A good place to stop and decide on their next course of action. Skylar nestled between two roots next to him.

From this position, Nash could see the ground continued to drop away for around a hundred meters below them. The landscape mainly consisted of dry, open woodland, tall eucalyptus trees scattered immediately, with plenty of scrubby undergrowth in between. This country would be straightforward to walk through, but would also make them easy targets to spot, with not much cover available. At the bottom of the slope the vegetation became thicker, and Nash wondered if a small creek or river ran along the lowest point. Nash's gaze followed the line of the valley floor to the right, noticing the vegetation change. He was no botanist and so couldn't name the plants he was seeing, but there were some type of palms and even a fern scattered in amongst the shrubbery, and it was somehow less dry and dusty.

Once they settled next to the tree, Nash tuned in to the surrounding sounds. The light swish of a breeze touching the leaves overhead, the ever-present hum of cicadas singing, heralding the heat of the day that was yet to come. Birds began to twitter in the branches above, ignoring Nash and Skylar as they hunkered down. It was almost pleasant, an outing in the bush on a summer's day.

"I'm beginning to wish I'd bought Dale something other than Bounty Bars," Skylar said with a wry smile, as he handed her breakfast in the shape of a candy bar and a bottle of water.

He gave her a tight smile in return. He was worried about what their next move should be, and his thigh was aching like a bitch.

As if on cue, Skylar asked, "How's your leg? Do you want me to look at it?"

"It's a little sore, but nothing I can't handle," he replied. "We've got more pressing issues to worry about. You heard the guy stalking us in the bush, right?"

"Yes," she acknowledged with a tilt of her head. "I still can't quite believe that someone would go to all this trouble. That guy sure has a hard-on for wanting us dead."

Nash nearly choked on his mouthful of water at her brazen choice of words. That was certainly one way of putting it.

"So, now you believe me that we can't go back to the top of the mountain?"

"Yes, you were right. But what's our alternative?" She finished her candy bar with a smack of her lips. "I could eat another three of those," she added.

Nash could too, but it was better than nothing. There were still four bars remaining in the bottom of his bag, but they should ration them, just in case they were stuck out here for longer than expected.

He'd asked Skylar before if she knew where they were, but

at the time, they'd been hoping to be rescued. Her knowledge of the area would be better than his. "Can you think of anything about this mountain range that might be helpful? Last night you said we're about sixty kilometers from civilization. But are there any farmhouses, hobby farms, or even plain old hippies living in the jungle out here?" He raised his shoulders in a helpless shrug.

Skylar tapped the top of the water bottle against her teeth. "Lamb Range is made up of a couple of different national parks. There's only one main road that runs through the middle. And being part of a National Park, there's not a lot of people living in the area, either."

"Damn," he said, sucking air in over his teeth.

"If I remember correctly, this range is different from one side to the other," Skylar continued. "The western slopes are in a rain shadow, and so the forest is dry, open woodland. But the eastern slopes get more rain and have a more tropical feel."

"That might explain the differences we're seeing now," Nash mused quietly.

"Yes, I think we're heading into the eastern side of the range, toward Cairns. I also vaguely remember there's a beautiful waterfall, somewhere on that side. It's called Davies Creek Falls, has water in it year-round, and is popular with the tourists. If we could get there, perhaps…"

Finding a waterfall in this terrain might be like finding a needle in a haystack. He didn't want to burst her bubble, so instead he said, "You mentioned a road that runs through the middle. Do you mean it runs north to south?"

"Yes."

"If we keep heading east, then we're bound to stumble over it sooner or later."

"That's a pretty vague plan, Nash," she said, eyebrows lowered in a frown. He couldn't disagree. But what else were they supposed to do?

He opened his mouth to say something along those lines when a noise froze the words on the tip of his tongue. He reached slowly for the backpack.

"Nash, honestly, don—"

He clapped a hand over her mouth. To her credit, she immediately became motionless, sensing the urgency in his touch. Her frightened gaze found his.

With his other hand, he felt around in the backpack until his fingers closed over the handle of the boning knife, the sharp edge still wrapped in rags.

There was another sound, off to their right. Ignoring the shooting pain in his thigh, Nash got to his knees, pulling Skylar with him, and moved slowly around the trunk of the enormous fig tree, careful not to stumble over the spreading roots. He handed Skylar the bag and held the unwrapped knife down low at his waist.

She caught sight of the knife and shook her head vehemently. Nash didn't want to do this, either. But if he got the chance, he would try and disable whoever was hunting them. The sound came again from higher up on the right flank. There was a flash of movement. It was only now that Nash realized all the birds and insects had gone quiet. He should learn to pay more attention to what was going on in nature. The birds had known before he did there was danger lurking in the bushes.

Following the sound of the huntsman's footsteps, it seemed like he was heading away from their hiding place beneath the tree, continuing to stalk the line of the ravine downwards, not noticing that Skylar and Nash had left the safety of the culvert. If Nash could sneak up behind the man and disarm him, then this might all be over.

He put his lips close to Skylar's ear. "You stay here."

She shook her head again, strands of honey-blonde hair

coming free of her messy ponytail. Real fear hovered in the depths of those crystal eyes.

"You have to trust me," he whispered. He was a cop, trained for these sorts of situations. Admittedly, he was an injured cop with only a knife as a weapon, going up against a criminal armed with a semiautomatic gun, but this was his job. It was his job to protect Skylar. To take down this gangster.

He was taking a risk by leaving Skylar completely unprotected, but it was a calculated risk. If he could take down the armed gunman, then she'd be safe. If he left the guy there to roam around freely, he might well sneak up on them and take them down next time. He had a chance to neutralize the gunman, and he had to take it.

"I'll be back soon," he promised, and then melted into the underbrush. Taking extra care not to make a sound, he headed on the same trajectory the gunman had taken, only slightly higher up the slope. Hoping to use his uphill position as an advantage. His leg hampered his movements, but the other guy must be going slow, as well, because Nash was gaining on him. Perhaps he'd realized his targets were no longer using the ravine. Sure enough, the man stopped up ahead. Using a eucalyptus tree as cover, Nash peered around the trunk. The gunman was now standing tall, craning his neck to see farther down the slope. Nash got his first good look at the guy. He was tall and muscular, dressed in long, dark, cargo pants, a black T-shirt, and combat boots. He wore a small backpack over his shoulders, a semi-automatic rifle held loosely pointed at the ground. Obviously well prepared. The man looked sharply to his right, and Nash saw his face was painted with ash and dirt. The term *gun for hire* flashed through Nash's mind. This guy was a pro. Who the hell had hired this man to come and kill them? Nash was determined to find out.

The man surprised Nash by suddenly turning around to retrace his steps, obviously convinced that he'd lost the trail. Heading straight toward Nash's hiding place. Nash stayed extremely still, hardly daring to breathe, not wanting to give himself away.

The man stalked like a black panther through the bush. Nash had to stop him before he backtracked too far. He couldn't take the chance that the commando might find Skylar. He waited as the man got closer and closer, knife held tight in his fist. He was going to pass within mere feet of the tree Nash was hiding behind. Nash carefully and silently worked his way around the tree, keeping the trunk between him and the huntsman. How was he going to do this? Should he wait until the man had passed by and leap out and take him from behind? He'd have to make his strike accurate. There'd be no second chances against a man with a gun. The commando was directly opposite Nash's tree now. He held his breath and tensed every muscle, hoping his leg wouldn't let him down, his senses on full alert.

A tiny sound filtered through the bush to his ears. A scrape and then a thump. It was Skylar, she'd peeked around the side of the tree, perhaps trying to see where he was; see what was going on. Nash cursed inwardly.

There was no doubt the commando had heard it, too. The other man stopped in his tracks.

Why had Skylar been so silly as to reveal herself? He couldn't see the gunman on the other side of the tree. So, he waited and listened, putting the knife between his teeth so both hands were free. The commando took one step in Skylar's direction, bringing his face and the barrel of the gun into view as he raised it. And Nash decided that this was the distraction he needed.

Nash pounced. He grabbed the weapon and twisted it sideways and downward, using all his weight to drag both gun and man to the ground.

Caught completely by surprise, the commando didn't react as quickly as he otherwise might've. That was probably the only reason Nash managed to orchestrate his maneuver, and both men rolled on the ground together.

The gunman let out a bellow of rage, trying to yank the gun free from Nash's grasp. He knew he wouldn't win a fair fight, not with his leg impeding him. He needed to keep this man on the ground, disable him as quickly as he could. Use the techniques he'd been taught on the job to wrestle this man into submission. The commando was on top, with Nash struggling on the ground. Letting go of the gun barrel with his right hand, he took the knife from between his teeth and plunged it down into the man's shoulder.

The man's bellow changed from rage to pain, and his grip loosened on the gun. That was the tiny slip Nash needed, and he wrenched the gun from the other man's hands. But the rifle was long and unwieldy, and he still had the knife in one hand. Before he could swing it around into a position where he could point it at the commando, the other man brought both his hands up underneath Nash's chin in a double-handed punch, sending the back of his head pounding into the dirt, and the gun skittering downhill through the dust, along with the knife.

Momentarily stunned, Nash shook his head to rid it of the bright lights flashing behind his eyes.

The commando was still on top of Nash, and he used Nash's split second of weakness to try and flip him over onto his back. Neither of them had a weapon now, and it'd come down to sheer brute strength. The other man's knee landed on the side of Nash's wounded thigh, and he let out a scream of pain. His injury had let him down, and now it looked like he was going to lose this fight. The man had used his weakness and gained the upper hand.

"Run, Skylar," Nash shouted. Even if he couldn't win, he needed to keep this man occupied long enough for Skylar to get away.

The man now had one kneecap dug into Nash's leg while holding Nash's left arm, dragging it behind his back. His other arm was practically useless, pinned beneath him on the ground. Nash drew in a deep breath. This was going to hurt. Instead of resisting the man's grip on his left arm, he leaned into it, arching his back. Then he bucked like a bronco horse, using his uninjured leg to swing backward, rolling them both sideways.

Taken by surprise, the other man grunted but didn't release his grip on Nash's arm. For a second, Nash was on top, but they continued to roll, both of them groaning with exertion as they wrestled. Then the commando had Nash in a headlock and was squeezing his windpipe so he couldn't breathe.

There was the sound of someone crashing through the underbrush nearby, and the commando lifted his head, easing his grip on Nash's neck.

"Why, you little…" The man's weight suddenly lifted off Nash, leaving him gasping on the ground. What the…?

Nash rolled over in time to see the commando racing toward where his gun had landed in the dust nearly ten meters away. But Skylar was also racing toward the gun. And she was closer.

"No," Nash screamed. "No!"

CHAPTER ELEVEN

Fuck. The man had seen her. He'd let go of Nash and was running towards her. Skylar was closer to the gun, but by the time she picked it up and pointed it—hoping to hell it was loaded and primed—the man would be on top of her. Wrestle the gun off her and then she'd be dead, as would Nash.

So, she did the only other thing she could think of and kicked the gun away. It skittered through the leaves and debris over the ground, coming to rest close to the edge of the ravine. Which still left the knife, lying on the ground nearby, half-buried in the leaf litter. The gunman stopped his headlong rush and stared at her, as if he couldn't quite believe what she'd just done.

Had he seen the knife?

They both crouched in a boxer's stance, facing off. Skylar could hardly believe she was capable of this. Of fronting up to some mad hunter, as if she'd actually be able to match off against him in a real fist fight. She knew she'd never win. Surely, he knew it as well.

Nash lay on the ground some way down the slope. She'd heard him scream in pain. Then he'd told her to run. But run where? She wasn't about to leave him here. The only other option was to get her hands on that gun. But she'd failed miserably at that attempt.

Should she go for the gun again? She could see it clearly, as if it was beckoning to her, the barrel glinting in the sunlight shimmering through the trees above. The gunman had his eye on the rifle, as well.

Or should she try for the knife? It was closer.

In the split second she wavered between the two weapons, the gunman sprang sideways, going for the gun.

In her peripheral vision, she could see Nash getting to his feet. It was as if things were happening in slow motion. The gunman was running, his back to her, intent on getting to that gun. Nash was yelling something at her, but she couldn't decipher his words.

The gun was right on the edge of the steep-sided gully. That's when she made her decision.

She charged after the gunman, her legs pumping as she sprinted through the woodland.

He bent down to retrieve the gun.

Just as he straightened, she cannoned into his back, using her hands as a battering ram to push him over the edge.

The man threw his hands forward, trying to save himself, sending the rifle tumbling through the air. There was a small cliff face, of around two or three meters, directly below them, the sides of the gully rising to meet the sheer drop. The gunman plummeted through the air, somehow managing to twist in the air like a cat and land heavily on his feet, but then the slippery slope gave way beneath him, and he was somersaulting down the steep, rocky gulch, tumbling over and over, yelling in fear and pain, until he finally came to rest with a thump against a large boulder near the bottom.

Oh, shit. Had she killed him? She hadn't meant to kill him.

Nash arrived at her side, breathless and grimacing in pain, and they both stared down into the dry creek bed. The man groaned and moved slightly. An absurd relief flooded through Skylar's veins. She shouldn't care if the man was dead, he'd been trying to kill them after all. But still, to have taken a life…Skylar wasn't sure she could live with that.

"Where's the rifle?" Nash barked.

"It went over there." Skylar pointed toward a rocky outcrop a few feet to the left, near the brink of the small cliff face.

"I got the knife," he said, holding it up for Skylar to see. "But we need that gun." He limped carefully along the edge of the cliff, not wanting to suffer the same fate as their hunter and tumble over the edge, while Skylar remained where she was, watching the other man. She couldn't believe what she'd just done. Couldn't believe she was capable of such violence.

"Shit." Nash was leaning over the edge of a jumble of rocks, looking into a small cleft in the limestone. "I can see it. But I can't reach it. The gun is jammed about five feet down in a crack."

Nash made his way back around to where Skylar was standing. "We might be able to rig up a stick or something to hook it out, but it looks like it's jammed in there pretty tight."

"Maybe we don't even need the gun," she said, turning to look at the spot where the man had landed. "If we can get down there and tie him up, then…" But the man was on his feet, dark eyes boring into them, filled with hatred.

His voice floated up to them from below. "No one gets the drop on me. You've made me mad. Really mad." The man turned his head to study his wounded shoulder, tearing at the ripped fabric in disgust. "I don't need that gun, I'll tear you fuckers limb from limb." He removed the backpack that'd miraculously stayed on his back during his fall and pulled out a small black box.

"You'd better watch out, you little fuckers, because I'm calling in my big brother. And no one gets away from Stan the Man. He was a sniper in the army. You guys are fucked, now." He held up a cell phone so they could clearly see him dialling.

"Is that guy for real?" Skylar could hardly believe her ears. "Surely, he's not going to keep coming after us?"

Nash glanced between the knife in his hand and the man at the bottom of the gully. Perhaps weighing up the chances of using it on the crazy guy below. Weighing up the chances of winning against that beast of a man. He reminded her of Rambo, or some equally muscle-bound bad actor out of a thriller movie.

"I wounded him," Nash finally said. "And he'd be lucky if he doesn't come out of that fall without at least being badly bruised all over. But that won't stop a man like him. And if it's true that he's calling in reinforcements, well..."

"What are you saying?"

"We need to keep running. It'll take him at least ten minutes to climb out of there. He might even need to walk farther down the ravine to get out. And he will try and retrieve the gun, he won't just leave it there unless he's sure it can't be rescued. We need to use that time to get ahead of him."

"You've got to be joking," she answered weakly. But even as she said the words, she knew Nash was determined. She just wanted this whole interminable disaster to be over. Wanted to be home, safe in her kitchen, dreaming up her next meal to astound her guests.

"Let's go back to our original plan. Head westward and see if we can find that road you mentioned, or that waterfall. I don't know if he's going to call in support, and God knows where they think they're going to land, with all the rescue aircraft up there, but we have to keep going."

Skylar merely nodded. It must only be around eight o'clock in the morning, and already she was exhausted. How was she ever going to make it through the day?

A quick glance showed her the man was already making his way up the slope. Shit, he was really coming after them again.

She followed as Nash led the way. He stopped to retrieve the backpack she'd forgotten all about from behind the tree. Nash had lost his walking stick during the whole debacle, but he was walking okay right now, perhaps adrenaline was keeping him going. If they were to keep walking, they'd need to find water soon. They were down to one less-than-half-full bottle between them. And food. Although, she knew people could survive for weeks without food.

She wanted to argue with Nash, tell him that he was wrong. All her instincts were screaming for her to head back up the mountain, toward the clear space at the top where one of those aircraft they could still hear occasionally buzzing overhead might actually find them. Skylar had heard stories of miracle survival; of people being found days after they went missing. And a lot of them recounted how they could hear the rescue service planes flying overheard but had no way of attracting attention. That they'd been left feeling terribly alone and abandoned. Exactly how she was feeling right now.

That wasn't quite her situation, because she had Nash with her. And Nash had been correct in everything he'd said so far. She had to keep remembering he was a cop. She had to start trusting his instincts. Because if she'd followed her instincts last night, they'd most probably both be dead.

They reached the bottom of the valley in record time, Nash half-jogging, half-limping, going as fast as he dared. Skylar kept looking behind, terrified she'd see the face of Rambo Man emerging out of the shrubs, bearing down on them with gun raised and teeth drawn back in a rictus of victory.

Another creek bed ran along the bottom, but this one miraculously had a trickle of water in it. Which was a good sign. Most creeks were parched and waterless by this stage into the dry season. But the water wasn't drinkable, not unless they wanted to get sick. It was barely moving and stagnant in some of the larger pools. Nash was correct when he said the vegetation was taking on a different hue, greener and lusher.

"We're not going to follow this creek," Nash announced.

"Okay."

"That's what he'll expect us to do."

Yep, probably. That's what she'd been expecting them to do.

"We're going to head down here for a little way, leave a few footprints, but make it look like we're trying to hide them by walking in the water."

Smart. Why hadn't she thought of that?

"But as soon as we see a good opportunity, we're going back up the mountain and skirt around the side, instead."

"That sounds like a good plan," she agreed. Skylar was impressed. Even on the run, with an injured leg and after fighting for his life with a madman, Nash was still able to think clearly. It was the mark of a true cop. No wonder he was good at his job.

She spent the next half an hour following his lead, stepping where he told her to, getting her feet wet in the puddles and shallow pools, a lot of them foul-smelling as they waded down the valley. All of a sudden, Nash held up his hand and then pointed up the slope.

"There," he said, indicating a limestone outcrop. "That should hide our footprints." Carefully, they left the safety of the sluggish creek and made their way up the rocky formation. The vegetation was much thicker up here, the air heavier and more humid.

"Can we stop for another drink?" Skylar pleaded.

Nash was pushing himself; she could see the pain etched

around his eyes. And even though he didn't say it, she knew he was grateful for the rest. Should she be worried about him? They should probably change the bandages on his leg. Try and keep it as clean and sterile as possible. Infection was a big worry out here.

"Just a quick one," Nash agreed.

They sat beneath the shade of a large cycad and passed the plastic bottle between them. The bottle was only a quarter-full by the time Nash put it back in his backpack.

"We'll climb up for a while," Nash said, standing and shouldering his pack. "And then we'll follow the contours around the side of the mountain range. Pity we can't keep following that creek down there." Nash looked back the way they'd come. "It'd more than likely to lead us out to a road or a waterfall." Nash shrugged and offered her his hand. "Onwards and upwards."

"Let me take the pack for you," Skylar offered, hoping to make this trek a little easier for him. It weighed a lot less now they'd drunk most of the water, and she figured she wasn't the one with the injured leg.

"Nah, I'm good," he said. But this time, she noticed Nash pick up a broken branch to use as a walking stick, to help him climb the increasing slope.

Walking became more difficult the farther around the mountain they got, as the forest turned into a tropical jungle. It was odd that two different landscapes could exist so close together. The dry, open woodland on the other side of the mountain, and now the tropical jungle, impeding their path. Strangler vines dangled from the branches up high, just waiting to trip up an unwary hiker. Sometimes the vegetation was so thick, Nash had to lead them around a patch of shrubbery, because it was almost impossible to beat their way through.

After a few hours of scrambling and slipping and cursing,

Skylar called for another halt. She was hot, sweaty, thirsty, and covered in scratches. There was one small silver lining to this forced march; there no way she could see that anyone would be able to follow them through this dense forest. Nash had chosen the best possible path to foil anyone tracking them.

He took a seat on a fallen log, lowering himself down with a grunt of pain. Skylar was shocked at how pale his face was. Rivulets of sweat ran freely down the sides of his face. His normally bright-blue eyes were drawn and dark with pain. The gash on his cheekbone looked red and inflamed. Shit, she should've been looking after him better. He'd been so stoic, not complaining, just kept plugging away through the bush.

She lifted the backpack from his shoulders and offered him the bottle of water. He needed it more than she did. He'd lost quite a bit of blood. And that wound needed attention. If only they had some painkillers. Or antibiotics. Or even some proper bandages.

"How's your leg?" she asked, keeping her voice deceptively light. "Should we take a look at it?"

"Nope." Nash waved her hands away, as she leaned in to peer at the bandages. Blood had completely soaked through them. "I don't really want to see what's going on under there," he admitted. "We don't have enough clean bandages to replace them, anyway."

Skylar opened her mouth to argue, but could find no justification that might convince him otherwise. He was probably right. There wasn't much they could do for him out here. They needed to get to civilization. That was the only real hope Nash had.

"We should have another one of those Bounty Bars," Skylar said. It was a small thing, but if Nash could keep up his food intake—even though it was one giant sugar hit—it might help him to keep going.

"I'm not really hungry," he said, but took the bar Skylar proffered and bit into it, as if his mind was working along similar lines to hers.

They sat on the log, side by side, eating their measly lunch, and stared out into the forest. It was frustrating, because they were up pretty high, but it was impossible to see through the dense canopy to the surrounding hills and ridges. If they could see the topography better, maybe they could locate a break in the trees that might indicate a road, or a denser patch that might take them to a watercourse.

"I haven't heard any aircraft recently," Skylar said after a while. "Do you think they've called off the search already?"

"No, it probably means they've found the crash site."

"That's a good thing. Isn't it?" Skylar sat up a little straighter, hope raising her chin, so she looked him in the eye.

"Yes. And no. It'll take them a while to figure out what happened, and that we're missing. Then they'll most likely organize a land search. Send out hordes of volunteers to flood the National Park. But these things take time to set up. They might not start the true search until late this afternoon."

"We could just stay here and rest. Camp the night and see what the morning brings. I'm pretty sure that lunatic will have lost our trail by now."

Nash shook his head. "We need to keep moving. Even if the gunman isn't hot on our tail, no one would ever find us stuck here, halfway up a mountain. We need to find that road you mentioned."

Skylar was beginning to wish she'd never said anything. That road could be at the bottom of this ridge, or it could be three ridgelines over. And she didn't think Nash was up for that kind of hike. He looked ready to fall right where he was and never get up.

That thought scared her. She needed Nash. Needed him to be strong, to help them both get out of this situation.

Nash heaved himself off the log and held out his hand for the backpack. His stamina was unbelievable, she would've given up hours ago and be a sobbing mess right now.

"My turn to carry it for a while," she said. Surprisingly, he didn't argue.

They continued to bash their way through the jungle, stopping to have a sip of water now and then. The heat was building, so it was almost unbearable; the humidity making the air feel like she was breathing cotton wool. It only got like this at Stormcloud during the wet season. During the dry, they had a reprieve from the life-sucking mugginess.

At one stage, Nash faltered, unable to lift his injured leg over a fallen tree in their path, and cursed out loud that the jungle had it in for him and was purposefully putting obstacles in the way. Skylar had waited for him to pick his way around the offending log, but when he stood staring at the ground, she'd taken things into her own hands. Taking the lead, she found a pathway through the strangling vines and palm fronds. And she took the role as guide from there on, Nash following behind, his head bowed as he struggled to find each new foothold.

Fear blossomed in Skylar's chest when she looked back to check on him. Nash was weakening, no matter how much he denied it, and she wasn't sure how much longer he could go on.

Without warning, Skylar broke through a hanging veil of vines and nearly stumbled down an embankment. Large fig trees straddled a rock-strewn culvert. And down the middle of that culvert ran a burbling stream.

"Water," she said. "Nash, we found water."

"Great," he replied heavily, and sat down on the nearest flat rock.

Skylar stood and studied the stream for some minutes. It flowed downhill; the vegetation getting more overgrown as it got closer to the bottom. But if they followed the stream, they could stick to the relatively flat ground. It might mean some scrambling over rocks, or wading through the shallow water, but it'd be easier than beating their way through the jungle.

"Drink this," Skylar demanded. It was the last of their water, but Nash needed it more than she did. He didn't seem to notice that she was no longer drinking, as he gulped it all down. His face had gone from merely pale to almost green in pallor, his eyes going a misty blue, as if he wasn't really seeing his surroundings anymore. And his breath was rasping in and out through his lips.

Without thinking, she leaned in and smoothed his sweaty curls away from his forehead. He barely lifted his head at her touch.

Skylar didn't let on how terrified she was, she merely slipped her arm through his and helped him to his feet. She wasn't going to discuss the direction they should take; she was just going to take charge.

"Come on, not far now." She didn't know if that was true or not, but it seemed to bring Nash to his feet.

They stumbled and bumbled their way down the creek bed. Skylar had no idea how long it took them, or how Nash negotiated his way over some of the larger boulders. But she managed to keep him moving.

Slowly, it became lighter, the jungle not quite as oppressive. The vegetation was opening up as they dropped lower and all of a sudden there was a gap in the foliage. The creek bed flattened and widened, the rocks clearing a pathway through the trees, and she could see sweeping views of the countryside below.

Twenty feet below them was a flat ledge. Skylar's heart did a double tap. Because below that ledge she could hear a waterfall dropping away into a pool deep beneath. They'd found a waterfall. Perhaps not the waterfall they'd been looking for, but a waterfall, nonetheless.

Skylar wanted to go and explore, but the next part before the flat area was steep and would require some rock-hopping.

"Stay here for a second, Nash," she said, leading him over to a rock and helping him sit. "I'm going to take a look. I'll be right back." She didn't want to get his hopes up, so she didn't tell him what she'd heard.

Nash didn't reply, but he lifted his head to stare down at the water disappearing over the edge. He swayed a little in his seat, and Skylar had second thoughts about leaving him. But she needed to check this out. She didn't think Nash would make it much farther, so if this was to be their camp for the night, she had to scout out the best place. And hopefully find some drinkable water.

Her muscles were aching from all the walking, and her mouth was parched. She didn't think she could go much farther, either. Taking care, as the rocks were slippery, and her arms were shaking with fatigue, she lowered herself down the steep incline. Eventually, she landed on the flat expanse of limestone.

And there, right next to the stream, ran a manmade pathway. She nearly fainted with delight. A flash of bright blue by the side of the path caught her eye. An empty water bottle. People had been here. It was late afternoon. If there had been any tourists visiting, they'd probably left for the night. But it gave her hope. Perhaps tomorrow the tourists would return. They just had to make it through the night.

She turned to tell Nash what she'd discovered and let out a scream of fright. Nash had fallen from his rock and was lying in a crumpled heap on the ground. She raced back up the bank, scraping her knee in her hurry, and turned him onto his back, taking his face in her hands.

"Wake up. We're safe now. Wake up," she sobbed.

But Nash was unresponsive.

CHATPER TWELVE

Nash groaned and rolled his head to the side. There was something wrong with his bed. It was as hard as a rock. He opened his eyes and then closed them again. Nope, that wasn't a good idea, his head was pounding, and the light only made it worse. But why were there trees growing on his ceiling?

"Nash? Nash, wake up."

It took him a second to remember who that voice belonged to.

Skylar. She sounded like an angel. He opened his eyes again to see her hovering above him. Mm, those lips looked decidedly kissable.

"Oh, thank God. You gave me such a scare."

A scare? What was she scared of? If his head hadn't felt like there was a hammer beating from the inside, he'd reach up and draw that gorgeous face down to his and devour those lips.

"Good morning, beautiful," he said. Why did his voice sound so raspy?

Skylar's lovely, blue eyes went wide. "Morning? Nash, it's late afternoon. Oh, God, did you hit your head?"

Maybe he had. Maybe that was why it was pounding so

loudly he could hardly think. He tried to sit up, but only made it onto his elbows before the trees above began to swirl alarmingly and his vision was filled with bright, sparking lights, and he fell back down.

He felt gentle hands lift his head, and then a bottle was placed on his lips. "Drink this," Skylar said. That's when it all came back to him. He wasn't safely tucked up with Skylar in his bed—which was a damn shame, and it'd been a nice fantasy while it lasted—they were lost in the jungle with a mad gunman on their tail.

Greedily, he slurped at the water. It was tepid and tasted earthy, but God, it was good.

"I found us some drinkable water. It's safe, it's filtering through the rocks at the bottom of this small waterfall. We can't drink from the main stream, though," Skylar warned. She was kneeling next to him, her beautiful face lined with concern and streaked with dirt.

"Mm-hm," he mumbled, laying his head backward and staring at the sky. "I feel like shit."

"Well, you look like shit," she quipped back. Then her face softened. "I think you're dehydrated, which is why you passed out. You've lost a lot of blood. You should be resting, not dashing through the jungle like an army of one."

"Tell me about it," he grumbled. "Where are we?"

"I'm not sure," she admitted. "We found a waterfall. It's not the one I was looking for, but that doesn't matter, because there's a path, leading down to a small parking lot and a road."

"That's great." His head cleared a little at that good news. He wanted to try sitting up again, but this time he raised himself slowly onto his elbows.

"Stay still," Skylar growled at him.

"I want to see where we are," he said, ignoring her hands pushing his shoulders down.

"Are you always this stubborn?" Skylar glared at him, and he liked the way her eyes went a dark indigo when she was mad.

"Yep," he said with a hint of a smile.

"Fine. Let me help you, then." She scooted around behind him and helped him into a sitting position, letting him use her legs to lean against.

A vista opened in front of him. They were on a rocky ledge, a small stream burbling along a few feet away. The stream flowed down a small waterfall directly in front, into a larger flat area below, before finally disappearing over a cliff edge farther down. He could see down the valley to where more green hills rolled away into the distance, where the sky was turning a bright orange as the sun set over the horizon. The whole view was framed by large fig trees leaning in on either side of the waterfall.

"This place is magic. Not a bad spot to spend the night."

"Yeah, we're *so* lucky." Skylar couldn't hide the heavy sarcasm in her voice. "Here, drink some more. I'll go and fill the bottle again. Before it gets dark."

Nash did as he was told. The water helped; his head no longer felt like it was going to split open. Skylar was right, he'd lost some blood and with all the walking and sweating they'd done over the past twenty-four hours, they hadn't drunk nearly enough water to counteract the life-sapping heat and injury. He glanced down at his leg, expecting to see a bloody mess. But it was clean and freshly bandaged.

He pointed to his thigh and turned his head to catch Skylar's eye. "How...?"

"You were passed out for over an hour," Skylar said. "When I said you scared me, I wasn't joking."

He shuffled forward so he could turn around properly and stare at her. "You cleaned it all up for me? While I was out cold?"

She nodded and scooted around next to him. "At least you didn't feel anything. You didn't even wake up when I poured the last of the whiskey over it. I cleaned up your face, too. That gash on your cheek isn't looking too good, either."

"Thank you," he said, reaching out to touch her arm. "I know you don't like the sight of blood."

"No, I don't," she replied with a small shiver. "But I was worried about you. Worried that it might be infected."

"And is it?"

"I don't know. It is swollen and puffy. But that could be because you've been tramping through the jungle all day instead of giving it time to heal."

"Could be." He was no expert on wound care, and they had no choice, anyway. Not while they were stuck out here. Then something occurred to him, and he frowned. "Where did you get the extra bandages? I thought we used them all up last time."

"I improvised," she said. And that's when he noticed her bare midriff. She was missing around a third of her tank top. She'd ripped up her own shirt to make him a bandage. For some unknown reason, that touched a chord deep inside him. This woman was amazing. Resourceful and determined.

As his mind slowly cleared, he began to analyze their situation. It sounded like they'd stumbled upon a hint of civilization. Was there a possibility they could be rescued tonight? If he could get Skylar out of here, then he should at least try.

He sat up straighter, pulling his injured leg into his chest to test its function. Would he be able to stand? Able to walk? There was only one way to find out. He drew his feet underneath him and began to push himself up into a crouch.

"What do you think you're doing?" Skylar was on her feet, towering over him, hands out, ready to catch him if he should fall.

"Perhaps we should we go down to this parking lot and wait there. Or walk down the road, see if we can find someone to help us."

"You're not in a state to go anywhere. Sit back down, now," she demanded, hands on hips.

Now she was standing right in front of him, her bare midriff was directly at eye height, and he got to fully appreciate her nicely toned stomach. Her cut-off shorts sat low on lean hips and the revealed skin was smooth and silky.

"Besides, I've already checked it out," she continued, oblivious to the fact he was checking *her* out. "I think the park closes at five o'clock. It won't reopen till morning."

"Right," he mumbled, lowering his buttocks onto the rock. She was right, his head was swimming once more, but he wasn't sure if it was the dehydration or the view of Skylar's stomach that was to blame. Perhaps it wouldn't be such a bad thing after all, to spend a second night out here with Skylar.

"It's going to be dark soon," she continued. "If you're up to moving, there's a spot a little farther back, away from the stream, which might give us better shelter."

"Good idea." He let her take his arm and help him limp over to a patch of flat ground beneath an enormous fig tree. The earth was covered with a layer of dry leaves and the lateral, spreading roots formed the sides of a natural bed.

He sat with his back against the largest root, while she fussed around him, gathering more dry leaves to form a sort of mattress they could both lie on.

"I'm going to refill the bottle," she said, after she'd finished their little homemade bed to her liking. "Will you be all right here?"

"Of course." He waved her away. Then watched in fascination as she tramped down the edge of the stream. She had to clamber over a large boulder, and it gave him the most delightful view of her very marvelous backside. She really did have an amazing figure. She was a beautiful woman. But that was nothing new to him; he'd been coveting her since the very first moment he'd seen her.

But being thrown together like this, he was learning a lot about the inner workings of this woman. And it made her all the more beautiful in his mind. She put up this screen of aloof determination to the rest of the world. But she was nothing like that on the inside. She'd shown him hints of vulnerability and even trauma. Traits she perhaps saw as a weakness. But those insights merely served to bring out his protective instinct, big time. He'd need to watch himself. He could feel a bond forming between them. A connection that couldn't be denied.

His male ego had suffered a beating this afternoon. It galled him that he'd been unable to guide Skylar to safety, that she'd been the one to take the lead in the end. And then, to top it all off, he'd passed out. His body had let him down, and he didn't like the feeling of limitation it gave him. But on the other hand, he quite liked Skylar taking care of him. That had some definite benefits.

He lay there, watching the last of the color drain from the sky. It was almost peaceful here. Nash mulled over the possibilities of the gunman finding them. Coming upon them in the dead of the night and murdering them in their sleep. He decided the risk was small. Skylar had only managed to find this waterfall by sheer luck. There really wasn't a lot he could do about it. He sat up and pulled the backpack closer. Then rummaged around and found the boning knife, which he put on the ground near his leg, within accessible reach if he needed it during the night. It wouldn't be much against a man with a gun, but it was all he had. He also pulled out the last two remaining Bounty Bars and balanced them on a thicker part of the root beside his shoulder. The drumming in his head had subsided some after he drank his fill of water, but the headache was still there. And his thigh throbbed dully, the pain radiating up his leg and into his hip. Probably not a good sign, but he decided not to mention it to Skylar. Hopefully, he'd be better after a good night's rest.

Finally, the weak light from his small penknife flashlight winked at him through the encroaching gloom. Skylar emerged up the steep bank, dragging an armful of palm fronds with her.

"I found us some blankets," she announced.

"It's not that cold," he said, confused.

"They're not to keep us warm, they're to keep some of these ravenous bugs away."

Aha. That was sensible. He had noticed an increase in the swarming little varmints since the sun had gone down.

Dropping the fronds on the ground, she sat next to him and unwrapped a candy bar, then handed it to him. "Dinner is served."

Again, Nash wasn't hungry, but he ate to appease Skylar. The bar had melted in the heat and was sticky and unappetizing. "I'd rather taste one of your gourmet meals. I hear they're quite good," he said through a mouthful of gooey chocolate.

"I will make that my mission. When we get back, I'll cook you the best three-course meal you've ever tasted." She leaned against the same large root, her shoulder touching his.

"That's quite a statement." He forced the last of the bar down his throat and shuffled down so he could use the root as a headrest. It was cool against his neck, the buzz of flying insects loud in his ears.

"I'm quite a good cook," she replied, a hint of sass in her tone.

"That's good to hear." He was quietly pleased that Skylar had such faith in herself. Some might call her conceited, but he could see through that to the way she clung to her belief. It was how she defined herself. And while Nash knew it probably wasn't good to rely so heavily on one part of her life, it was all she was capable of right now. Perhaps he could offer her a distraction. Something else besides food to think about.

Skylar had finished her meager meal as well, and flicked off the little flashlight.

"Come here," he said gently, holding out his arm. He was looking forward to this. To sleeping side by side, like they had last night.

She fussed around with the overlarge palm fronds, draping them over their legs and then laying some more over their bodies. "I don't know if this will work," she said, "but I've seen them do it on that *Survivor* show."

Nash snorted. "Tell me you don't watch that?"

"I do. And I'm proud to admit it," she said, finally laying down and snuggling into his chest. "Oh, wow, you're hot."

"Why, thank you," he said with a grin, even though she wouldn't be able to see it in the near-dark.

"That's not what I meant." She slapped his chest. "I mean your body is hot."

"Don't I know it," he teased.

"Nash, take this seriously."

"Sorry." But he wasn't, really. He was enjoying the feel of Skylar's body next to his, way too much to be sorry.

"It might mean you have a fever. Which might mean you have an infection."

It was quite possible. He did feel a little dreamy, as if he wasn't really here. From this vantage point, they had a perfect view of the darkening sky.

"Look," he said, reaching out a finger. "The first star of the evening." A tiny pinprick of light sat alone, high in the indigo sky. It was so cold and alone and beautiful. "Shall we make a wish?"

"I wish we would be rescued," Skylar said, quick as a whip.

"Hm, I'm not so sure," he replied meditatively. "I might wish that we could lie here together like this forever. It's kinda nice."

"Oh." Nash could hear he'd surprised Skylar by his statement. Surprised her so much, she had nothing more to say, it seemed.

He tilted his head down so his chin rested on the top of her head. "The other thing I wish, is that I could kiss you. But I'm scared you'd run away if I did that."

Her head came up and banged his chin.

"Ow," he laughed.

"What are you saying, Nash? Now I'm definitely convinced you have a fever and you're delirious." Her profile was in silhouette against the dark-magenta sky. He traced the outline of her eyebrows, lowered in a frown, down her delicate nose and over her lips, pursed into a pout of indignation.

"I'm not delirious. I like you, Skylar. I want to get to know you better. I want to kiss you, to see if you taste as good as my imagination says you do."

He heard the intake of air over her teeth as she absorbed his words. "I'm not...you're not..."

"What, Skylar? What are you so afraid of?" He brushed a gentle finger down the slope of her cheek. Her skin was soft and plump. "It's just a kiss. It's not the end of the world."

"I haven't kissed anyone since..." He wished he could see her eyes, then he might be able to gauge what was going on in her head. Without that information, he had to go on intuition. And his gut was telling him that someone had hurt Skylar. Damaged her so badly that she no longer trusted anyone.

"You can trust me, Skylar. I would never do anything to

hurt you, you have to believe me." He tightened his grip around her shoulders as he felt her tense beneath him. She was as skittish as a cat beneath his fingers, as if she was about to get up and flee. But he'd started down this course, and now he had to follow it through and hope like hell she didn't run away. "I don't know what happened to you. And you don't have to tell me, if you don't want to. All I can say is that not all men are the same. We're not all like that bastard Dan Sanders."

She was still rigid beneath his hand, like a steel trap about to go off. He stroked his other hand down her upper arm, a soothing touch to let her know he was there for her.

"I know you're not like him." Her voice was so low he could barely catch her words. "And I know you're not like Craig, either."

At last he had a name to attach to the reason for Skylar's pain. He tucked that gem away for further analysis later. He was a cop. He could find people. And make their life a misery.

"At least my head knows that," Skylar continued. "But it's hard to...get past it all. Especially when I trusted him so completely. And then he...well, never mind, you don't need to know what he did."

She'd just confirmed his worst fears. That a man from her past had treated her badly. Had made her wary and guarded and want to hide away from the rest of the world. There were so many things Nash wanted to ask. Like what had this monster done to her. Had she sought help from anyone? Nash doubted she had. Skylar was the type who'd suffer in silence. Think she could handle her pain alone.

"I'm so sorry that some asshole mistreated you," Nash said softly.

"Me, too." Her voice was soft and full of anguish.

All he wanted was to wash that pain from her life. If she let him, he could give her a new baseline with which to measure all men.

"And I know you're a good man, Nash." She lifted her head from his shoulder and balanced on one elbow. "And believe it or not, I've been wanting to kiss you, too. But I'm not sure how to…"

"It's easy," he whispered. Then he lifted her chin with his thumb and dropped his lips to hers.

At first, she flinched, but he kept the pressure soft and firm. She could move away if she wanted to. But she chose to stay. He let her take the lead, and her mouth was tentative to begin with. He let her explore his lips with hers, kept his mouth closed as her velvety lips pressed harder, and inhaled the scent of her as she ran her fingers down his cheek, brushing against his two-day stubble. Then she nibbled at the corner of his mouth and little pulses of electric heat shot through his chest, straight to his groin. He ran his tongue along the seam of her mouth. Then he couldn't help it, he opened his mouth and invited her in. And she took his invitation, letting her tongue dart inside his mouth, deepening their kiss, taking it to a whole new level. This was way better than even he'd imagined. She tasted of sweet chocolate and also of something deeper, hints of darkness swirling within.

He went to roll onto his side, wanting to get as close to Skylar as he could. But the movement jolted his sore leg, and he let out an involuntary grunt of pain.

Skylar immediately withdrew. "Oh, sorry, I forgot all about your injury."

Shit, he didn't want this to end. He wanted to keep kissing her all night. "What about my leg? My leg is fine. I can no longer feel my leg," he said. But it was too late. Skylar had gone into caretaker mode once more. She sat up and rearranged the palm fronds that'd fallen away in their throes of passion. Then she put a gentle hand on his forehead.

"You're still hot. You should try and get some sleep."

He wanted to say that he was hot because he was burning up for her. But it was no use, the spell was broken. But at least Skylar snuggled back down into his arms, draping her legs along the length of his. She was finally at ease with him, which was all he truly wanted.

After a few moments' silence, Skylar spoke into the darkness. "It's the reason I couldn't let Dan get away with it. Not once I knew for sure that he was hurting his wife. When women are caught up in that kind of vicious cycle, it's really hard to see a way out."

"I know," he replied. "But that took a lot of courage. You're a much stronger woman than you know, Skylar Williams."

She huffed in reply, but he could feel her smiling as she lay her head on his shoulder.

CHAPTER THIRTEEN

Skylar scratched at her face. Then she scratched at her neck. The bloody bugs had eaten them alive last night. Her palm fronds might've helped a little, but the mosquitoes seemed to have found every square millimeter of bare skin and honed in on it.

At least it was morning now, the sky turning a light purple on the horizon. Soon the hot sun would drive away the remaining insects.

Nash lay beside her, and she snuggled in a little more, not wanting their contact to end. It was so nice to lie here with a man all night, have him cradle her in his arms, offer his support and protection, and not require anything in return. Enjoying the heat of his body so close to hers.

Actually, now that she thought about it, Nash wasn't just warm, he was hot. She sat up so she could look at his face. His breathing was ragged and uneven.

"Nash." She shook his shoulder gently.

He mumbled something but didn't open his eyes.

"Nash," she said a little louder. "Wake up."

He frowned but still didn't open his eyes, and then tried to roll away from her touch. He cried out in pain then and mumbled something more incomprehensible.

She put a hand on his forehead. Shit, he was really burning up. There must be an infection in his leg. The feelings of contentment and peace fled, and she suddenly felt useless and helpless. What should she do? She had no drugs to help bring down his fever. Not even anything as simple as paracetamol.

There was always the old-fashioned way to reduce a fever. Cool water. And she had plenty of that.

"I'll be right back," she told him, even though he couldn't hear her.

She filled two plastic bottles with water from the stream and ran back to Nash, pulling the fronds away from his body. There were no rags left in the backpack, so she resorted to tearing another strip off her tank top. It now barely covered her bra and was filthy from her having spent two nights in the open, but it couldn't be helped. Dousing the fabric in water, she leaned down and dabbed it over Nash's face. Again, he mumbled something incoherent, and tried to bat her hand away. But she persevered, tipping a little of the water over his sweat-soaked scalp and combing her fingers through his blond hair. The gash on his cheek had stopped bleeding, but it was crusty and red; it didn't look too good, either.

But this wasn't enough. She needed to cool his whole body if she were to have any hope of reducing his fever. She leaned in, and without a second thought, began undoing the buttons on his shirt. Spreading his shirt open, she was surprised to see an amazing set of tanned abs. The abs weren't the surprising bit, he was fit and muscular—although they were definitely drool-worthy—it was the deep, even tan that had her stopping to stare. Where would he get a tan like that? But she was forgetting herself. She poured more water onto her rag and patted it over his chest, down his sternum, and over his impressive abs.

Nash rolled his head from side to side at her touch.

"Please open your eyes," she begged him. But they remained firmly shut.

She pulled up the hem of his ragged shorts and sponged the top of his legs. Should she remove the bandages from his injured thigh? There was minimal blood soaking through, and she decided against it, for now.

Moving the wet rag down, she gently ran it over his knees, and then over the scars on his lower legs. They fascinated her, as did the story of how he received them. What a horrible thing to have happened to him. Yet, he'd survived the trauma and possibly become a better man because of it.

She continued to administer her damp cloth to his exposed skin, hoping and praying it was helping. At least he'd stopped thrashing around. That was a good sign, wasn't it?

Skylar had no idea how long she persevered with sponging Nash down. She emptied both bottles of water and went back for more. But as she knelt next to him and lay a hand on his forehead, he finally opened his eyes. Oh, thank God. Those bold, blue eyes pierced her to her very soul.

"Hiya," she whispered.

"Whatcha doing?" he asked groggily, lifting his head to peer down the length of his nearly naked body.

"You're burning up," she replied. "I'm trying to cool you down."

"I know. You said I was *hot* last night." He gave her a wobbly smile.

"That you are," she replied. "Where do you get time to get a tan?" she teased gently.

"Surfing," he said. "I love to surf."

Skylar knew that wasn't the case, because where he lived in Dimbulah was hours away from the nearest beach, but she didn't argue with his fantasy. He might be speaking nonsense, but at least he was awake.

"Thirsty," he said, reaching for one of her bottles.

She snatched it away from him just in time. "This is not the drinking water," she told him. She'd scooped this up directly from the stream. If he drank that, he might get sick—sicker. "I'll get you something to drink. Promise me you'll stay here."

He gave her a lopsided smile that nearly broke her heart. Even while he was sick, burning up with an infection and delirious, he was doing his best to keep her morale up. He was a good man. She already knew that, but something warm flooded her chest as she stared down at him, as if her heart was finally catching up with her mind. His smile turned to a grimace, and he reached for his leg, as a spasm of pain seemed to shake him. He was really sick. If they didn't find help soon, he could even die. Her hand flew to her chest at that thought. She couldn't lose him. Not now.

Heart beating wildly, she scrambled down to the small spring where the clean water seeped from the rock, nearly falling and spraining her ankle in her haste. She caught herself just in time. The last thing Nash needed was for her to get injured, as well. He was relying on her.

Unable to wait for the bottle to fill completely, she sprinted back up the hill with a half-full container. He was still lying exactly as she'd left him.

"Here," she said, landing on her knees by his side. "Drink this." She held it to his lips as he slurped greedily. It might not be good for him to drink it all in one go, so she drew back and let him take a few breaths.

"Oh, no," he complained. "Can I please have some more?" He sounded so much like a petulant child, Skylar had to smile. "I'm really thirsty, and that tastes so—"

"Shh," she said suddenly, putting her finger to his lips. She'd heard something that was out of sync with the birdsong and insect life buzzing around them. A human voice. Fear flooded her veins. Had the gunman found them, and come to finish the job?

Nash let out a quiet giggle. "Are we playing hide and seek?" he whispered.

Oh God, he really was hallucinating. How was she going to keep him quiet? If it was the gunman, there was no way Skylar could hope to move Nash to safety now. She scanned the ground, looking for a weapon. That's when she remembered the knife. She'd noticed Nash had placed it beside him at some stage last night, probably in a vain hope that he could use it to protect them if need be.

"Shh, baby," she entreated. "We need to be really quiet." Holding her finger against his lips, she retrieved the weapon and crouched above him, knife in one hand. She had no idea how she was going to protect Nash; all she knew was that she wasn't going down without a fight.

This time, she definitely heard a voice.

A man's voice.

Then it was answered by a second voice. This one female.

That made no sense, because if it was the gunman, he said he was calling in his brother.

It sounded like they were down on the path to the parking lot. Skylar craned her neck to try and see through the tangled jungle.

"Hello," the female voice drifted through the jungle. "Anybody here?"

A bright flash of yellow shimmered in a gap between the leaves. Yellow. The SES wore that color, so they could be seen easily. A flood of relief swept through Skylar's veins so strong it nearly knocked her off her feet.

She stepped out onto the flat rock beside the stream at the same time as a petite woman, dressed head-to-toe in fluro yellow-and-orange, appeared at the bottom of the small waterfall.

"We're here," Skylar shouted, waving her arms.

"Holey moley." The small woman took an involuntary step back. "Hey, George," she yelled. "I think we found them."

Skylar sank down onto the cool, rough limestone.

Rescue. They were being rescued.

* * *

Skylar paced back and forth across the small hospital room.

"Why don't you sit down, honey? You need to rest," Daniella said. Her mother patted the hospital bed, as if hoping Skylar might take her advice.

Daniella had chartered a helicopter to be at her daughter's side the second she heard they'd been rescued. Skylar was grateful for her mother's concern. It was one of the very few times she'd ever seen her mother show such depth of emotion. When she'd burst through her hospital room door and taken Skylar into her arms, sobbing into her neck that she thought she was dead, Skylar got a glimpse of the true Daniella she kept hidden beneath her veneer of professional aloofness.

But right now, her mother's concern was suffocating.

"I'll sit down when I know Nash is okay," she snapped. And then immediately regretted her words. It wasn't her mother's fault that Nash was still in surgery. All Skylar wanted to do was to run through the hospital hallways until she found the operating theater and burst in there, so she could be by his side.

"Nash will be fine," her mother said in a surprisingly soothing tone. "The doctor said the wound wasn't life-threatening. They'll clean it up, stitch him up, and put him on some strong antibiotics and he'll be right as rain."

"I know." Skylar stopped her pacing long enough to glare out the window for a second. Cairns Hospital was right on the beachfront, and Skylar stared out at the Coral Sea. But she wouldn't feel completely rational again until she saw Nash for herself. Was able to touch him, and look into those brave, blue eyes.

It was late afternoon, and Skylar had spent the last hour pacing back and forth across her room.

Daniella's arrival had distracted her for a while, and she had to fill her in on the short version of their frightening ordeal. Dale, Daisy, Steve, and Julie were all terribly worried about her, and she had to speak to Dale over the phone before he believed that she truly was safe. Dale's fear made her more aware of how distressed her family had been over the crash and her subsequent disappearance. When she'd been lost in the jungle, her thoughts had been on survival and staying one step ahead of that crazed gunman. But now she was safe in the hospital, it was beginning to dawn on her how much this episode had affected her family, as well.

Much like when Dale and Daisy had been taken hostage by their employee, Sally, and her boyfriend. Skylar had been terrified that her only brother was going to be taken from her. So, she could sympathize with how overwrought they must all be feeling right now.

But all that paled into comparison when she thought about Nash. Maybe she was being selfish, but she didn't seem capable of calming her family's fears until she calmed her own fears about Nash's wellbeing.

Around the same time her mother arrived, a serious, middle-aged female cop had come in and taken a statement from her, but she wouldn't answer any of Skylar's questions as to whether they'd found the gunman who'd been chasing them; or even if she believed her story.

Senior Sergeant Robinson had poked his head into her room briefly to check on her safety and tell her he'd be back at some stage to debrief her fully. He also said he was stationing a police guard outside her room, which shocked her at first. But much like the first police officer, Robinson wouldn't be drawn into a conversation about what was going on regarding the gunman, and so she assumed he was still out there. And she was still at risk.

Skylar's vision glazed over, and her mind drifted back to this morning. By the time the SES volunteers had called in an ambulance, Nash had been completely delirious. It was scary to watch him hallucinating. He would giggle and talk loudly to someone who clearly wasn't there. Then, in the next second, he would curl into a ball and moan incessantly, like an animal in severe pain. She felt like he was going to combust every time she touched his feverish skin.

The petite SES lady who'd first spotted her was calm and efficient, telling Skylar that they were safe now, checking on Nash even as her partner called it in to HQ. It seemed like an eternity as they waited for the ambulance, and then once the paramedics arrived it was another eternity until they loaded Nash into the back of the ambulance. She tried to warn the SES people about the gunman who was after them, but they both looked at her as if she was hallucinating as well, so, after a while, she stopped. All she truly cared about was getting Nash to hospital.

They'd allowed her to ride in the ambulance with him. There was no way she was letting him out of her sight, and the older male paramedic seemed to understand how important it was to her. They wanted to check her out as well, but she brushed them aside, telling them it was Nash they needed to concentrate on. Nash hadn't wanted to lie peacefully on the stretcher, he'd thrashed and cursed at the paramedics, not realizing they were trying to help him. At one stage he'd told Skylar to run away, while he distracted the gunman, and they said they'd have to sedate him. It wasn't until she'd been allowed to sit next to him and lay her hand on his cheek, and whisper to him that they were safe now, that he'd let go. In a moment of brief lucidity, his blue eyes cleared, and he stared at her with such a look of tenderness that her heart lurched in her chest.

"Is it true, Skylar? Are you safe now?" he'd asked.

"Yes, baby, I'm safe. You let these lovely people help you now, okay?"

And he'd calmed down and lay peacefully on the stretcher as the paramedics fussed around him.

It wasn't until she got to hospital and caught sight of herself in a mirror that she understood what a dreadful sight she looked. Her face was covered in red welts from the mosquito bites, and she was filthy, streaked with dirt and blood. But she knew Nash looked just as bad and so she'd shrugged, thankful she'd never been too hung up on her looks. The bites and bruises would fade in a few days. She smelled bad, too. She felt a little sorry for the paramedic who'd shared the back of the ambulance with them on the trip down to Cairns.

Now, three hours after she was first admitted to hospital, the bullet graze on her shoulder had been cleaned and dressed, as had all the other scrapes and bruises. She'd been encouraged to drink as much water as she could, and she'd eaten a meal of sandwiches and fruit. Then, she'd had a shower and washed the dirt and bugs out of her hair and was now dressed in a clean pair of pyjamas her mother had brought with her. The myriad bug bites all over her body were driving her crazy, but the nurses had given her an anti-inflammatory, and smothered her with calamine lotion and the itch had dulled to a low-grade annoyance.

The nurse had told Skylar that she'd need to stay in overnight for observation. And Skylar was fine with that, because it meant she could stay close to Nash.

But worry still gnawed at her guts.

There was a knock at the door, and Skylar whirled around. The policeman on guard let a young doctor in blue scrubs through the door, then closed it behind him and went back to his guard station. Daniella stood up, and they both stared at him expectantly.

"How is he?" Skylar asked at once.

The young doctor fixed his steady gaze on her. "He's out of surgery, and recovering nicely," he replied. "The wound was deep and left a nasty incision in the muscle of his thigh. And infection had also set in."

Skylar felt like telling the doctor to get on with it, she already knew all this. But she held her tongue and smiled sweetly.

"The infection was spreading fast; it was lucky the SES found you when they did. The poison was already in his bloodstream."

"But he's going to be all right?" Skylar demanded.

"Yes, we've got him on strong antibiotics, they should knock the infection on the head within twenty-four hours. He should be up and walking around by this time tomorrow."

"Oh, that's great news." Skylar sagged against the bed. "Can I see him now?"

The doctor hesitated. "Technically, we should only let close family in…"

Skylar opened her mouth to object, and doctor held up a hand.

"But he's been calling for you non-stop since he came out of the anaesthetic. And we think that for his mental wellbeing we should let you see him. Follow me."

"Thank you," Skylar said, grabbing a light robe her mother had brought for her and wrapping the tie around her middle.

The doctor stopped as Daniella also made to walk through the door. "Sorry, just your daughter at this stage, ma'am."

Daniella looked about to argue until Skylar shot her a quelling glance. She wasn't about to let her mother ruin her chance to see Nash.

The doctor had a quick word with the police officer, who nodded, then followed them down the hallway. They were really taking this shit seriously, if the policeman had to follow her around. But Skylar didn't care if ten police followed her thorough the hospital, as long as she got to see Nash.

"What about his family?" she asked the doctor, as she hurried after him down the hallway.

"I believe one of his sisters is flying up from Brisbane this evening," the doctor replied. "That's all I know," he added, as she opened her mouth to ask him more.

She followed the doctor's blue scrubs through a maze of hallways until they finally reached a double door that had intensive care splashed across it. There was another police officer stationed outside this door, and she nodded to Skylar and the doctor and let them through.

A row of hospital beds stretched down the length of the room, but only two were occupied. A nurse looked up from studying a chart in surprise. The doctor led her past a man in the first bed, who Skylar barely glanced at, toward the one at the very end. She could see Nash lying very still beneath the stark, white sheets.

Then she was by his bedside, looking down into his familiar face. A white bandage covered his left cheek.

She took his hand, and he opened his eyes. They were fuzzy, as if he was still affected by the anaesthetic, but they cleared as he saw her face.

"Hi." She smiled at him.

"Hi." Those delectable lips curled up at the edges, and he smiled back.

Her heart did a backflip as he squeezed her fingers.

"Right, I'll leave you in the capable hands of Sarah." The doctor indicated the nurse farther down the room. "You shouldn't stay too long."

Skylar lifted her gaze from Nash's for an instant. "Thank

you…" She didn't even know this young doctor's name. "Thank you," she said again, hoping to convey how much this meant to her. But he was already on his way out.

"How are you doing?" she asked softly.

"I'm magnificent, now that you're here," he replied, and her heart did two backflips this time. Everything was right once more, now that she was close to Nash again. As if her world had tipped on its axis while they'd been apart, and now her world was whole again.

CHAPTER FOURTEEN

Much later that night, Nash sat up in his hospital bed. Skylar was sitting quietly by his side. He wanted to reach out and take her hand, but resisted the urge. Because senior sergeant Robinson was staring at both of them. Nash didn't want his boss to see that sort of PDA. It was hard enough to look strictly professional while he was wearing a hospital gown and sitting in a hospital bed, with Skylar was still dressed in her pyjamas and robe.

He was feeling better. The wonder drugs they were pumping into his body were doing the trick. He couldn't actually remember a lot about this morning's rescue. All he really remembered was pain. Like his whole body was bathed in boiling-hot lava, and it was burning him from the inside out. And Skylar. He remembered her touch; her face coming close to his, telling him he was going to be all right. And he'd believed her. Clung to her presence.

He'd been released from intensive care a few hours ago and been given a private room. Skylar had been at his bedside ever since, refusing to leave. Her mother, Daniella, had hovered around, coming and going. She was now sitting in the visitor's chair in the corner. Skylar had told her she could stay on one condition, and that was she didn't say a word. So far, Daniella had kept her promise.

"After we spotted the helicopter, and we discovered that you were missing, we widened the search, sending volunteers to all parts of the park accessible by road," Robinson said, and his mouth turned down as he frowned. "You have to understand, the messages coming in were garbled at best. We had reports of shots being fired, but we weren't sure why or what had happened. The dispatcher only got part of your message, Nash. At first, she had no idea if it was a hoax or not. When we tried to get your location off your phone's GPS, it was no longer online. It must've been smashed in the crash." Robinson scrubbed a hand over his face. "There was a lot of confusion, which is one reason it took us a while to find the wreck site. Then, when you weren't at the site, we thought you become dazed and confused and had just wandered off."

"Which is probably exactly what the gunman wanted you to think," Nash replied meditatively.

"Yes." The senior sergeant tapped his nose and captured Nash's gaze with his. "But after Skylar filled us in on some of the details, I had two officers go back to the site. They found some discarded shell casings."

"That's good." Nash nodded.

"Why is that good?" Skylar asked. She'd remained quiet up until this point, but he could see the beginnings of an indignant pout to her mouth. "Of course, there were shell casings. Why does he sound so surprised? Didn't they believe us?" Skylar stood and crossed her arms. "Didn't you believe me?" She stared directly at Robinson, and Nash winced inwardly. It was a pretty crazy story. If he hadn't been intimately involved, he might've been skeptical, as well. He didn't blame Robinson for checking the facts.

"Of course, they believed you," Nash said, taking Skylar's hand to console her, and then immediately regretting his move when his boss's gaze flickered to their joined hands and then back up to his face.

"Anyway," Robinson continued, ignoring Skylar's interruption. "We haven't located the rifle yet. But I've got a guy with a metal detector going on-site tomorrow morning."

Again, Nash nodded. If they could find the gun, that'd be the hard evidence they needed. "No sign of the suspect, then?"

"No," Robinson admitted. "But we're trying to find the pilot of the helicopter that shot you down, as well as following up on the lead Skylar gave us. That guy slipped up when he mentioned his brother was called Stan the Man. Someone will know who that is; it's only a matter of time before we find him."

"Yes, but how much time?" Daniella said, finally entering the conversation. She'd clearly come to the end of her patience. Her promise to Skylar forgotten in the heat of the mounting questions burning on her tongue. "Because I'm assuming that my daughter isn't safe while that man is still out there? Am I correct?"

Daniella's shrewd mind didn't miss much.

Robinson shifted on the spot, uncomfortable with the question. "Well, now, we still don't know who the target was, exactly," Robinson admitted. "We think it most likely they were after Senior Constable King. We're going through his list of convictions right now, trying to narrow down any suspects who have a grudge against him."

Daniella said nothing, merely tapped her foot impatiently on the linoleum floor.

"But we can't rule out Skylar as the target, either," Robinson added.

"I haven't got any enemies, apart from Dan Sanders," Skylar scoffed. "And I told you that he threatened me again at the court case," she added.

"I know…" Robinson started to say, but Skylar wasn't finished.

"And if it is Dan, then aren't we both targets?" she asked, hands on hips, gaze shooting between Nash and the senior sergeant.

"We don't know. It's all conjecture at the moment. Perhaps that gunman was after both of you. Or it might've been the pilot they wanted, and they were just tying up loose ends, getting rid of any witnesses when they went after you," Robinson replied. But Nash caught something in the sarge's countenance that made him frown. Like there was something he wasn't telling them; a piece of information he was holding back. Nash knew better than to question his boss in front of Skylar and Daniella, however.

"Well, that's not good enough," Daniella huffed. "We need answers, because I want to know that when I bring my daughter home, she'll be safe."

"That's the thing, Mrs. Williams." Robinson stroked his chin, a sign that Nash was familiar with. It meant bad news was coming. "I haven't told Skylar this yet, but she'll probably need to go into protective custody, at least for a while. As will the senior constable," he added as an afterthought.

Nash understood on some level that it was probably inevitable, but he still felt a flash of frustration at the news.

"That's not going to happen," Skylar declared, at the same time her mother said, "I won't allow that." At least they agreed on one thing.

"I'm not sure you have any choice," Robinson replied gruffly, extending his already-tall frame to fill the room.

"I do have a choice," Skylar said, letting go of Nash's hand and stalking toward the senior sergeant. "I can refuse to go into protective custody. And what does that mean, anyway? I just want to go home." She turned beseeching eyes in Nash's direction. "I need to get back to my kitchen. Back to… normality."

He understood what she really meant was back to the safety of her ordered and non-confrontational life. Where she could bury herself in her work again, and forget about Craig and all the bad things he'd done to her, as well as the trauma of two days spent in the jungle being hunted by a madman. It was her way of coping.

All of a sudden, there was a knock on the door, and a constable Nash recognized from the Mareeba station poked his head around the door. "Sorry, Sarge, can I have a word?" The constable's demeanor was inscrutable, but Nash got a sudden bad feeling in his guts.

"I'll only be a second," Robinson promised, disappearing through the door. Was that a hint of relief Nash saw on his face as he escaped?

As soon as Robinson had gone, Daniella rounded on Nash. "You need to stop this. Skylar needs to come back to Stormcloud. This is your problem, and you need to solve it. Without putting her in any more danger."

"Now, hold on one minute, Daniella." Skylar moved to stand between her mother and the bed. "Don't you take this out on Nash, he had nothing to do with it. He's as much a victim of this as I am."

Her mother took a surprised step back, then narrowed her eyes.

"Oh, I see how this is going."

"What the hell does that mean?"

"You were holding hands before," Daniela accused.

"And so what if we were?" Skylar wasn't backing down.

Great, he was about to become embroiled in a Williams family disagreement. Nash wished that Steve was here. He was usually the calming presence to Daniella's hot temper.

Nash was slightly distracted, however, because Skylar

looked stunning as she argued with her mother, her blue eyes flashing, blond hair falling around her shoulders as she stood between him and Daniella, like some kind of avenging angel.

Robinson barged back into the room, just as Daniella shook her finger in Skylar's face. He took in the dynamics of the room in a split second and said, "I'm not sure what you're discussing, but you need to take a seat. I've had some news you need to hear." Pulling back his shoulders, Robinson seemed to fill the room with his commanding presence.

Robinson's aura of control did the trick, and Daniella lowered her finger, retreating to the visitor's chair with a scowl. Skylar returned to Nash's bedside. Nash fixed his boss with a steady gaze. This didn't sound like good news.

"I don't know how else to put this, but we responded to a triple-zero call early this morning. A woman was found dead in her hotel room in Cairns. It was Patty Sanders."

Daniella gasped and stood. "Dan's wife? Dead?"

"Yes," Robinson said. "We weren't sure at first—which is why I didn't mention this to you earlier—but Constable Newman just confirmed to me it has been ruled as a homicide."

Oh, shit. Nash reached for Skylar's hand. She remained still as a statue, and he wondered if she'd even heard Robinson's words. Then she let out a small noise, like that of an injured animal. And turned to face him.

"No," she whispered. "It can't be true. We helped her. She was getting away from him. How can this happen now?" Her face was a mask of despair.

The silence in the room was deafening. He had no words to comfort Skylar. After all she'd done, after her sacrifice to try to help the other woman, it was all for nothing.

"Are you saying that her husband did this?" Daniella asked. "Are you saying Dan Sanders had his wife murdered? Because she dared to take him to court?"

"It's starting to look like it," Robinson agreed.

"Does that mean…" Daniella stopped and gaped at Skylar as if she could barely believe the idea forming in her head. "Does that mean he was the one behind the attempt to kill my daughter?"

Robinson held up his hand. "Look, we can't go jumping to wild assumptions here. We need to wait until we have definite proof. But—"

"Yes. That's what you really mean, isn't it, Senior Sergeant? This madman is somehow able to extend his reach from inside his jail cell and try to kill my daughter. To what end? To silence her, so his trial is terminated?"

Robinson held his other hand in the air, both palms forward. "We don't know the answers to that, Daniella. He might be operating under some kind of illusion that if he kills all the witnesses, then the trial will be forfeited, and he'll be a free man. Which is definitely not the case. We have enough evidence to convict him. There might be a re-trial, but he will still go to jail for a long time. Dan Sanders is an intelligent man; I think he'd understand that."

"Then what's his reasoning? I don't understand." Daniella hugged her arms in front of her chest, her confused gaze flicking from Robinson to her daughter and back.

"I know why he's doing this," Skylar said dully. Her face had gone blank, as if the news of Patty's death had shut down all her emotions. "I think it's much more basic than that. I think it's out of plain old spite. He wants payback for being sent to jail, simple as that. He's a man who thinks he can control everything. Including his wife. He's the sort of man who lives by the rule that if he can't have something— meaning Patty—then nobody can." There was a bitter twist to Skylar's mouth that Nash had never seen before.

Nash studied Skylar for a few moments. She was probably right. The sad part was that once again, Skylar was using Dan as justification to fan the flames of her belief all men were bad. All men were control freaks who weren't to be trusted. He was worried that all his hard work over the past few days to break down her barriers was all for nothing. Because now those barriers were back up, higher than ever.

Robinson gave a noncommittal lift of his eyebrow. "Sanders is refusing to talk, but don't worry, we'll get to the bottom of this. Meanwhile, I think it prudent if Skylar stayed somewhere safe. Where we can keep an eye on you." He directed his last statement at Skylar, intentionally ignoring Daniella.

Daniella opened her mouth to say something, then, as if realizing this wasn't her choice to make, shut it again and turned to stare at Skylar.

"I really want to go back to Stormcloud," Skylar said. "Couldn't you organize a police guard to keep an eye on me out there? Surely, that's the safest place? I've got Dale and Steve, and even Wazza, who will all protect me."

"I don't like it," Robinson's nostrils flared, and Nash knew it was a sign he was trying to hold on to his temper. "The station is far too open, with too many entry points. Anyone can just come and go as they like. You also have up to twenty guests at any given time. How do you know one of those guests isn't really a hitman? I'm assuming you wouldn't close the lodge?" He looked at Daniella.

Daniella hesitated. "I suppose we could, but…"

Nash was surprised she'd even considered the idea, but he knew it wasn't an option. Not when they had no clear timeline, and no clear suspect. It could take days to find the gunman, or weeks, or even months. They couldn't afford to close the lodge for that long.

"No, you're not closing the lodge for me. That's not an option, and we both know it," Skylar said. She was becoming agitated, pacing back and forth between his bed and the wall.

"We have places we can take you. Houses that no one knows about where you'll be safe," Robinson interjected.

"Where are they? Cairns? Brisbane? No. I need to be near my home. I'm not going to be locked in some police safe house like a naughty schoolgirl." She stopped pacing to glare at Robinson, like this was all his fault, which really it wasn't.

"You're blowing this out of proportion," Robinson replied. "Your life could be at stake here, isn't that more important?"

Nash scoffed quietly. Robinson didn't know Skylar very well. Her cooking was the most important thing to her. She wouldn't want to give that up for anything. He had another idea, but he wasn't sure how Skylar would take it.

"I'm blowing this out of proportion, am I?" Skylar stamped her bare foot on the linoleum floor. "Well, you can just take your protective custody and shove it up your a—"

"Whoa," Nash said loudly, holding up his hands to get their attention. This was getting out of control. "Sarge, what if Skylar came to stay at my place for a few days?" Skylar swiveled to face him, blue eyes flashing with barely controlled anger.

"I don't need your charity," she snapped.

"Skylar," he said, a warning in his tone. "This isn't about charity; this is about keeping you safe. And you'll be helping me, as well. I'm going to need assistance over the next few days with my convalescence. We can stay safe together."

That seemed to stop her in her tracks. She probably hadn't thought about how he was going to cope once he was discharged from hospital. He knew he was stretching the truth, but if he needed to play the invalid for a few days, that was a hardship he was prepared to endure.

"It'd be easy to post a guard outside my place," he said to Robinson. "And I'm assuming you'll fill my position at the station while I'm on sick leave?"

Robinson nodded, a thoughtful glint in his eye. "Yes, I was

going to keep Constable Willow on to act in your position. He's already been inducted into your station, so it makes sense to keep him there." He rubbed his chin. "That might work. With you protecting her on the inside, a cop out the front, Willow doing a regular drive-by. It's not quite as good as a safe house, but it's not bad. An interesting solution to keep her safe."

"Hello!" Skylar waved her hand in the air. "I'm right here. Please don't talk about me as if this is already decided."

"We're not." Nash hit her with one of his best grins. One he knew would melt most women's panties right off them. But Skylar wasn't most women. "But you did promise me you'd cook a meal once we were safely out of the jungle. Well, this is your chance."

"Really? You'd stoop to that? Play on my conscience? Use the promise card? Use the invalid card?" She threw her hands in the air.

"You bet?" he said with a wicked smile. If making her feel guilty would get her to say yes, then so be it.

"It's actually not a bad idea," Daniella said. He could hardly believe she was backing him up on this one. But she threw him a look that told him he wasn't off the hook yet, and he sobered quickly.

"It seems you're all in on the conspiracy," Skylar huffed.

"So, is that a yes?" Nash held his breath.

"I guess so. But only for a few days, no more." That was okay, Nash would take whatever small win he could get.

* * *

"There's no food in this house." Skylar slammed the refrigerator door shut. "I can't believe you managed to cook anything with so few ingredients."

They'd only been home an hour, and she was already pacing like a caged lion. Nash wisely kept his mouth shut. The life of a bachelor cop was a lot of living on TV dinners and two-minute noodles. He'd never learned to cook properly, scrambled eggs and maybe spaghetti Bolognese, if he wanted to impress someone.

"There's ten packets of noodles in here and nothing else. I need to go to the supermarket to get some fresh ingredients."

He winced. She was probably right. He couldn't remember the last time he'd stocked his shelves. But going outside wasn't really on the cards.

"That's not in the protocol. We shouldn't leave the house, but I can send…" he began to say.

Skylar's eyes turned the color of ice. "I don't care what the *protocol* says. You know I'm only here because I don't really have a choice. And I *need* to go to the supermarket."

They stared at each other unblinking; at an impasse. Her words sounded a lot like an ultimatum, which was why he was the first to back down. Because the last thing he needed was Skylar storming out of his house after less than an hour under his protection.

"Okay," he said, raising his hand. "Let me run it by Robinson."

It shouldn't be too hard to organize a trip into town. His little wooden cottage was on the outskirts of Dimbulah. A quick, five-minute walk to the Main Street, or in their case, a one-minute drive.

"I'll get my shoes on."

"You don't need to come. You're supposed to be convalescing," she said, the snark clearly evident in her voice. "Why don't you stay here with your feet up and I'll run into town, like a good little woman."

Nash sighed. She wasn't taking this seriously. It was almost as if she was blaming him for her situation. Of course, he needed to come. He might be injured, but he was also part of her security detail. She still didn't seem to get how much danger she could be in.

He got up off the couch, reaching for his walking stick. They'd given him plenty of painkillers when they'd discharged him this morning after two days in hospital, and his leg was feeling pretty good, considering. But he still needed a stick to help him get around. The thick bandage on his face had been removed this morning, replaced by a few butterfly strips, and he was happy to see the gash on his cheekbone was healing nicely. They'd kept Skylar in hospital with him, after a special request from Robinson, so they could keep her safe and under police guard until he was ready to leave.

His replacement phone was on the kitchen countertop, and he hobbled over to pick it up. Even after the police had scoured the crash site, his old phone hadn't turned up. Which meant it'd been a good decision not to waste any time looking for it when the gunman had been after them.

"I can't believe we have to phone in and ask permission to go to the shops, like we're some irresponsible children who can't be trusted to do anything on their own." She glared at him, arms crossed, and hip planted against the countertop.

"That's not how this is, and you know it." Nash was already beginning to regret his suggestion to bring Skylar home. If she was going to be this difficult and bitter the whole time, it was going to be a very long few days. This Skylar was nothing like the woman he'd come to know in the jungle. That woman had been vulnerable and scared, but also feisty and determined. And then, for a while during their stay in hospital, Skylar had been solicitous toward him, concerned about his welfare. Now the walls were back up, and the old, aloof, reserved Skylar was firmly back in place.

Daniella had brought in some of Skylar's clothes to the hospital, and she was back in her normal uniform of blue jeans and a loose, linen shirt, sleeves rolled up to the elbows; hair drawn back into the tight ponytail she normally wore for work.

Nash understood she felt lost, out of place here in his house, and she was searching for familiar ground. He put the call through to Robinson, who wasn't at all happy with the break in procedure. But he eventually agreed to the trip, on two conditions. That the cop stationed at their front door go with them as backup—which Nash was going to do, anyway. And if Nash even thought he glimpsed someone who looked out of place, then the mission was to be aborted. Skylar wouldn't like that, but it was something she was going to have to get used to.

The media had swarmed all over the story of the chopper being shot out of the sky. It was front page news; a pilot killed, and two passengers injured and lost in the jungle for a day and a half. Images of the crash site had taken up so much of the early news reports that Skylar had asked Nash to turn it off, as she didn't want to keep being reminded of the horror of being hunted and the heartache of losing Paul.

Robinson had managed to keep Nash's identity away from the media. So far. But everyone knew the chopper had been headed for Stormcloud, and a couple of diligent news crews had driven out to the station and hounded Skylar's family for information. Steve and Daniella asked Nash not to tell Skylar about the media harassment, as it would only worry her more. Steve had succeeded at keeping the paparazzi at bay, locking the large, wrought iron front gates, and warning them that they'd be arrested for trespass if they dared even put one toe over the fence. This was now the third day after their rescue and Steve had reported that the last of the crews had given up this morning as interest in the crash waned, probably returning to the city and more up-to-the-minute stories. There was a small possibility someone from the media might yet be prowling around Dimbulah, searching for locals who knew a juicy tidbit or two. He was taking a risk, being seen with Skylar in town. The last thing they needed was the paparazzi camped out the front of his place. But it was a calculated risk. Nash also knew the locals had no love for the media, and hopefully, they wouldn't give too much away.

Robinson had most of his team working on finding the gunman who'd shot them out of the sky. But as of this morning, they still had no concrete leads. Even though Nash had wounded the man and he must've been hurt from his fall into the ravine, the gunman had disappeared. Like a ghost. Almost as if he and Skylar had made the whole thing up. And it was the same with the pilot of the helicopter that'd shot them down. There'd been no flight plan listed and no evidence that another chopper had even been in the vicinity of Lamb Range. Thank God they'd retrieved the rifle lodged in the cleft in the rocks. It certainly helped corroborate their story. But the gun had given up no more leads, as the serial number had been filed off. It was obviously bought on the black market, but it was turning up nothing helpful.

Dan Sanders had been interrogated three times over the past two days, while Nash had been in hospital. But the smug shit was refusing to talk. Pretending ignorance about the helicopter shooting, and feigning concern over Nash and Skylar's well-being.

Nash retrieved his gun—thankfully, the police had located his bag, with his lockbox still safely stowed inside—from the drawer in the dresser by the front door, and slung his holster over the top of his T-shirt. Normally it was kept in a gun safe in his bedroom, but with a potential threat out there, he needed it to be more accessible. He opened the front door and spoke to the cop on duty today. Nash had only met this constable for the first time this morning; they'd sent her up from Cairns. There was going to be a guard on his door around the clock for the next few days at least, in a rotating shift of eight hours each. He didn't envy the poor bugger who had to stand guard duty for that long. It was a shit of a job, but someone had to do it. Constable Schroeder was her name, and he briefed her on the upcoming outing.

She frowned and looked about to argue, and he merely held up his hand. "Robinson has agreed to this. So, let's just get it over as quickly as possible."

"We'll take the police cruiser, then," was all she said in reply. Smart lady.

"Let's go," he called to Skylar, and she appeared at the end of the hallway. "Please don't tell me we're going to be driven around in the back of the police car?"

"It's either that, or we don't go." Nash had had about enough of her attitude.

"Everyone in town is going to see us. Especially with you wearing that." She stared pointedly at his gun. "They're going to wonder. We're going to be the talk of the town."

"Probably," he admitted. He was used to being stared at, pointed at. People usually saw a cop and got out of their way, then gaped as they walked by. But Skylar valued her privacy, she wasn't used to people talking behind her back. The police cruiser was a necessary evil. A show of force, if you like. If there was someone still out there gunning for them, it showed that Nash and Skylar were under police protection and they'd hopefully think twice about trying to get to them.

This trip into town was going to be interesting. Not only did he have to hope they didn't bring themselves to the attention of the rogue gunman, but also pray they weren't spotted by any media.

Nash ushered Skylar to the rear seat of the police cruiser parked in the driveway. He was becoming better at using the walking stick. He could probably get by without it, but it might make for a good weapon. And it helped keep him firmly in the invalid category in Skylar's eyes. Because at the moment, that was the main reason she was justifying her stay at his house to herself. She'd said more than once she was determined to help Nash recover. And as soon as he was better, she was out of there.

165

CHAPTER FIFTEEN

Skylar strode ahead of Nash, not stopping to wait and see if he followed her into the supermarket. An anger that she couldn't explain burned deep in her belly. She knew it wasn't really Nash that she was angry at, but she was taking it out on him anyway, because she couldn't help it.

This whole situation sucked. All she wanted was to be back in her kitchen at Stormcloud. Not worried about who might be stalking them down the main street of a small, country town in the middle of a hot, summer day. And not thinking about going to Paul's funeral in a few days' time; a man who'd died, possibly because of her. And definitely not feeling like she was going to suffocate being locked up in a house with Nash for the next however long it took.

She pulled things off shelves and shoved them into her basket, without care or thought.

A quick glance backward told her that Nash had asked Constable Schroeder to stay outside the small IGA. Good. The last thing she needed was an armed policewoman trailing her around the supermarket aisles. Everyone was already staring as it was. Nash stayed near the front counter, keeping a wary eye on every customer and every staff member in the store. But the mere fact that he was also sporting a gun while dressed in civilian clothes would have tongues wagging. They were all locals, of course, and they all nodded a greeting to her, albeit with a question hovering behind their gaze. But at least they had enough manners not to ask. Everyone was local, except one woman Skylar didn't recognize. Nash followed her with his astute gaze as she strolled up and down the aisles. Most likely she was a tourist; there were a couple of caravans hitched to four-wheel-drives parked on Main Street. Nash narrowed his gaze in the tourist woman's direction. Really? Did he really suspect that middle-aged lady in flip-flops and flowery shorts to be a killer for hire?

She snorted her frustration. She needed to calm down. This was doing her no good. And in truth, maybe Nash was right to suspect everyone. Perhaps that ordinary-looking lady was on Dan Sanders' payroll and was right now reaching for a gun strapped to a hidden holster beneath her shirt.

Skylar whirled around to stare at the retreating woman's back. She disappeared around the end of the aisle, and Skylar let out a breath. Now she was becoming paranoid. She was better off leaving it up to Nash and the others who knew what they were doing. Taking a few deep lungfuls of air, she calmed her buzzing nerves and headed for the fresh produce section. Their range wasn't the best, but for a little town, hundreds of kilometers away from any big city, they didn't do too badly. Lifting a plump, red tomato to her nose, she drew in its distinctive smell. That was better. It calmed her, centered her. Food was reliable, it never let her down.

A few minutes later, she strolled back to the checkout, feeling a little more serene and in control. She'd decided what she was going to cook for Nash tonight, and the simple act of planning the meal in her head was a good distraction.

"Hello, Skylar. Senior Constable King." Kim was on checkout today, and he nodded his greeting to them both. She gave him an anemic smile, hoping he'd get the message that she didn't want to talk. Kim was tall and lanky, the owner's son, and normally Skylar enjoyed talking to him about any new products they were bringing in, or what fresh fruit was in season at the moment.

"Looks like you've got something delicious planned," Kim said conversationally. When neither she nor Nash answered, he must've got the hint, because he scanned her items without further comment, shooting one quick, curious glance in Nash's direction.

"Thanks, Kim. I'll see you soon," Skylar said, helping him pack the last of her ingredients into a reusable carry bag.

"Yes, thanks." Nash echoed her words. He hesitated for a second and then speared the younger man with a steely gaze. "By the way, Kim, has anyone been in here asking questions?"

"Ah, like what sort of questions, Senior Constable?" Kim blinked rapidly at Nash as he kept his laser focus on him.

"About me. Or about Skylar," Nash answered gruffly.

"Oh, ah, no, sir." Kim shook his head vehemently.

"That's good. But if anyone does…well, I'd like to keep this little shopping trip between you and me, if you know what I mean?" Nash's smile didn't reach his eyes.

"You got it, sir. My lips are sealed." Kim made a zipping motion with his hand across his mouth.

"Thank you." Nash nodded.

Skylar could feel Kim's stare burning a hole through her back as she exited the shop, Nash by her side.

Keeping her eyes pointed forward, she strode down the street, ignoring Constable Schroeder, who slotted in behind them. After two or three strides, she noticed Nash struggling to keep up with her. She'd forgotten all about his leg. He was so bloody stoic about the whole thing. She knew he didn't really need her help to recover. It was all part of the story to convince her to stay at his place, where she'd supposedly be safe. Nevertheless, a large part of her had been terribly relieved when the doctor had said he would suffer no long-term damage, and he'd be back to full duties within a month to six weeks. That was great news for Nash. It meant he could keep doing the job he loved so much.

"Was that really necessary?" she asked, once they were out of earshot of the doorway.

"Yes, it was," Nash said roughly. "We need to stay vigilant. And you need to stay behind me." He hobbled past her and put her between himself and Constable Schroeder. Had Nash really just snapped at her? She was about to answer back with an equally snarky response, when Nash stopped so abruptly in front of her that she ran into the back of him.

"In here." Nash dragged her into the mouth of a narrow alleyway.

"What the…?" But she never finished her question as Nash forced her behind a large dumpster, pushing her down so she could no longer see the main street, his solid body rammed up against her back, the bag of groceries squashed in between them.

"Over there. The guy with the baseball cap and dark shirt," she heard him say. It took her a second to realize he was directing the constable, who was still out on the street.

"Stay down," he hissed as she tried to poke her head above the dumpster.

"What's going on?" she squeaked, but he didn't answer.

Two anxious minutes later, Schroeder's voice echoed down the alley. "False alarm, sir. Just a tourist from Sydney. You can come out now."

Nash's large hand under her elbow helped her up to standing, and he led her out from behind the dumpster and into the street.

"Sorry," Nash apologized. "I saw someone who resembled the gunman," he admitted.

Skylar's glance took in everything around them. The street was still that of the same sleepy little town, but it now had an air of menace that'd been missing when she'd entered the supermarket. All she wanted now was to get back to Nash's cottage and out of sight.

"You don't have to apologize for doing your job," she replied.

They hustled the rest of the way to the police cruiser, and Skylar remained silent on the trip back to the house, vaguely aware that both Nash and the young constable were super vigilant, checking the street as they drove down it, making sure no one was following them. The constable made them stay in the car until she'd checked the house thoroughly, both inside and out, and then let them in through the front door. It'd been a false alarm, but it'd made Skylar more aware that she was still in danger. That Nash was still in danger.

"Can I get you anything before I start dinner?" she asked Nash as she placed her haul on the kitchen countertop.

"No, thanks. I'm gonna take it easy on the couch for a while." His face had gone a tad pale, and Skylar suddenly felt like a right witch for the way she'd been treating him. Even though he was uncomplaining about his wound, it was clearly still causing him pain.

She took him a glass of water and some paracetamol and put them on the table next to him.

"Thanks," he said, laying his head back against the cushion. "Can I ask what you're cooking tonight?" He sounded hesitant, as if she might bite his head off at the question. She mentally reprimanded herself for behaving like a she-devil, and was determined to make up for it.

"It's going to be quite simple tonight, I'm sorry."

"Don't you dare apologize. Anyone who cooks food for me is definitely an angel in disguise," he said. "I don't get too many home-cooked meals."

Judging by the minimal ingredients in his cupboards, she believed him. "Good. Well, I'm doing a roasted-cherry-tomato, basil, and goat cheese pasta, with some home-made damper and garlic butter."

"Sounds divine," he said, a spot of color coming back to his face. "Especially the damper. I haven't had homemade bread like that in ages."

"I hope you like it. You rest there, and let me know if you need anything." She made her way back to the small kitchen. Nash's house was an old weatherboard cottage that'd been renovated. The main living space was open plan, and had enough room for a comfortable couch and two wing chairs, a TV, and a dining table with four chairs. She could see the top of Nash's head from where she stood in the kitchen as he leaned back into the couch. There were two bedrooms, and only one bathroom, with a small porch to sit on out the front. A wall-mounted air conditioner kept the main living area cool, as the heat of the afternoon swirled outside. It was cute and comfortable, and like he'd said earlier, it was all he needed right now. Skylar tried for a moment to imagine herself living here. But the kitchen wasn't nearly big enough for her needs, and after living at Stormcloud for so long, she'd gotten used to the rustic luxury and the open spaces.

Half an hour later, the damper was in the oven, along with the tomatoes to roast for the pasta sauce. She put a saucepan of water on to boil on the stove. Everything else was prepared. It was an easy meal, as she'd already told Nash.

She glanced over at the couch. Nash hadn't moved, his blond hair falling over his eyes as he watched the TV.

A few faltering steps took her to the edge of the rug in the small living area.

"Nash?"

"Hm?" He looked up at her, eyes lidded, as if he'd almost been asleep. She took a second to appreciate his poor, battered face. The scar on his left cheek was healing well, but that, combined with the other small nicks and bruises, still gave him the look of a prize-fighter freshly returned from battle.

She took a seat at the other end of the couch. "I'm sorry I've been so…difficult." It was time she apologized. He'd been nothing but obliging and hospitable toward her. She'd been the one spitting at him like a cornered cat.

And she knew the reason why, but she wasn't about to reveal that to him.

She was scared. Scared of being alone in this house with him. What it meant. Because she had no idea how she was supposed to react to him. It was as if her skin had a million tiny gnats underneath it, and they buzzed and tingled whenever he came close. And they weren't lost and alone in the jungle, anymore. As funny as it might sound, she felt like she was on unstable ground with Nash now. In the jungle, they'd only had survival on their minds. A clear objective. And she'd allowed her emotions to be controlled by that need. To overrun all her natural senses of caution and let herself get carried away with her feelings for Nash.

But now they were back in civilization, in his house, and her feelings were all mixed up, a jumble of emotions. Her attraction to Nash was as strong as ever, there was no denying it. But she'd soon be going back to her life, and he to his. There was no point in continuing with this infatuation she had going. Was there? She'd sworn off men after Craig, was determined to live the rest of her life without male companionship. And then Nash had slammed into her world, giving her heart palpitations, and showing her that he was different. That he could be trusted.

She hated to feel like this. She had no mechanism with which to cope with these conflicting emotions.

She stared out the window, unable to meet his gaze.

"Difficult, is that the word?" he asked, but his broad smile belied his words.

She frowned at him. She was trying to apologize and all he could do was mock her?

"I don't see you as difficult, Skylar." He moved closer, shifting down the couch so their knees were touching. His voice was tender, not what she'd been expecting. "I see you as a woman who knows her own mind. Who's been through a terrible ordeal, but faced it with courage and humor." Nash lifted a hand to her chin, forcing her to look at him. "It's okay if you're struggling to find a way to deal with the past few days, you're only human, after all." His thumb traced softly down the line of her jaw, and it felt so good she wanted to lean her cheek into his palm. "But you'll get through it. We'll get through it, together. If you'll let me help."

If she'd been standing, she was sure she would've gone weak at the knees at his words. How did he know exactly what to say? And how could she argue with that? He was letting her off the hook. Giving her an excuse for her bad behavior.

His other hand came up to cup her face as he stared into her eyes. Goddamn, he had the bluest eyes. Always with a hint of a smile behind them. And those lips. She already knew how generous and giving he could be with those lips. What would it be like to kiss him right now? Without the jungle as their bed and without fear driving her emotions? Skylar had dismissed their kiss at the waterfall that night as a one-off. Something borne from shared adversity, as a way to put into action some of those emotions that'd been threatening to overwhelm her.

But she *really* wanted to kiss Nash again. Here. Now.

She leaned toward him, right at the same moment he drew her chin up to his face.

"You're beautiful," he murmured, and then his mouth

closed over hers.

Oh, the sweetness of him. He was gentle, yet she could feel the tension thrumming through him as he held himself back. He wanted more, but he was letting her take the lead.

And so, she did.

Reaching a hand around the back of his head, she let her fingers twine in all those glorious golden curls. Her mouth demanded more from him, and she shuddered as he ran a hand up beneath her shirt, grazing the skin on the small of her back. For a fleeting second, she remembered the young policewoman guarding their house. But she wouldn't be able to see what was going on through the solid wooden door.

"Mm, you taste fresh, like a sexy nymph straight out of the garden."

"Basil," she said. "I ate some of the basil." She laughed and nipped at the tip of his nose.

"I like it," he murmured, claiming her mouth again, and she was lost in her lust for Nash. It was a deluge of longing. A liquid pull deep in her belly answered the passion in his kiss. Taking care not to bump his wounded thigh, she pushed him gently down onto the sofa, deciding to ignore the constable's presence outside.

Nash lay along the length of the couch, head propped up on the armrest, eyes indigo-dark with longing as he stared up at her.

Her fingers found their way to the top button of his shirt. She'd already had more than a good look at his amazing abs, but this time she wanted to play with them, stroke them, run her fingers tantalizingly close to the waist of his jeans. Each button came undone with a flick of her fingers, revealing more of all that lovely, manly chest. Finally, the last one gave way, and she spread his shirt wide, just like she'd done the other morning in the jungle. But this time, her intentions were different. Not honorable in the slightest. And from the hunger radiating from his gaze, Nash was completely on board with her thoughts.

She leaned down and used her tongue to explore the hard planes of his chest. Mm, just the right amount of muscle there, not overly pumped from excessive use of the gym. But firm and tanned, with a light sprinkling of blonde hair. On impulse, she licked each nipple in turn, then watched as they puckered in the cooling airstream from the air conditioner. He gasped, his eyes going almost black with heat.

"Woman, what are you trying to do to me?" he growled.

She wasn't sure; all she knew was that she wanted to keep doing it.

Nash's phone pinged from the coffee table with an incoming message. They both looked at it, then returned to what they were doing. Skylar found the top button of Nash's pants and undid it slowly. He was wearing shorts today, a concession to his wounded thigh. But he hadn't seemed to notice that he'd also exposed the scars on his lower legs. She'd caught a few of the locals staring at them in the supermarket, but Nash had either ignored them, or was perhaps too preoccupied with staying vigilant to notice. Whatever the reason, Skylar hoped this might be the beginning of Nash slowly coming to terms with his scars. They were part of him, and he shouldn't have to hide them. Perhaps telling her about how he got them had been cathartic, in some way.

She'd ask him about it later. But right now, she was wondering if she could get those shorts off without hurting his wounded leg. With precise care, she slowly slid the zipper down, watching his face as she did so. His features, which were normally schooled into a genial half-smile, had lost all that professional veneer. His blue gaze bored into her, intense and full of a fire she'd never seen before. A barely veiled hunger evident in the slant of his mouth. His hands reached up to grab her hips and pull her closer.

Her phone, which was over on the kitchen countertop, pinged with a message, as well—her mother had brought her a new one while she'd been in hospital. Skylar lifted her head and glared at it with annoyance. Who the hell would be texting her now?

"Do you think—" Her words were cut off by a knock at the front door, which had her scrambling off the couch quicker than a mouse with a cat on its tail. Nash sat up swiftly and began doing up his shirt buttons, an unimpressed grimace on his face.

Skylar ran a hand through her hair to tidy it, but she knew she still looked disheveled. "Oh, ah…wait a sec. I'm coming," she called. It could only be the young constable; she wouldn't have allowed anyone else to come to the door unannounced.

Skylar drew in a deep breath and cracked the door open, keeping Nash, who was still doing up his buttons, out of sight.

"Sorry to interrupt." Constable Schroder looked decidedly uncomfortable. Shit, she knew what she and Nash had been up to. Skylar felt color rising up her face, but kept her gaze fixed on the young woman, determined not to let embarrassment take over. "But there's a man in the car over there," Schroder pointed to the road and Skylar rolled her eyes, "who says he's your brother, and is demanding to see you."

It was indeed Dale, leaning out the window of his four-wheel-drive, making hand signals that were obviously meant to encourage her to convince the police officer to let him in.

"Yes, that's my brother," Skylar sighed. "You can let him in."

"I'll need to clear it with Senior Sergeant Robinson first." The constable reached for the radio in her shoulder holster.

There went her and Nash's little interlude out the window.

"Dale's coming," she said to Nash, who was doing up the last button on his shirt and straightening his hair.

"That's a shame, just when things were getting interesting," he said with a wicked grin.

Yes, they had been. And who knew where it might've stopped, if Dale hadn't decided to visit? But perhaps Dale's interruption was a good thing.

CHAPTER SIXTEEN

Nash stood up from the couch, running his hand quickly through his hair. Would Skylar's brother be able to tell what he'd been up to with his sister?

Too late to worry now, because the door swung open, and Constable Schroeder ushered Dale and Daisy through.

Schroeder shot him an unreadable glance, and said, "Robinson has agreed to this visit, but he doesn't want any more unannounced family or friends arriving." Then she shut the door firmly behind her. She was pissed at this break in procedure, but she was professional enough not to ream him out in front of Dale. She also probably knew what he and Skylar had been up to. He needed to get his game face back on. And stop being so unprofessional. The problem was, when Skylar was around, he seemed to lose all logical thought.

Dale strode over and wrapped Skylar in an embrace. "I needed to see for myself you were okay."

"I'm fine," she said, struggling to break out of his hold. She slapped him playfully on the arm. "Put me down you big oaf."

"He's been like a bear with a sore head," Daisy said, also stepping in to give Skyler a hug. "When Daniella told him he couldn't come to the hospital to see you, he was *not* happy."

Nash stood back and watched the interplay between the three. Dale and Skyler were obviously close. And Daisy had an easy manner with them both. Dale and Daisy had connected after Dale had rescued her from a flooding river, and then he'd fallen head over heels in love. But Daisy was originally from Perth and had gone home to continue her life at university. Love had won out in the end, however, when Daisy had returned to the area to follow her dream of introducing native bush foods to everyday people. She and Dale were now engaged, and by the looks of them, as happy as two cats who'd got the cream. She was also helping Skylar create a kitchen garden, stocked with all kinds of native foods that she could use in her amazing creations. Daisy and Skylar had become close over the past six months, and it was good to see Skylar had a girlfriend she could rely on. Nash wondered if Skylar had confided in Daisy about her relationship with Craig. He somehow doubted it.

"Sorry, mate, I almost forgot you were there," Dale said, finally letting his sister go. He came over and shook hands with Nash. "It sounds like you came out of this a little worse for wear." He glanced at Nash's face and then down at his bandaged leg. He did a double take when he noticed the scarring on his lower calves, but didn't comment, so Nash left it alone.

"It's not as bad as it looks. I was lucky." And that was the truth. If the SES volunteers hadn't found them when they did, the infection might've been much worse. But at least they'd survived and had lived to tell their tale. "If it wasn't for your sister here, things might've turned out quite different."

Skylar was in the kitchen, pulling things out of the oven. She looked up and gave him an exasperated stare. "We were running for our lives. We both did things we're proud of... and not so proud of. But don't you dare give me all the credit." She waggled a finger at Nash.

"Mm, that smells good." Dale wandered closer, his nose in the air.

"It's our dinner," Skylar retorted. "And no, there's not enough for you."

"Oh." Dale screwed his face up in a pout

"It's okay. We were going to have a meal at the pub before we head home," Daisy said, scowling at Dale.

"But I love Skylar's homemade damper," Dale grumbled, licking his lips as he spied the warm bread on the countertop.

"Stop it," Skylar said. "I'll be home soon enough. Then, I'll make you whatever you want."

"Good." Dale seemed to sober at that, his handsome features lowering in a frown. "And speaking of coming home…" He took a seat in one of the wing chairs. "…when do you think that'll happen?" His gaze landed squarely on Nash. "Now that the papp—" Dale stopped himself just in time before he mentioned the media, shooting a glance in Skylar's direction, but she was concentrating on the food and didn't seem to have heard him. Daniella still thought it was better if Skylar didn't know they'd been harassed by the press.

Of course, Skylar's brother wanted his sister at home. The problem was, Nash had no clear answers. He re-took his seat at the end of the couch. Daisy came over and perched on the arm of Dale's chair, and he wrapped a casual arm around her waist, smiling up into her face. They were clearly very happy together. Nash suddenly had a longing for that kind of intimacy. To know somebody so well that being together was easy, effortless. It'd be nice to have someone to share his life with. But his job made that hard at times. His last long-term relationship had been over four years ago, back when he'd been working in Brisbane. Tonya had been fun, a free spirit who'd wanted to change the world with her herbal teas and protest marches. But she'd never understood his commitment to his job, or the long hours he had to put in. They'd drifted apart, and Nash had only had a few sporadic, short-lived affairs after that. He was thirty-one years old. He'd never thought time would run out for him to find the right person. But perhaps he needed to start looking a little harder.

Nash glanced up and saw Skylar staring at him.

"Did you hear me?" Dale asked.

"Sorry, what?" Nash had been lost in his contemplations.

"When can Skylar come back to Stormcloud? Now that, you know…"

"Yes, I'd really like to know that, as well," Skylar said, taking a seat at the other end of the couch.

Talk about putting him on the spot. Three pairs of eyes were trained on him.

"That really depends on how our investigation goes over the next few days."

"I'm not going to hide out here, forever," Skylar warned.

"I realize that," Nash said. Although his heart squeezed tight at the thought he might not be able to keep her eternally safe. "Robinson is throwing everything he has at locating this man called Stan the Man or the chopper pilot. If he can find one of them, then they could lead us to the first gunman."

"But what happens then? Even if they capture the gunman and his brother, what's going to stop Sanders sending another hitman after Skylar? And another after that? And yourself?" Dale added, almost as an afterthought.

"If we can pin this first hit on Sanders, then a judge can freeze all his assets. He won't have access to his money, and then hopefully we'll become less of a priority as he adjusts to life behind bars with no chance of parole, and no one to do his bidding."

"Hm." Dale didn't sound convinced.

"Well, I've made a decision," Skylar declared into the

awkward silence that followed. "I'll stay with Nash up until Paul's funeral on Friday. I want to go and pay my respects. After that, I'm going home. Whether you've caught Stan or not." She looked him directly in the eye, daring him to argue.

Which he was definitely going to do. "That's only three days away. You can't—"

Skylar held up her hand. "That's right. But like Dale said, I can't hide out here forever. And by then your leg should've recovered enough so that you can cope on your own."

Three days. Could Robinson's team find the men they were looking for in that time? It was asking a lot. But he knew that look on Skylar's face. She was one determined woman. Paul's funeral was in Cairns, and it was only right that Skylar wanted to go and pay tribute to the man who'd lost his life in part because of them. He wanted to attend as well, although Robinson had advised against it. But if Skylar was going, so was he.

He hung his head. "I'll talk to Robinson, see what he says."

"You can talk all you like; my mind is made up," Skylar said.

He was sure it was. His problem would be his boss. Nash also understood that if he and Skylar attended the funeral, it'd be a logistical nightmare for Robinson and his men. But he also knew Skylar would go, whether she had police protection or not, so Robinson would have to make this work.

"We'll be going, too," Daisy interjected. "Maybe we should drive over in a convoy. If that'd help?" She turned her emerald-green gaze to Nash. Daisy really was a stunning lady. With her coffee skin, green eyes, and long, caramel hair down to her mid-back, she'd make most catwalk models jealous. However, she was a bit like Skylar, in that she never flaunted her beauty. Most of the time, it seemed as if she were actively trying to hide it—or at the very least ignore it—under her regular work attire of baggy jeans, button-up shirts, and boots. This evening, she'd changed into denim shorts and a sky-blue, silky blouse that contrasted nicely against her brown locks and skin. Dale was one lucky man.

"That might be a good idea," Nash mused. There was safety in numbers. With Dale and Daisy, as well as a police car tailing them and perhaps even Daniella and Steve, if they were going, a show of force might make the gunman think twice. If indeed, he was even still out there.

"I must, say, this is the most relaxed I think I've ever seen you look." Daisy changed the subject, waving a hand up and down, encompassing Nash's surf shorts and short-sleeved shirt. Then her eyes widened slightly as she suddenly caught sight of his scars. He could see as things became clearer in her mind. Why he always wore long pants and long sleeves. But, to her credit, she merely said, "It suits you. Hopefully, we see more of this relaxed you around the place." This time, her gaze shot to Skylar. The hint of a raised eyebrow was the only giveaway that Daisy suspected there was something else going on. She was an astute lady.

Dale frowned, as if realizing he was missing some subtlety in the conversation, but not understanding exactly what it was. Nash was sure Daisy would fill him in later. He winced at that thought. Dale was a very protective brother. He might not like the idea of Nash and his sister being together. But that was a bridge he'd have to cross if he ever came to it.

Skylar spent the next ten minutes interrogating Dale and Daisy on how Bindi and Julie were coping with the cooking while she'd been away. She gave them plenty of hints to pass on, and ended up by saying she would call Bindi and help her with this week's menu.

"We'll let you get to your dinner," Daisy finally said, standing up and dragging Dale with her. "I'm really happy that you both survived." She went over to the couch and gave Skylar a heartfelt hug. "We were so worried about you." She leaned back and stared at her friend. "You make sure you listen to the senior constable here. He's only trying to protect you. And I know what you're like, you'll argue something is black until the cows come home, when it is clearly white." Daisy cast Nash a sympathetic glance.

"Humph," was Skylar's only reply. But she pulled Daisy in for one more quick hug, before releasing her and taking Dale by the elbow to lead him to the front door. "Have a nice dinner at the pub," she said, wrapping her arms around her brother's neck.

"Yeah, well, I bet their chicken snitty won't be nearly as nice as whatever you're serving up here." Dale made puppy-dog eyes at Skylar.

"Get out, you big oaf." Skylar pretended to push him through the door.

Nash and Skylar stood in the doorway to wave farewell to the other couple.

Schroeder came up the steps onto the porch as Dale opened the door of his four-wheel-drive for Daisy. She stood beside Nash as they waved goodbye. Her uniform was immaculately pressed; the pleat running down the middle of her trousers was so sharp you could slice a cut of beef on that edge. Her blonde hair was scraped back into a severe bun at the nape of her neck. She might be pretty if she ever relaxed. She was clearly a stickler for protocol; one of those cops who reveled in the military-style rules of the force. Nash hoped she was as good at her job as she was at following the rules. She hadn't said much during their trip into town, or while she'd been on duty all afternoon. But she watched everything with keen eyes and remained alert and on guard the whole time.

"I've just finished a perimeter run," Schroeder reported, watching Skylar as she retreated into the house. "Senior Sergeant Robinson has someone coming to relieve me in a few hours," Schroeder continued quietly as Nash observed the other couple drive away. "I'll be back tomorrow."

"Right." Nash scrubbed a hand through his hair. "Thanks for everything," Nash added belatedly.

"Do you want me to do a quick run through the house before I go?" Schroeder kept her eyes pointed forward.

"No, I've got that covered, thanks." Nash had already checked that all the other windows and doors were locked, but her careful vigilance reminded him he should probably do it again, just to make sure. Skylar had complained about having to keep everything closed up, as she wanted to let the late-afternoon breeze run through the house, until it finally dawned on her why he was locking everything. They'd have to make do with running the air conditioner all night, instead.

He closed the door behind him with a click and limped over to the dining area, where Skylar was laying out two plates. He hardly ever sat at the small table. Most nights, he'd eat his microwave dinners on the couch in front of the TV, or even leaning up against the countertop in the kitchen.

"This looks great," he said.

Skylar had set the table with proper plates and cutlery, the plates piled high with what could only be called gourmet-style pasta. The damper sat in the middle of the table, with a pat of real butter next to it. She'd even found a candle somewhere in the depths of his kitchen, and there were two wine glasses, waiting to be filled from a bottle of chardonnay. She must've bought all this from the shop because there was no way she found it in his kitchen. It was all very grown-up.

Skylar shrugged off his comment and took a seat, looking up at him expectantly. Even though Nash knew this wasn't supposed to be a date, he decided that they needed music. Something to complement this wonderful meal. He limped over to his stereo and flicked it on. The last CD he'd been listening to started up. Keith Urban. It'd have to do, for now.

This wasn't supposed to be a seduction, just two friends having dinner and listening to some music.

Nash went over and sat, tucking into the plate of pasta. "Oh. Holy cow. This is…amazing, Skylar."

He half expected her to do one of her shrugs of indifference again, but her face lit up with a bright smile.

"Do you really like it?" she asked, and he suddenly realized that his reply truly mattered to her. Why on earth would she need his seal of approval?

"Yes, I really like it, Skylar," he said, meeting her gaze and holding it. "You're an awesome cook. And an awesome woman." Skylar blushed at his words, but perhaps she needed to hear them. Maybe she didn't hear it enough. People took it for granted that she could cook, and she was a resilient woman who could look after herself. But by the look on her face, he could see that she was still terribly uncertain deep down inside. How could a woman as beautiful and talented as her not realize what she had?

Skylar was rubbing her wrist again, and he reached for her hand, covering it with his own. "I mean it." Her blue eyes widened at his touch. "And I meant what I said to Dale. I don't think I would've survived without you out there in the jungle. You need to give yourself credit for that."

She bit her lip and stared at him, then her gaze dropped to the table. The muted tones of Keith drowning out what would otherwise have been an awkward silence. Right at that moment, Nash wanted to find this Craig guy and take him into a private room, away from all prying eyes, and teach him a lesson he wouldn't forget. How could any man treat Skylar so badly that she doubted herself at every turn? It was a crime that needed to be punished.

"I do give myself credit," she replied, but there was a lack of sincerity in her answer. "Do you want a glass of wine?" she asked, removing her hand from beneath his. Which was a shame. Because now they were alone again, the buzz of anticipation had started up along Nash's skin, and his mind went back to that hot kiss they'd shared before Dale had appeared.

"Yes, please." He watched as she poured them each a generous glass. As she passed it over to him, his fingers grazed hers and his awareness of her shot up another level. They locked gazes over the rim of their glasses, and he suddenly felt an altogether different type of hunger fill him.

Skylar began to eat, breaking him off a piece of damper and buttering it for him. He watched her nimble fingers work the butter knife and wished he were that piece of cutlery. She shot him a look, almost as if she could hear his thoughts, and their gazes locked for uncounted seconds, until she finally broke away to take another sip of wine.

Nash bit into the damper, which melted in his mouth, and ate a few more mouthfuls of pasta, but his mind was no longer on the food. He was unsure of where this was going with Skylar. He wanted her badly, but that was nothing new. He'd wanted her from the first moment he'd laid eyes on her. But she'd rejected him with her cool manner and uncompromising words. Now, however, he could see that she'd only been protecting herself.

During their time together in the jungle, he'd broken down so many of her defenses. She wanted him, too, that much was abundantly clear. But she was a complicated woman, and with her, he was pretty sure a simple case of lust wouldn't be enough to entice her into a fling. But on the couch earlier, their scorching kiss had set him aflame, and she'd seemed keen to get him undressed. To go that one step farther. But now, he wasn't so sure what her intentions were as she picked at her meal.

One thing he was sure of, however, was how much his body hummed with pleasure when she was near. How a fire lit in his belly every time he touched her. How much he wanted to lay her down in his bed and explore her body, slow and languorous, until she purred like a contented cat. There was a chemistry between them that he wasn't sure he'd ever encountered with another woman.

If he took her to his bed now, where would it lead? Would he be happy with one night with Skylar? Would she be happy with one night?

They were going to be locked up together for the next three days. Could they take these next three days as a sort of interlude? An escape from reality. The idea had merit.

He'd never know unless he put it out there. She could always say no. Which might make their enforced time together uncomfortable. But he had an inkling she might not say no.

Pushing his chair back, he walked around the table and held out his hand. "Ever since that one dance we had at the ball, I've wanted to do it again. Would you do me the honor?" He waited as she considered his hand. This was the make-or-break moment, and he almost held his breath.

Her dark eyes suddenly softened. "Why, yes, sir. I would love to dance to Keith Urban with you." Skylar gave a girlish giggle and took his hand.

Nash silently thanked Keith; he owed him big time for giving him this opportunity.

Urban was crooning a ballad, his voice soft and smooth. Nash took Skylar's right hand in his and pulled her left hand around his waist, tugging her hips in close to his own. He could dance a passable waltz when required, and they began to sway their hips in time with the music, gliding their bare feet across the floor. He liked the way Skylar felt in his arms. Liked the heat of her radiating through his shirt, her soft body held against his chest. He would've been happier if she was wearing that skimpy little dress she'd had on at the ball, the one that'd let him feel each and every one of her curves. But at least with what she was wearing tonight, he could run his hand underneath her shirt and find the warm skin at the small of her back, and run his finger around the waistband of her jeans.

He almost forgot about his injured leg, instead revelling in the moment, losing himself in the undulating rhythm, as he and Skylar moved as one.

At first, Skylar held herself a little apart from Nash, but he drew her closer, laying his chin on top of her head, and with a sigh that sounded a lot like that of deliverance, she lay her cheek against the crook of his shoulder and let her body meld to the shape of his.

CHAPTER SEVENTEEN

Skylar let Keith Urban's voice roll through her, his dulcet tones washing away any remaining vestiges of worry. Laying her cheek against Nash's chest, she could hear the beating of his strong heart beneath his shirt. It felt so right to be held by him. She decided she was just going to enjoy dancing with Nash and go with whatever happened tonight. Why was she continuously fighting with herself? Fighting with her hunger for another human's touch. For Nash's touch. Her head was constantly arguing with her heart about what was best for her. Well, maybe tonight she was going to let her heart and her body lead the way. To hell with it all.

Were things about to *get interesting again*, as Nash had so succinctly put it, when Dale and Daisy had interrupted their kiss on the couch?

She hoped so.

And by the feel of Nash's growing erection against her hip, Nash was hoping so, too.

Nash kept his shirt untucked from his shorts, casual style, and this allowed Skylar easy access to what she wanted most. She ran her hand beneath his shirt, following the contours of his lower back, finding each bump of his vertebrae as she worked up his spine. His warm skin felt wonderful beneath the palm of her hand.

"Hmm, this is nice," she hummed on an exhale. "I'm a closet Keith fan," she added.

"Oh, for a second, I thought you meant that dancing with me was nice?" Nash feigned a hurt expression.

"Maybe that, too," she said demurely, raising her head so she could look him in the eye.

He captured her jaw with his fingers and held her gaze. "Where do you want this to go?" he asked.

It seemed there'd be no beating around the bush tonight. Skylar's heart rate soared at his question. Where *did* she want this to go?

"I'm going to be completely honest with you, Skylar. I want to take you to my bed. I want to make love to you." He took her hand and put it on his chest, right above his heart. "Can you feel that?"

Yes, she could feel the thrumming in his chest, and see the pulse running through his neck. It made her stomach do all kinds of strange flip-flops, to think she had this effect on him. This man, with the compelling blue eyes, who seemed so serious and proficient when he wore his police uniform, was now surrendering himself to her.

"My heart is thumping like crazy at the mere thought of you. You set my soul on fire from the very first time I saw you. But I know you might be hesitant, after what your ex-boy—"

Skylar shushed him with a finger to his lips. She didn't want to think about Craig. He wasn't part of her world now. Nash was here, and he was real, his flesh and blood beneath her fingers, hunger burning in his eyes.

Without speaking, she took his hand and led him toward his bedroom.

The room was dark, Nash had secured the windows and drawn the curtains earlier in the afternoon, before it had even got fully dark. But she preferred it that way. If she was truly going to go through with this, it'd been a long time since she'd made love with a man, and perhaps the lack of illumination might help with her self-confidence. A beam of light streamed down the hallway from the main living area, and it was enough to see their way to the bed.

Skylar had briefly glimpsed Nash's bedroom when he'd first shown her around the house. Her own room—the spare room—was down the hall and to the left, and it was smaller, with just enough room to squeeze in a double bed and two side tables. Nash's room had been decorated in dark, masculine colors, in shades of chocolate and tan, with white walls. His large, king-sized bed took pride of place in the middle of the room, with a walk-in closet on one side and a door to the shared bathroom leading off the other.

Her bare feet found the rug beneath the bed, and she turned around to face Nash, meeting the edge of the bed with the back of her legs.

He said nothing, merely stared at her with those intense eyes, following her lead.

She sucked in a breath.

Her fingers found the buttons of his shirt and worked their way down the line, undoing each one with delicious anticipation. Then she slipped the shirt over his shoulders and let it drop to the floor, like she'd just unwrapped a Christmas gift, revealing the much-anticipated present inside. Even in the dim light, Skylar could see the hard planes of his chest, the angular lines of his shoulder muscles as they sloped up to meet his neck. His narrow waist and sinewy hips.

He stood perfectly still, letting her run her fingers down his chest, investigating every bump and contour, his gaze never leaving her face.

She'd been meaning to ask him again about his amazing tan, but the words evaporated in her mouth as his lips came down to claim hers.

Her hands roved over his shoulders, down his back, becoming twitchy with hunger, wanting to feel him all over; all at once.

Without realizing quite how it happened, while she was busy devouring his mouth, her shirt ended up next to his on the floor. And so did her jeans. His nimble hands removed them without fuss or fanfare, and she was left with only panties and bra on. She should feel exposed, vulnerable, because he was seeing her body for the first time. But the way his gaze raked down her legs and then up over her breasts made her feel the exact opposite.

His shorts were the only thing standing between her seeing him fully naked. She fumbled with the top button and zip, drawing them down his hips before she suddenly remembered.

"What about your leg?" She glanced at the white bandage wrapped around his thigh quickly and then away. It still made her a little queasy to think about it. And it still surprised her she'd been able to deal with his wound out in the jungle when she'd had no other option.

"It's fine," he reassured her. "And I know you'll be gentle with me." He raised one corner of his mouth in a cheeky smile.

Skylar wanted to be anything but gentle, but she'd control herself for Nash's sake.

"Let me do it," he said, taking over the removal of his shorts. He carefully shimmied them down over the bandage, and then her wish came true. He was standing in front of her, naked. And, oh, he was a glorious sight to behold, his erection pulsing out his need for her. Then he smiled, his teeth white in the muted light of the room, and something sparked hungrily deep inside her.

She pushed him backward toward the bed, taking care of

his leg. Then, with an uncharacteristic abandon of all propriety, she flicked off her bra and panties and crawled onto the bed after him. No man had seen her naked in four years. But she suddenly didn't care. In a flash of faith, she knew that Nash appreciated her for what she was and would like what he saw. Otherwise, he wouldn't be with her here tonight.

Settling her head onto the pillow next to him—on his uninjured side—she let her legs drape gently down the length of his. All that naked skin. It was so good to feel the warmth and aliveness of Nash next to her. Why had she left it this long to find human connection again? She'd been kidding herself when she decided she could live the rest of her life without a man. She hadn't even realized how much she was missing until this exact moment.

Her hand roamed over his torso, down, down, following the trail of hair, leading to…Oh, hello. She stroked his erection with gentle fingers. It throbbed beneath her touch, and Nash let out a gasp. She certainly hadn't realized how much she missed *this* part.

Nash's hungry mouth found hers, and he rolled up onto his elbow so he could cradle her head in his is hand. But the move elicited a grunt of pain.

He'd said his leg was fine, but he was probably lying. There was only one thing for it. She pushed him down onto the bed and straddled his hips to make sure he stayed there. Taking control.

This time, she let her tongue do the exploring, tasting, and licking all the way down his magnificent body. Until she found the tip of his erection. Could she do this? Craig had often demanded she give him a blowjob, but very rarely reciprocated, using the misogynistic excuse that men needed it more than women. Men liked it more. She'd come to despise that particular act even more than the rest of it.

Nash groaned. "Oh, Jesus, Skylar." He feathered his hand down her back. But there was no suggestion of coercion. He didn't place his hand on the back of her head and push her down, like Craig used to do. She could feel the urgent need drumming through Nash. But he let her make the decision.

Taking him in her mouth, she began a gentle rhythm.

He groaned again and began to move his hips along with her. She felt in control. Powerful. This was nothing like the demoralizing performances she'd been forced to carry out with Craig.

His gasps of passion as she moved lit a fire between her own legs. She was going to combust with need if she didn't have him soon. After a few moments, she stopped and sat up.

Nash lifted his head, his dark eyes boring into her.

"Your turn now," he said huskily, and levered up to his elbows, as if he meant to do exactly that. He even turned his head to hide the grimace of pain as he sat up. But she saw it.

"Next time," she promised. Wriggling along the length of his body, she lay on top of him, breasts pushed into his chest, hips hovering over the top of his hips.

"God, Skylar, you're so beautiful. Do you know that?"

She didn't answer, because she wasn't sure she did know it. But if he thought she was beautiful, then that was enough for her.

Instead, she dug her knees into the bed and sat astride him, her core hovering over his erection. Slowly, she lowered herself until the tip was just touching. The heat of his cock surged through her. She wanted him inside her so bad.

"In the side drawer," Nash croaked. "We're going to need it."

What? Skylar straightened. Why was he interrupting her now? When she was so close to...

Oh. It finally dawned on her. It'd been so long since she'd had sex that she hadn't even had to think about protection.

The idea almost seemed absurd. At least Nash was thinking straight. She reached over and pulled out the drawer, finding a box and pulling out a wrapped condom. The notion of him having a whole box in his side table made her hesitate for a second. But then again, why wouldn't he? He was a good-looking, single man. And tonight wasn't about asking him about his previous love-life. It was about fulfilling a need. Her need, and his need.

She took her time slowly rolling on the condom. He bucked beneath her touch, as if he almost couldn't bear to wait a single second longer. And neither could she.

Regaining her position above him, she locked her gaze with his and then dropped onto him. That second when he entered her was sweet torment. So long. So long since she'd given herself permission to feel this. She let her body take control. It knew what she needed. As did Nash. Big hands grabbed her hips, urging her on. She wanted to watch his face, to see if he was soaring as high as she was on this untapped emotion, this fervent need.

"That's it, Skylar," he murmured. "Take me, I'm yours."

It was the sound of his voice that toppled her over the edge. That deep growl urging her on, telling her to take what she wanted, because he was right there with her. That he would never hurt her.

She let out a small scream of pure pleasure and rode the wave of her shuddering orgasm, higher and higher, until she collapsed onto Nash's chest, breathing so hard she could've just run a marathon. Somewhere in the vague recesses of her mind, she registered Nash's cries of passion as he, too, reached his peak.

Skylar had no idea how long they lay together like that. With her draped over his chest, his hands still resting on her hips. At last, her breathing returned to normal. Gently, so as not to hurt Nash, she clambered over to his uninjured side and lay down, still hardly able to believe what she'd just done.

"I'm sorry that was so quick," she apologized. Skylar had thought men were the only ones capable of climaxing that quickly. In her previous life, it'd taken lots of foreplay and plenty of time and attention for her to orgasm. And with Craig… it'd happened rarely, if ever. "It's been a long time between drinks for me," she added.

"You have nothing to apologize for," Nash retorted. "Fast, hot and dirty does it for me every time."

"Oh, okay." Skylar drew absentminded circles on his chest with her finger. "I was going to say we could try again. You know, get it right next time. Try for long, slow, and sensual. And if that didn't work. We could try again. But if you don't want to…" She let the words hang in the air.

She could feel Nash's smile in the dark. "When you put it that way…" He rolled up onto his elbow to stare down at her. "I've got all night."

He kissed her deeply, then rolled away, and it took Skylar a few seconds to work out that he was removing the condom.

But he was soon back in her arms, and she snuggled down into the crook of his shoulder. "I hope Schroeder didn't hear us," Skylar said sleepily into his chest.

"It's probably the new guy from Cairns out there now. They change the police guard every eight hours." Nash replied, just as sleepily.

"Oh, great. I'm not sure how reassuring that is," Skylar groaned. "I think I'd prefer if Schroeder was the one who overheard us." At least Schroeder was a known entity. Would she even be up to look this new cop in the eye in the morning?

She wondered about the propriety of what they were doing. Would Nash's boss frown on him, consorting with the very person he was supposed to protect? Nash didn't seem fazed by it, so she'd follow his lead.

Skylar almost giggled. In some ways, this was the ultimate form of protection. There was no safer place than lying in the arms of a police officer. Was there?

CHAPTER EIGHTEEN

Nash went to roll over in bed and remembered his injured leg as a jolt of pain shot through his thigh. All the activity last night hadn't helped. But he wouldn't change a thing. Last night had been so worth it.

He rubbed a hand across his eyes. It was still dark in his bedroom, but a glow of light could be seen along the bottom of his curtains, heralding morning. He was awake now, and as his leg began to throb, he realized there would be no going back to sleep. Pain killers and food, in that order, was what he needed.

But first, he turned his head on the pillow and came face-to-face with the most gorgeous woman he'd ever had the pleasure of knowing. She was fast asleep; her face peaceful in repose. Mouth a plump rosebud, with a hint of pink about her lips. He liked to think that was from all his kissing. He hadn't noticed before, but her eyelashes were slightly darker than the hair on her head, reminding him of the dark, sugary surface of a crème caramel. Strands of her honey-blonde hair fell across her face, and he gently tucked them behind her ear. She stirred but didn't wake.

He would let her sleep. Get up and make some breakfast. Poor woman needed some rest, after what they'd been through in the past few days. As well as what they'd got up to last night. A shiver ran through him at the memory of her body melding to his. Of the way she'd thrown her head back in abandon as she climaxed on top of him. A single touch from her, and his mind went to mush as his body lit up on the inside. It was a little scary, the way she affected him.

As gently as he could, he slipped out of bed. But his leg almost gave way the second he put his weight on it, and he had to grab for the side table to stop himself from falling.

The sound must've woken Skylar, because she sat up with a start.

"What?" Her sleepy eyes took a second to focus. "Are you okay? Is something wrong?" She swiveled her head, her gaze searching the room for trouble.

"Nope, nothing's wrong," he said, enjoying the sight of those wonderful breasts suddenly bared for him to see. Then she seemed to come to her senses and dragged the sheet up to cover herself.

"I thought for a second…"

"No, we're safe," he soothed. "The guard on the door would let us know if there was anything wrong." Which reminded him, he needed to go out and introduce himself to the new constable.

"You go back to sleep. I'll make us some coffee and breakfast."

"I thought you said you couldn't cook," she said, snuggling back underneath the blankets.

"I can manage toast and coffee," he quipped. The one piece of equipment he did know how to use in his kitchen was the coffee machine. He prided himself on how good his coffee was. Nash tried to hide his limp as he headed for the bathroom, but it was no good.

"Nash King, your leg is bad, isn't it?" She was out of bed and beside him in a second, grabbing his arm to help him across the room.

"Now that's the best view I've seen in a long time," he said appreciatively, taking in the spectacle of her slim legs, and pert breasts bouncing in front of him. She'd jumped out of bed, ignoring the fact she was completely naked. Her long hair was a tousled mess, her face creased with lines from where her head had rested on the pillow. He was also baring his naked ass, but Skylar seemed not to notice. She'd have none of it, she was back to her officious nurse persona.

She helped him to the bathroom, then left him to do his ablutions. When she came back, she was fully clothed, and Nash gave a small sigh.

"Come and sit in the living room. I'll make breakfast. I'm supposed to be looking after you, remember?" He did remember, but he also vowed to himself that one day soon, he would return the favor and bring her coffee and toast in bed.

She helped him get dressed, making him sit on the edge of the bed so she could get his shorts on. And even though he grumbled about it, he was finding it harder to hide the pain from her. He wondered what his doctor would say, if he knew the sort of exertion he'd put his leg through last night. But even the thought of the look on his doctor's face wasn't enough to dull the pain.

Skylar led him to the living room and sat him down on the end of the couch. Then he gratefully accepted the two little white pills she dropped in his hand, and gulped them down with a shot of water. Then she handed him two more, pink this time. The antibiotics his doctor had prescribed.

"You missed both doses last night before you went to bed?" she said, half accusing.

"I did have other things on my mind," he replied with a twitch of his lips.

"Yes, well," she huffed, a red tinge drifting up her neck. "It's probably why your leg is so sore this morning."

"That's definitely not the only reason, babe." He raised one eyebrow, daring her to argue.

She glared at him, and he wondered if she was going to tell him off for the term of endearment. But he remembered quite clearly, she'd called him baby more than once, back in the jungle. She probably hadn't even realized she was doing it, and maybe she didn't remember. But he did. Was it too soon to be using terms of endearment? He wasn't sure, but after all they'd been through, the strong connection they'd made, he felt like perhaps he had a right to use it.

"I'm making eggs Benedict for breakfast," she said instead, turning toward the kitchen.

"You are?" That sounded a lot better than the toast and honey he'd had on offer.

"It's the least I can do, while I'm cooped up here with you," she said, turning back to face him. "Cooking relaxes me. There are no surprises in the kitchen. Well, very few bad ones, at least. Food is something I understand."

"Okay," he replied.

Then he remembered he was yet to meet the new constable, and went to get out of this seat.

"Ignatius King," she called him by his full name, and he grimaced. Damn, she'd remembered. "Sit down. Tell me what it is you want, and I'll get it for you."

"All right," he agreed. "But don't think you get to order me around like this all day." And certainly not later tonight. He didn't voice that thought, however, but he sincerely hoped they'd have a replay of the previous night's activities. "Could you ask the officer at the door to come in for a second, please?"

"Sure." She strode over and unlocked the door, pulling it open. Nash enjoyed watching her figure, silhouetted in the morning light pouring through the gap. Her jeans snug enough to show off her lovely ass, and the linen shirt flimsy enough for him to see the lace of her bra.

The surprised face of an officer stared back at her. "Hello," she said sweetly. "Do you mind coming inside for a second? The senior constable would like to see you."

"Yes, ma'am." The young cop followed Skylar inside.

Nash recognized him from the hospital. "Constable Newman." Nash stood and extended his hand. "Thanks for this."

Newman shook his hand and stood back, looking a tad uncomfortable. "Sorry to hear about your injury, sir. I hope your recovery is a swift one."

"Me, too." And wasn't that the truth; but for more than one reason.

Nash spent the next five minutes debriefing the constable. It'd been a quiet night, with no disturbances and nothing unusual to report. Nash didn't envy the poor young man; he'd probably been bored to death with this guard detail. And perhaps it was all in vain. They might not even be targets, anymore. But they couldn't take that chance. The smell of freshly brewed coffee wafted past Nash's nose, and his stomach rumbled loudly.

"Constable Newman, was it?" As if on cue, Skylar came over, two plates in her hands. "I've made you breakfast."

The other man's eyes lit up at the sight of two perfectly poached eggs on toast, smothered in yellow Hollandaise sauce. But he took a step backward. "Thank you, ma'am. But I can't, I'm on duty."

"Please don't call me ma'am," she said with a scowl. "And I don't care if you're on duty or not. This is my way of thanking you for the unenviable task of standing guard all night. Now come on, you can't tell me you're not hungry."

Nash hid a smirk. It'd take a stronger man than Newman to resist Skylar's cooking. And that determined look on her face. In the ensuing silence, they both heard the young constable's stomach declare loudly that he was indeed hungry.

Skylar smiled at him. "See. I'm always right."

Newman finally conceded, stepping forward and accepting the plate of food. "Thank you. But I'll eat this outside, if that's okay."

Nash watched the young man retreat out to the porch. Willow might do a drive-by at any moment, and Nash knew the last thing the young constable would want, was to be caught not doing his job correctly.

"Here's yours." She placed Nash's plate on the coffee table and went back to the kitchen to retrieve her own plate and two cups of coffee. His stomach nearly turned itself inside out at the smell assaulting his nostrils, and he remembered that they hadn't had a chance to finish Skylar's meal from last night, after they got distracted by the dancing. And the bedroom.

Nash shoveled a forkful of egg into his mouth. "Holy shit." He stared up at Skylar, who gave him a secretive smile. "These are fucking fantastic."

"Can't beat fresh, homemade hollandaise sauce," she said, taking a seat and tucking into her own eggs.

"If this is the sort of food you serve up to the guests at Stormcloud, it's no wonder they rave about you."

Skylar opened her mouth and looked as if she were about to say something, then changed her mind and said, "Thanks, Nash. I'm glad you like it."

They ate in companionable silence until both their plates were completely clean. It was nice to see Skylar enjoy her own cooking. He'd already noticed she enjoyed eating, enjoyed food. He'd watched her devour her meal the night they'd spent at the Shangri La Hotel in Cairns.

"What's on the schedule for today?" Skylar asked, shooting him an expectant look. That's right, he'd almost forgotten she was practically hyperactive. Ever since he'd known Skylar, she'd always been on the move, flitting around her kitchen, ordering her staff around. And if she wasn't cooking, then she was out in her garden, pruning, or weeding, or planting. Her mother, Daniella, seemed to have some of the same tendencies.

Skylar's mind was constantly on, thinking, dissecting, coming up with the next new plan. How was he supposed to get her to sit still for the next three days? Because they were effectively under house arrest. Supposed to keep a low profile and stay out of sight so that Robinson could do his job.

There was one thing Nash could think of that would keep them entertained. He glanced down the hallway toward the bedroom. He'd be quite happy to spend the next three days in bed with Skylar. Would she go for that plan?

Before he could formulate a reply, there was a knock at the door. "Come in," he said.

Constable Schroeder pushed open the door. "Morning," she said brightly. "Just letting you know, I'm taking over from Newman."

"Morning, Sally," Skylar replied. When had these two got on a first-name basis? "Would you like some eggs Benedict? I can make some more, it's easy enough to do."

Schroeder hesitated. "Is that what Newman is raving about? He said he's just had the best eggs he's ever tasted."

"Sure is." Skylar beamed.

"Yes, please. As long as it's no trouble."

"No trouble at all." Skylar picked up their empty plates and went back to the kitchen. "I was just asking Nash what the plan is for today?"

Schroeder looked a little confused and Nash felt an absurd sense of relief that it wasn't just him in the firing line now. "Ah, it's much the same as yesterday," she replied, looking at him for confirmation. "You need to sit tight until Robinson and his crew tell you it's safe."

Skylar looked up sharply. "You mean stay cooped up in here all day?" She banged the metal bowl down on countertop. "Can I at least take a trip out to Stormcloud to check on my staff? Make sure everything is running smoothly?"

"I strongly advise against that," Schroeder replied. "You're supposed to be keeping under the radar. Stay at home and stay safe. Protocol states that all requests need to be passed by Robinson, anyway."

Nash grimaced and glanced at Skylar. How was she going to react to the word *protocol* today?

She made a sound of annoyance and glared at Nash. Why was he getting the look? This wasn't his fault. But she didn't seem ready to storm out of the house, like she had yesterday.

"Well, then, I'll have to make some calls." Skylar said, whisking the sauce with a frustrated twist of her wrist. "I'll need to finalize the menu for the next week. Order in supplies. I hope Julie is okay with taking up all my slack. I should talk to Daniella." Her last comment was said almost under her breath, meant more for herself than anyone else.

Schroeder glanced at Nash and gave a little shrug, as if unsure how to answer that. "I'll be outside if you need me."

"I'll bring your food out in a second," Skylar said, with an absent-minded wave. "Wait." She stepped around the counter. "Can I at least go to the supermarket again? If I'm going to be cooped up here all day, then I may as well make myself useful."

Nash wanted to tell her not to worry about it. To take it easy. But that wasn't Skylar's way. She needed to feel productive. To stay in motion, almost like a shark—if they stopped moving, they died.

Schroeder sought Nash's gaze, almost as if asking him silently how he coped with her demands. Nash bristled slightly at her implied criticism. Skylar was in a unique situation, and she was only trying to survive the best way she knew how. If he could do this one little thing to help her through, then it was worth taking the risk. Willow had confirmed in his report last night that all the media had now left town, so they shouldn't be a problem. Although what Skylar needed to buy from the supermarket was beyond him; it seemed as if she'd bought enough to keep them fed for a week yesterday.

"Can you see if you can clear it with Robinson, please?" He said, making it abundantly clear this wasn't a request.

"Yes, sir." She knew a command to a junior officer when she heard one. "Right away."

Skylar came back to sit on the couch once Schroeder went out the front door. She lay a hand on his knee. "Thank you. I know I'm still being...difficult." Her lips quirked up at the word. "And I don't mean to put us in any more danger. It's just..."

"I understand," he said softly. "We'll get through this." He ran his hand down the side of her cheek, just to feel the glorious softness of her skin beneath his fingertip.

Skylar leaned into his hand for a second, then she said, "I don't want this bastard to win. And after that fright yesterday...well, it made me start second-guessing myself. But if I'm too scared to go into town, then he wins. Do you understand?"

"Completely," he replied.

Skylar got up to take Schroeder her eggs with a smile on her face.

The trip to the supermarket an hour later was uneventful. Nash strapped on his gun holster and stood guard at the register the same way he'd done yesterday, posting Schroeder out the front. By then, the painkillers had kicked in, and his leg was feeling better. Almost good enough so that he could hide the limp. The locals still stopped to either stare or wish him a good morning. And Nash returned their greetings, trying not to resent their curiosity. It was only natural they were curious about the goings-on in their little town. Especially when it included the district cop and a reclusive chef from the renowned luxury lodge. He could see the questions written all over their faces, but he closed down any further queries with his brusque tone and serious manner. This wasn't the time to curry the favor of the community. He could do that later, mend his bridges later, if need be. His only priority at the moment was to keep Skylar safe.

Same as yesterday, he saw nothing unusual. Nothing to make him think there was anything out of place in his little town. But Nash couldn't shake a vague feeling of unease. There were more tourists wandering the streets today, eating ice cream and waving away the flies. But none of them looked remotely like they meant to do him or Skylar harm. They were just individuals, minding their own business.

Skylar heeded his request and kept her shopping trip brief, but she still returned to the cash register with an overflowing basket. He didn't ask, he merely helped her pack the items and carry them to the waiting police vehicle.

He scanned the street as they made their way back to the car, searching for the reason behind his illogical agitation. The same as yesterday, he got Schroeder to clear the house and surrounding garden before he let Skylar out of the car. But such was his unease that he even questioned Schroeder quietly as they helped Skylar to unload the car, asked if she'd seen anything out of place. Her blank look and shake of her head told him he must've been imagining things. Perhaps he was being hyper-vigilant because it was Skylar's life at stake. And his own; he had to keep reminding himself of that small detail.

Following Skylar up the stairs onto his porch, he noticed a

small quantity of red stones scattered near the edge of the wooden platform, partially hidden by one of the pot plants that sat each side of the door. Where had they come from? Had one of the guards walked them up on the bottom of their shoes? He kicked at the stones, sending them cascading over the edge. They reminded him of something, but he couldn't put his finger on exactly what.

He shrugged and took the shopping bag inside, soon forgetting about the stones, when Skylar asked him to put the milk away in the refrigerator.

Later, Skylar made her phone calls while Nash pretended to read a book on the couch. He was supposed to be recuperating, after all. And he had a vested interest in getting his leg healed as quickly as possible. He hated feeling like a burden, and if this phantom gunman ever did turn up, he wanted to be as fit as possible to be able to fight him off.

She made them a lunch that she called *simple sandwiches*— they were anything but. Dark-rye bread with Swiss cheese and honey-smoked ham, carved straight from the bone. They were delicious, melting in his mouth.

She said she had something of a surprise for him for dinner, and anticipation simmered in his belly all afternoon. But it wasn't merely anticipation of the food that was giving him an appetite. It was the thought of what might happen after dinner that intrigued him the most. There was an air of tension in his house. Could Skylar feel it, too? Every time she passed by him, his skin buzzed with unrequited need. He was extremely aware of wherever she was in the room. His gaze followed her swaying hips as she sauntered through to the bedroom, talking on her mobile.

Skylar had been a surprising delight last night. So unfettered and uninhibited. After her revelations about her ex, Nash had been expecting to have to take it slow with her. To treat her with kid gloves, in case he inadvertently triggered an adverse memory for her. He'd been more than ready to stop at any stage, if she'd merely looked at him the wrong way. He still didn't know the extent of Craig's mistreatment of Skylar. He suspected it was physical as well as mental abuse, but she'd been insistently vague about any details. But it was almost as if she were a different woman last night. He wondered if that'd be true all the time? Or if it was a one-off thing, where she'd put Craig away in a box inside her head and decided to forget he even existed?

Nash had experience enough with trauma to know it was never as easy as that.

Later that afternoon, Nash watched Skylar putter around his kitchen. If she kept feeding him like this, he was going to need to do some serious exercise to lose all the extra weight he was going to put on. He could get used to having her in the house. Having someone to fuss over him was nice. He'd opened his pantry door earlier, to find it stuffed full of items he'd never use in a million years; wouldn't even know what half the ingredients were.

He had to keep reminding himself that she was only here for the next three days. They were not living in some sort of domestic bliss; this would all end soon.

CHAPTER NINETEEN

Skylar stretched, letting the sheets slide down her naked body, feeling as languorous and satiated as a cat who'd got the cream. Nash lay flat on his back beside her, his chest rising and falling in a soft rhythm. His eyes were closed, but she knew he wasn't asleep. It shouldn't have come as a surprise, after the sexual tension hovering around them all day, but Skylar could still hardly believe it when Nash had led her to the bedroom again after dinner.

For some reason, she'd been loath to bring up the subject of their lovemaking the night before during the day, almost as if talking about it might taint it somehow. Nash must've caught her vibe, because he seemed to be avoiding the topic, as well. So, they'd never discussed their intentions, whether it would happen again, or if it was just a one-night fling. Last night, Skylar would've been happy with just that one sweet moment of release. A chance to get outside herself. But this morning, her treacherous body had craved more; she wanted more of him.

So, when he took her hand this evening and asked with his eyes, she knew her answer would be yes.

Nash was a revelation. He was such a giving lover, making sure she felt safe, making sure she got everything she needed, and more. Not once had she felt threatened or vulnerable. In fact, it was the exact opposite. Nash made her feel powerful and cherished.

Of their own accord, her fingers moved up to find the smooth shape of his collarbone, then eased up to the heavy muscle of his shoulder. She loved that she was learning his body, the contours of it, the way the hair on his chest curled, all golden and soft, even the scars on his arms and legs.

Nash stirred and opened his eyes. "Hey, gorgeous."

Her heart did a stupid pitty-pat at his sweet talk. For some reason, when he called her gorgeous, she really did feel like she could live up to that name.

It must be nearly midnight by now. They should try and get some sleep. But her body didn't want to sleep, it wanted more of him. As if she just couldn't get enough. Which was probably true—no sex for nearly four years was making her want to binge on him like she hadn't eaten in weeks, and he was an unending packet of chocolate cookies. She'd discovered what the word *insatiable* meant in the past few hours.

When they first hit the bed earlier tonight, she'd been determined that she would do all the work to save his leg from any more pain. And the first time they'd made love had been the same as last night, with her on top, riding him to an explosive orgasm that nearly blew her mind. But that resolution had gone out the window fifteen minutes later, when he'd got up onto his hands and knees and sank his head between her legs. Oh, the pure extravagance of his tongue inside her had driven her to heights she'd never dreamed of with Craig. Nor with anyone, if she truly thought about it.

The third time, they had somehow ended up on the floor; him taking her from behind. Afterwards, they'd lay on the rug as he spooned her, then she'd had to help him back into the bed, both of them giggling like two teenagers.

"Hey, yourself," she replied. Her hand slithered from his shoulder, slowly down his belly, then lower, to find his cock, already at half-mast, ready to do her bidding. It seemed Nash was a little insatiable, as well.

Perhaps it was time to give him a break. She didn't want to wear him out.

"I'm hungry," she said, sitting up suddenly. "Do you want dessert in bed?" Skylar had made a self-saucing chocolate pudding. But they'd barely made it past the main course; Skylar knew Nash had only stayed at the table long enough to eat her steak with blue cheese sauce, and edamame and nori salad to be polite, because she'd spent so much time preparing it. They'd spent most of the meal trying—and failing—to ignore the boiling sexual tension around them.

"Mmhmm," he mumbled. "Sustenance would be good. Need to keep my blood sugar levels up, so I can keep up with you." He winked at her, and she slapped his shoulder.

She slipped Nash's shirt over her head and padded down the hallway to the kitchen. Five minutes later, she was back, bearing two desserts and a glass of milk each. Nash was already sitting up in bed and she handed him his warm pudding, then took off the T-shirt and hopped in beside him.

The decadence of sitting in bed naked with Nash by her side, gorging on chocolaty heaven, suddenly hit Skylar. She'd missed this simple act. The intimacy of it all. Such a normal thing for many couples to do. How would it feel to be able to do this whenever she wanted?

"Oh. My. God," Nash moaned. "This is the best thing I think I've ever tasted."

Skylar felt an absurd flush of pride.

They both leaned back into their pillows, hands over bellies, with a sigh of satisfaction. Yep, the chocolate pudding had been delicious. She licked the last bit from her lips, enjoying that final taste.

"I forgot I made one for Constable Newman. It's probably too late to take it out to him now," she said with a chuckle.

"Yes, you're much better off staying here with me." Nash gathered her up into his arms and they snuggled down into the bed.

But talk of the police guard had Skylar thinking. Nash had had an update from Robinson earlier in the evening, and while some of it had been hopeful, it still hadn't been the report she was hoping for. The police had found Stan the Man and taken him into custody. Skylar had been ecstatic at the news, but then Nash told her Stan was refusing to talk, and they were still no closer to finding the gunman who'd hunted them through the jungle. Robinson said it was only a matter of time before they cracked Stan; it was a waiting game. And she and Nash were still in limbo.

Robinson had also confirmed what they all feared. Rumors were abounding in the darker underbelly of society— supposedly Robinson had heard from a couple of trusted undercover sources—that Sanders had indeed put out a contract on her and Nash. And by all accounts, it was a large amount of money. Skylar wasn't sure whether to be flattered or insulted by that. But Sanders was still refusing to talk.

"Whatcha thinking?" Nash asked, propping up on his elbow and stroking the hair away from her face.

How did he do that? As if by magic, he could tell when her mind was elsewhere. It must be a knack that police officers developed. Or maybe, it was just Nash.

"I was thinking about Robinson's call this afternoon." There had been one silver lining to it all. "At least the courts have enough evidence to put Dan Sanders in jail." Robinson told them Sanders had been convicted of both the charges of domestic abuse of his wife, as well as the assault on Skylar, and was now he was awaiting sentencing.

"Yes, thank God for that," Nash replied. "We're still putting the case together for Patty's murder, but all the evidence points to Sanders and hopefully, once that's gone to trial, he'll spend the rest of his life in jail. I know it'll never bring Patty back, but at least he's getting what he deserves."

Grief surged through Skylar at the memory of Patty. She'd thought she was doing the right thing by forcing Patty to confront her predicament. Confront the monster that was her husband. But in the end, it'd cost her life. Was there no fairness in life? Patty certainly didn't get what she deserved. Even Nash's continued stroking of her face wasn't enough to alleviate her distress over the other woman's fate.

"But is he? Getting what he deserves?" Skylar sat up and leant against her pillow, no longer feeling peaceful enough to lie there and let Nash soothe her. Nash followed suit. "I'm not sure any of these bastards ever get what they deserve," she said. "It's one of the reasons I never told anyone about Craig. Maybe I never truly believed he'd get his comeuppance."

"And that's how they continue to get away with their crimes," Nash said softly. "It's not until a strong woman, like you, decides to stand up for themselves, they finally get caught out."

Skylar rubbed her wrist as she considered his words.

"You always do that whenever we talk about Craig," Nash said, capturing her fingers in his. "It's like a nervous tic, or something." She didn't pull away from him, because he was right.

She'd never told anyone that Craig had broken her wrist. Even when she took herself to emergency, she said she'd fallen down a set of stairs. It was a busy Saturday night at the Cairns hospital and the attending doctor hadn't even questioned her; he'd been so distracted by a flurry of cases of minor stab wounds after a drunken party that'd gotten out of hand.

Nash brought her hand to his mouth and gently kissed her knuckles. That small gesture gave her the strength to say the words.

"The part that hurt the most, was the fact he didn't even apologize afterwards," she said in a small voice. "It was as if it never happened."

"I'm so sorry he hurt you," Nash said, and the irony wasn't lost on Skylar. Nash thought nothing of showing his compassion; the exact opposite of how Craig had responded.

"Thank you." She glanced up into his blue eyes. "I really don't know what I saw in him." She bit her lip and then decided to tell him it all. "Craig was older than me. He was head chef in an up-and-coming trendy restaurant. And at first, I think I was blinded by his celebrity. I couldn't believe he'd want to be with someone like me."

Nash snorted, but kept his words to himself, encouraging her with a tilt of his head to continue with her story.

"But that night when he smashed his boot down on my wrist, I decided to leave him. It was the last straw." It wasn't the first time Craig had been physically violent toward her. Over the year they'd been together, his drunken outbursts had slowly become more and more frequent. But that was the first time he'd broken a bone.

"The problem was, it took me another year to finally work up the courage to walk out the door. I kept thinking he was going to change, you know?"

"But they never do, do they?" Nash still held her hand, his thumb tracing comforting circles on her wrist.

"No," she answered softly.

"So, you never told anyone about how Craig treated you? Not even your family?" Nash asked.

"No. When we broke up, I told them he left me for another woman, and I didn't want to talk about it. And they respected that."

"They never suspected anything? You seem close to Dale. You didn't confide in him?"

"No. I especially didn't want him to know."

"Why not?"

Skylar had never told anyone about how Craig had raped her as revenge when she finally left him. She'd buried it, along with all the other terrible things Craig had done to her, deep in a box within her mind, never to see the light of day again. It was just one more thing amongst a whole litany of assaults—both verbal and physical—he'd rained down on her.

"Lots of reasons. The main one being because I didn't want Dale to avenge me. If he knew Craig raped me, he'd probably try and kill him. I couldn't have my brother go to jail for me."

"Wait." Nash straightened and looked her directly in the eye. "Craig raped you?"

Shit. The word had slipped out. That was the problem when you let yourself get too familiar with someone. You said things you shouldn't.

"Um…" She withdrew her hand from his, the mood well and truly broken now. She raised her eyes to the ceiling. What should she tell him? In for a penny, in for a pound, is that how the saying went? And was raping a woman really a worse act than breaking her bones? Sometimes she didn't know. "If I tell you, will you make me a promise?"

"Yes, of course. Anything you want."

"I want you to keep the information to yourself. And I don't want you to talk me into reporting it to the police…to you," she said hurriedly. "And most importantly, I don't want you tracking down Craig and harassing him, or taking some sort of revenge out on him. I want you to leave him alone."

He hadn't been expecting that, she could see the shock written in his eyes.

He hesitated, before finally saying, "Of course, I'll honor

your wishes, if that's truly what you want. But you never told me he raped you. That changes things." There was a slightly accusing tone in his voice. "That makes me want to…" He curled his fist into a ball.

Skylar sucked in a breath. Why did all men react in the same way? With violence. Clearly, in Nash's mind at least, the rape was the worst of Craig's crimes. But why did he want to repay violence with more violence?

"I won't ever break your confidence, Skylar. But, Jesus, you should report this bastard. He needs to pay for what he did to you. I can help you to get him locked up. Get him off the streets, where he can't hurt anyone else."

She shut her eyes. That last comment hurt the most. Didn't he realize how many times she'd thought the exact same thing? Because of her weakness, other women might be hurting, as well.

He hadn't realized that she'd become as still as a statue next to him. "Please let me help you, Skylar. You can't keep something this big a secret." He was a cop. It was what cops did. They put bad people in jail. But this wasn't so clearly black-and-white for her.

Nash was sitting up in bed, a frown marring his handsome face. He'd moved away, no longer touching her, as if trying to understand how she could be so ignorant. Not able to comprehend why she refused to turn Craig in.

A sob tried to burst loose from her constricted throat, but she swallowed it down.

She'd broken something fundamental between them. The connection she thought she'd had with Nash was gone. She knew he felt he could no longer trust her. That this secret was too much for even him to bear.

And she could no longer trust him. Even if he never brought the topic up again, she'd know that he'd be frustrated with her lack of courage, would be constantly wondering why she didn't just grow up and report this monster.

"I'm going to sleep in my room," she said flatly, slipping out of bed and gathering up her clothes.

"What? Skylar, wait. Stay. Please. I'm sorry." The entreaty in his voice hurt her heart. "Don't walk away." He got out of bed, but stumbled as soon as his wounded leg hit the floor. He grabbed for the corner of the bed to steady himself. "Don't shut me out, please. I shouldn't have pushed you."

"Sorry." It was the only word she could force through her frozen vocal cords.

"Please don't run away. Take a chance and stay with me. We can sort this out." His voice followed her down the hallway.

How could she make him understand that was the way she was? It was how she coped. Running away might be the coward's way out, but at least it kept her heart safe. Why had she ever thought this was a good idea? She fled to her own room and shut the door behind her.

CHAPTER TWENTY

Skylar's last, anguished word echoed through his head. *Sorry.* She had nothing to be sorry about. He was the dickhead who'd fucked everything up. What should he do? He couldn't leave things like this. One minute they'd been making love, in a cocoon of warm desire, and the next, he'd been acting like a complete ass, demanding she do something because of his expectations. Skylar had enough of men telling her what to do, of trying to control her. No wonder she ran away from him.

He limped down the hallway and knocked softly on her door. "Skylar, can I come in?"

Silence.

He knocked again. "Please let me in. We can talk about this. We need to talk about this."

Still no answer.

He could just barge right in there, there was no lock on the door. But something told him Skylar wouldn't appreciate that. If she needed her space, then perhaps the least he could do after his monumental screw-up, was give it to her.

Nash hobbled back to bed. He lay on his back, staring at the ceiling.

Fuck.

His body was craving sleep, and his leg ached like a bitch, but he knew his mind would give him no rest.

An hour later, Nash was still staring at the ceiling, still with no clarity on how to approach his problem with Skylar.

There was a noise outside his window. Nash sat up, listening intently. There it was again. A thump, followed by a shout. Something was going on.

Quickly, he pulled on some shorts. And then reached for his nightstand, retrieving his weapon from the top drawer. He'd taken to keeping the loaded gun in his bedside table at night for easy access. He slid quietly out of the bedroom and walked down the hallway, making sure that Skylar's bedroom door remained shut. Holding his weapon in both hands, pointed at the floor, he stood in the middle of the living room, listening.

There were no more noises, and no more shouting. He wanted to check outside, but he dared not leave Skylar unprotected. So, he waited, staying away from the windows and the door, knowing that Newman would report if there was anything amiss. He flicked on the light switch for the backyard spotlight, knowing it'd light up the whole of the yard. The small light above the front porch was left all night as extra security, but he left all the internal lights off, except for the kitchen, which'd been on the whole time.

Just when he could no longer stand the suspense, there was a quiet knock on the front door, and Newman called out, "Senior Constable King, it's me, Constable Newman. May I enter?"

Recognizing the other man's voice, Nash lowered his weapon, but kept it ready, just in case. Limping to the front door, he unlocked the deadbolt. "Come in," he muttered.

"Sorry to disturb you, sir." The young man seemed out of breath and agitated. He took one look at Nash's state of undress and the gun in his hand, and said, "But I guess you heard what was going on outside."

Nash nodded. "Give me the rundown, Newman." He was in no mood for chitchat. Newman looked abashed, and Nash fleetingly wondered if he'd been caught dozing on the job.

"There was someone outside," Newman said. "I heard something, but I wasn't sure at first. It's hard to hear anything over the crickets and the cane toads at night sometimes."

Nash nodded impatiently for Newman to continue.

"I'd just finished a perimeter check fifteen minutes beforehand, and I was standing in the front driveway. There were a few odd noises, but I checked the road and saw no unusual cars, or other activity, so I ignored it, at first. It wasn't until I heard a definite thump and then a scraping sound, like maybe someone was trying to jimmy a window open, that I decided to investigate. I crept around the side of the house. But whoever was there must've heard me coming. They took off before I could get a good look at them. I gave chase, but they disappeared into the bush over the back fence."

Nash's house was on the outskirts of town, and while it had a neat little grassy yard, it backed on to an area of surrounding bushland. Dirt trails crisscrossed the area like a maze. The guy could be anywhere by now.

"I should've investigated earlier. I'm sorry," Newman said.

"Are you sure there was only one person?" Nash asked. He was playing out scenarios in his head, trying to figure out if they were indeed safe now. They'd all become a little too casual about this whole threat, not quite believing the gunman would try again. Newman wasn't the only one to blame for his lack of urgency, Nash was also culpable.

"I can't be sure, sir. I didn't really see much of anything. It was too dark. I heard someone clamber over the fence and saw the fleeting impression of a lone figure disappearing into the trees. That's all."

"Okay," Nash said slowly. It seemed like the threat was

gone. For now.

"I'm sorry, sir," Newman apologized again.

"No harm done. You did a good job," Nash replied gruffly, placating the young constable. He hadn't done anything wrong. And perhaps if he hadn't been so vigilant, whoever was out there may well have got inside.

There was a noise, and both men swung around at the same time to see Skylar come down the hallway, hair tousled and eyes bloodshot. Thankfully, she'd donned a pair of pyjamas. "What's going on?"

"I'll fill her in," Nash said to the constable. "You get back outside and do another patrol. I'll come out as soon as I get dressed. Report this incident to HQ, as well."

"Yes, sir." Newman closed the front door behind him.

Skylar fixed Nash with a fearful gaze. "What's going on?" she asked again. "Was someone trying to break into the house?" Her voice rose an octave on the last word.

"We don't know." Nash took a step toward Skylar, meaning to pull her into his embrace, but she moved backward, out of his reach, her eyes going cold. All he wanted was to comfort her because he knew her bloodshot eyes were from crying. And he was the dickhead who'd made her cry.

Instead of taking her into his arms, he stepped back with a sigh while she stood with arms crossed, glaring at him. She hadn't forgiven him. Didn't look like she was about to forgive him anytime soon. How was he supposed to redeem himself?

"Newman heard something outside, and he chased someone away. But we're not sure who it was, or what they wanted," Nash said.

"What do you mean, you're not sure?" Skylar sent him an incredulous look. "It can only be one person. Can't it? No one else would take the risk of poking around here. Not with an armed policeman out front."

Nash wanted to argue with her. Could it possibly be just a nosy local thief? Unaware of the guard out the front? Or willing to take the chance even if he was? Nash doubted it. But without any concrete evidence, they had no way of knowing who'd been out there, or what they wanted.

"We need to stay extra alert, that's all. I'm pretty sure whoever was out there won't come back."

"Don't treat me like a child," she hissed. "At least pay me some respect. I spent two days and two nights with you in the jungle, being hunted by that crazy fucker."

She had a point. He was trying to shield her from the truth. Not wanting her to worry. His protective instincts and his cop persona taking over. But they'd been equals while they'd been on the run. She was a strong, fierce woman, and could look after herself. Had indeed helped to save his life.

"You're right, Skylar. I'm sorry."

"I'm going to make some hot chocolate." She stomped toward the kitchen. "It's going to be a long night. Do you want some?"

"Yes, please. But I'm going to give Newman a hand to make sure the house is secure first. I won't be long."

"Do what you need to do." Skylar turned her back and pulled out mugs, and the milk from the fridge, as if none of this was her concern. But he could tell by the tense line of her shoulders she wasn't happy.

He hurried to his bedroom and threw on a shirt and a pair of shoes, grabbed a flashlight, then dashed back down the hallway. He needed to check for himself that the area was clear. Look for any clues the intruder might've left behind. Not that he didn't trust the young constable, but he may well have missed something. He was half-way out the door when he remembered to say, "Please don't open the door to anyone but me."

She threw him a derisive glance.

Nash descended the stairs, weapon drawn and at the ready, and stood at the end of his driveway. Then he did a slow three-sixty turn, taking in the road, his front yard and finally his house, set back from the curb. Nothing looked out of place. The air hummed with the song of night insects, some of them throwing themselves futilely at the porch light. It was warm out here, compared to the air-conditioning inside. Cane toads croaked from numerous places around the garden. An especially brazen one sat in the middle of his driveway, surveying him, throat slowly pulsating, not scared of Nash in the slightest. A slight breeze shifted the branches of the tall eucalyptus trees at the rear of his property, rustling the leaves together in a soft sigh. Newman was correct; there was a lot going on out here that might hide the sound of a prowler. It was a big ask to expect a single guard to monitor the whole house and garden. Nash wondered if Robinson might find money in the budget to post a second cop on his house. He'd probably say no, but Nash was going to ask, anyway.

A shadow broke away from the side of his house and Nash tensed for a millisecond before he recognized Newman's distinctive profile—the young cop had one of the largest Roman noses Nash had ever seen.

"This is where I think the prowler was trying to break in," Newman said as Nash approached. Newman had his own weapon out, pointed at the ground. "I made sure I didn't compromise the crime scene, sir," Newman reported.

The constable had stopped right beneath the window to his bedroom. Nash swallowed a rush of fear. Had the intruder known that was where Nash slept? Thank God he'd heeded policy and kept all the windows and curtains closed. At least he hadn't attempted to enter Skylar's room, which was on the other side of the house. Nash flicked on his flashlight and explored the ground around the window. His little cottage was set up on stilts, in case of flooding, like many

Queensland houses. There was enough space underneath the house for a man to crawl beneath it. He assumed Newman had already checked, but force of habit made him bend down and direct the beam of light under the house, just to make sure. Nope, no one under there. He straightened again.

Nash wasn't much of a gardener. He didn't have the time or the inclination to do more than make sure the lawn was neat and relatively green. The area beneath his window was supposed to be a garden bed, but right now it was bare, dry earth. The flashlight showed lots of scuff marks in the dirt. Then Nash's blood ran cold as he spotted a single, fresh boot print in the red earth.

Because his cottage was on stilts, it meant that all the windows were higher off the ground than most houses. Even a tall man would have to stretch to see inside. The window surrounds were made of wood, with two panes of glass opening out from the middle. Nash directed his flashlight at the wooden casing. There were marks on the white paint, as if someone had tried to push a crowbar underneath.

The intruder couldn't have been in the yard for long. Newman reported that he'd done a perimeter walk only fifteen minutes before. Had the prowler been watching and waiting for his chance? He could've stood in the bushland by the back fence for hours and not be seen. How long had he been watching the house?

Was it the same man who'd hunted them through the jungle? It was just lucky that the prowler had made a mistake and given away his presence. Nash didn't like to think about what might've happened if the man had managed to get in.

A sudden memory of the pile of small, red stones on his front porch the other day came back in a rush. He remembered where he'd seen those stones before; in the ravine where he and Skylar had spent the night. The same ravine where the gunman had ended up at the bottom, after

Skylar had pushed him. Nash's blood turned ice-cold. Had that been a sign? Had the gunman been to his house the other day, and left the pebbles to taunt Nash?

Nash spent the next ten minutes stalking around his house, he and Newman checking every nook and cranny before he finally declared the area clear. Newman followed him up the stairs onto the front porch.

"You should up your perimeter patrols to every ten minutes," Nash instructed. "I'm going to leave all the lights on. That might act as a deterrent, in case he's thinking of coming back."

"Yes, sir."

"I'm going to contact Robinson first thing in the morning and ask if he can send another officer," Nash continued. "We have a clear and present threat now; he needs to increase the guard patrol."

"Yes, sir." Newman's replies were stilted, and he stood to attention as he spoke.

"Relax, Newman. This isn't your fault," Nash said. The poor guy was blaming himself, when none of this was his fault. But Nash knew how he felt, because he was also berating himself for being less mindful than he should've been.

Maybe it was a good thing Skylar wouldn't be spending any more time in his bed. She was one huge distraction, and he needed to concentrate on keeping them both alive, not be led astray by that luscious body and keen mind. He'd been lulled into a false sense of security, not dreaming that the gunman would continue to hunt them down. Overcome by his lust for the gorgeous woman staying in his house.

It was time he put his cop face firmly back in place, and remember his duty was to keep Skylar alive, not to feed his own libido.

CHAPTER TWENTY-ONE

The past two days had been a living hell. Having to stay in the same house with Nash had been a sheer nightmare. After sharing his bed for two nights, tasting that sweet elixir and then having it all ripped away from her, it was a special kind of torment. Living so close to him, yet having him out of bounds.

She should've known better. Should never have let him kiss her. Never let him lead her to his bedroom. Thank God it was soon to be over.

They were going to Paul's funeral this morning, and then she'd be back at Stormcloud Station tonight.

Home. She was going home.

Nash had tried to talk her out of it, of course. But she was sticking to her guns. There was no way she could spend even one more moment cooped up in this house with him. Nash had been polite, cool, and highly professional over the past two days. Ever since Newman had chased away the prowler, Nash had become a different man. The warm, gentle soul she'd been coming to know was firmly hidden behind the wall of the officious policeman. He'd taken on the role of protector, and it didn't matter how much she disagreed with him, told him that she was capable of looking after herself, his persona never cracked.

None of that really mattered, anyway, because she'd already made a decision the night she'd revealed Craig had raped her. She and Nash could never be together. Because his male ego would always try and dictate her feelings. He wouldn't be able to help himself, he'd exert his influence—it may be subtle, but it'd be there—to control her. And he was proving her point right now, with his overbearing attitude and seeming lack of empathy for her position.

The night of their fight, he'd entreated her not to shut him out. To let him help her. But Skylar knew no other way to keep her heart safe. Perhaps she was using their argument as an excuse, a way to block him out of her life. Because she could never trust him completely not to coerce her to turn Craig in, or even go after Craig on his own. The rape, and how it affected her, would always hang like a knife blade about to fall between them.

There'd been no sign of any more intruders after that night. Perhaps it was the second policeman Robinson had stationed at the house, acting as a deterrent. Whatever it was, it was almost like that night had been a dream, like there'd been no intruder, and it was all a made-up story to keep Skylar locked inside. Maybe a part of Skylar wanted to believe there had been no prowler, that Newman had imagined it all, because then she could go home safely with a clear conscience.

That was a knock on the door. "Are you ready to go?" Nash's voice came through the wooden panel between them.

"Yes. Be with you in a sec," she replied, forcing her voice to sound light and breezy. She took one more quick look at herself in the mirror above the dresser. Daniella had delivered her clothes this morning; she'd asked her mother to find something suitable for a funeral in her wardrobe and bring it along. The black dress was simple, knee-length, with lacy capped sleeves. Plain black pumps and a dark blue handbag her mother had found at the back of her wardrobe finished off her outfit. They'd never recovered her favorite handbag from the crash site, and Skylar wondered if that meant it was lost forever, or if someone had picked it up. A shiver ran up her spine at the thought.

No makeup for her today. This was going to be hard enough without having to deal with mascara running all over her face.

Taking a deep breath, Skylar opened the door and walked down the hallway. Everyone was waiting for her in the living room. Daniela and Steve were seated on the couch, looking uncomfortable in their funeral outfits. Steve was even wearing a suit, and Daniella, a dark blue dress that hung down to her ankles. Dale and Daisy stood next to the kitchen countertop, also dressed in mourning attire. Dale acknowledged her with a nod of his head. But there was no laughing or joking; a subdued air of sorrow hung over the small gathering. They were going to drive in a convoy to Cairns for the funeral. Dale was driving Daisy, Daniela, and Steve in his four-wheel drive, and he would take the lead. Nash and Skylar would follow in Nash's private vehicle. Constable Schroeder and the other constable—she could never remember the third one's name—would bring up the rear in her police cruiser. Effectively sandwiching herself and Nash between the two other cars, just in case the gunman thought to make an attempt on their lives as they drove to the funeral.

Nash stood as she appeared in the hallway and came forward, no longer walking with the cane, the limp hardly evident now. Her heart jolted at the sight of him. His black trousers and a long-sleeved dark-gray shirt made him look handsome and debonaire; set off his sky-blue eyes. She longed to reach out and touch his face; trace the healing scar along his cheekbone. And tell him she missed him.

But then she noticed the gun in his shoulder holster and flinched away. It was a reminder that they still weren't safe.

"Shall we get moving?" Nash suggested, surprising her by taking her elbow and steering her toward the front door, gathering up his black suit jacket as he went. "We don't want to be late."

Skylar let him lead her down the stairs, where Schroeder and the other constable were waiting, keeping their watchful gazes directed up and down the street.

Skylar wished that she could ride with Dale and Daisy. Being stuck in a car with Nash for close to two hours would be excruciating.

But she needn't have worried. Nash seemed fixated on the road, almost as if he was actually expecting the gunman to jump out in front of the car at any second. And he kept his mouth shut, which suited her fine. But this hypervigilance was beginning to annoy her. He wasn't normally like this. What the hell had changed so much on that night? It was as if a switch had flicked inside him. Her thoughts turned down a darker path as she brooded, staring out the window. Perhaps it was more than that. Maybe Nash despised her, now that he knew she was spoiled goods. She'd thought Nash wouldn't be the type to let that worry him. In fact, she thought he'd been the exact opposite. But people were fickle. Men were untrustworthy.

The drive was uneventful, apart from Skylar's spiraling thoughts, and they made it in record time, in just over an hour and a half.

Skylar's brain switched from analyzing Nash's motives to nervous worry, as the outskirts of Cairns appeared. She was dreading having to face Paul's family; having to face the finality of Paul's death.

Nash turned off the main road, following Dale, and Skylar was surprised to see a media scrum at the entrance to the cemetery. She hadn't been expecting that. Bright flashes of light filled her vision as cameras were forced against the windshield and the side windows. Two police officers, obviously stationed there to keep the pack at bay, were being overrun. Nash made a noise of annoyance, but continued to drive slowly, but surely, through the throng, following in the wake of Dale's large four-wheel-drive.

"Sorry about that," Nash said. "We'll have to run the gauntlet on the way out as well. They've been sniffing around at the station, too, but Steve told them in no uncertain terms they weren't welcome, and when they discovered that you weren't there they got discouraged and left. Robinson kept my name out of the media, so at the moment, they still have no idea I was the other passenger in the chopper. Which is the main reason we allowed you to stay at my house."

"Really?" The media hounding her had never even crossed Skylar's mind. Nash had never mentioned it. Neither had Steve nor Daniella. Probably not wanting to worry her.

"They're not allowed into the cemetery, so they won't interrupt the ceremony."

"That's good," Skylar said faintly, not sure how much of a salvation that really was.

Nash pulled his car into a parking spot beside Dale. Schroeder and her sidekick were already out of their car, scanning the surrounding gardens and buildings.

"We should be fairly safe here," Nash said, when he saw Skylar glance nervously out the window. "Robinson is attending, along with four other officers. This case, and this funeral, are now high profile. The media are already going crazy with all sorts of conspiracy theories about what happened to us up there on the mountain." Nash stared straight out the windshield as he related the reality to Skylar. "Robinson has only released the bare facts of the crash. He hasn't made the details available of how the chopper was shot down, or the fact that someone pursued us through the jungle in an attempt to kill us. He doesn't want it known that the police are hunting a crazed gunman, or that he has Stan the Man in custody."

Skylar felt uncomfortable when she realized she'd been condemning Robinson as not doing his job properly to protect her and Nash. But perhaps she'd been too wrapped up in her own selfish bubble. They'd kept the TV and the radio off while they had been cooped up at Nash's place. That sort of thing only helped to fuel her paranoia. She got all the behind-the-scenes news she needed from Nash.

"Wait," Nash demanded, as she went to open the passenger door.

He got out, pulling on his suit jacket as he moved swiftly around to her side of the car, taking her arm and helping her out, hovering beside her as they walked up the path toward the crematorium. It took her a second to realize he was shielding her with his body. She swiveled her head around, looking for a threat. Shielding from what? Did he really expect the gunman to jump out of the bushes and open fire on them? Did he know about some threat he hadn't told her about? It was obvious he was prepared to put his body on the line for her. Skylar grunted in frustration and walked a little faster, so that he struggled to keep up with his injured leg. It was petty; she knew. But his overprotectiveness was fast becoming frustrating and downright annoying. Even if a small voice in the back of her head kept telling her how sweet and courageous it was, at the same time.

The crematorium was packed with people, and Skylar dropped her gaze to the floor as she walked up the aisle. Even so, she could still feel people staring, their gazes boring into the back of her head. She passed Robinson seated in the back row, and spotted the other officers stationed in the corners of the room. Nash led her to a chair three rows back, and she sat down just as the rest of her family arrived. Daniella took the chair next to her. Then her mother did something completely out of character. She took Skylar's hand in her own and patted it, in an awkward, comforting gesture. Her first reaction was to pull her hand away. But she forced herself to leave it resting in her mother's palm. Daniella had never been an overly affectionate mother, and this sort of public display was almost unheard of. She was clearly trying her best to help Skylar, even though she had no idea where to start.

Nash glanced down at her lap, where her mother still held her hand, and then shot her a sympathetic look, as if he knew how much this was costing her.

Paul's family filled the first two front rows. There was his girlfriend, Sonia. Paul had showed Skylar a picture of her on the flight over just the other day. They'd only been seeing each other for six months or so, but Paul had said she was the one. Panic filled Skylar's veins, and she suddenly found it hard to breathe. What must they think of her? Did they even know the full story? Had the police told them everything? She must ask Nash later on. None of the family looked back at her, however, and her trepidation began to subside after a few moments.

Skylar glanced at the front of the chapel, where a priest was milling around a podium, getting ready to start the service. A large, framed photo of Paul sat atop a wooden coffin, draped in flowing bunches of Australian wildflowers.

Paul stared at her from out of the photo. He was smiling, but she could see the censure in his eyes. *I would be alive, if it wasn't for you,* they seemed to say.

Oh, shit.

Then the priest began to speak, and the hushed voices of the gathered mourners fell silent. He talked about Paul's love of flying, how he'd known, even as a boy, it was all he wanted to do.

The room started to close in around Skylar. The sound of gunfire pinging off the metal of the chopper rang in her ears. Paul's voice, loud and terrified, calling in the Mayday, haunted her. The image she could never clear from her mind, that of Paul's body crushed beyond recognition by the boulder. Paul hadn't done anything to deserve this. He'd just been doing his job that day, expecting to go home and lie in the arms of his girlfriend that night. He'd tried to land the chopper safely, to save them all. Where was the fairness in all of this? He was the innocent bystander who'd been killed. While she and Nash, the intended targets, had survived.

She couldn't do this.

Her hands began to tremble. Then her whole body started to shake.

Daniella looked at her in bewilderment.

Then a strong arm snaked around her shoulders, and Nash pulled her into his chest. "It's okay," he whispered, passing her a handful of tissues. "I'm here. You're safe. We're both safe."

Nash understood.

She hadn't cried for Paul. For the loss of an innocent life. For all the things he had yet to do. She'd kept the emotions from those few days in the jungle locked away in a vise in her mind. Now all those feelings came tumbling out, like an avalanche rolling downhill, gathering speed, until she was weeping silently.

"Let it out," Nash said into her ear. There were tears in his eyes, as well. She sobbed into his shoulder.

The rest of the ceremony passed in a blur, as Skylar struggled in her fog of sorrow and guilt. Vaguely, she was aware of Paul's brother speaking, but she couldn't remember what he said. Other people around her also dabbed at their eyes with a tissue. Paul had been well liked, and would be sorely missed. She finally managed to get her tears under control and pulled away from Nash's chest. He let her go, but rested his hand on her thigh, instead.

Slowly, her head began to clear, and she realized the ceremony was over. People were standing up and heading toward the exit, paying their respects on the way out.

The family was holding a wake at Paul's parents' place. They were all invited, but Skylar already knew she wouldn't be able to face them.

"Are you okay, sweetheart?" Her mother never called her sweetheart. It was that, more than anything, that finally brought Skylar back to reality.

"Yes." She nodded. "I really want to go home, though."

"Of course, you do," her mother replied, and shot an expectant look at Nash. "You'll take her, won't you?"

"Yes," he replied stiffly. "Of course, but—"

"Good." Daniella didn't want to hear Nash's reasons for Skylar not returning home any more than she did. They'd rehashed it so many times. Skylar was prepared to take her chances at Stormcloud, and her whole family backed her up on that decision.

Nash shut his mouth with a snap.

"Dale and Steve would like to go to the wake," Daniella continued. "They want the family to know that Paul meant a lot to us. He was a great pilot, and he gave us an important lifeline between the station and civilization. Is it okay if we don't come straight home with you?"

"We'll still have the police escort to see us back to Dimbulah, so that's fine," Nash replied, but he continued to glare at Daniella, and she continued to ignore his stare.

Skylar was glad the rest of her family was going on to the wake. It made her non-attendance a little less obvious. She knew she wouldn't be able to cope with all the questions and the sympathy, and perhaps the reproach she'd have to deal with, if she went.

"Great, we'll see you at home soon, Skylar. Then this will all become a distant memory." Daniella put a protective hand on Skylar's shoulder before she turned back to Steve and Dale to let them know what was going on.

Nash spoke quickly to Robinson, then rounded up Schroeder and her sidekick, and they were back in his car inside of five minutes, following the police cruiser through the media throng at the front gate.

Nash had lulled her into a false sense of security on the drive up to Cairns by keeping the conversation to a minimum. Keeping his manner strictly professional, calm, and polite. And for the first part of the trip home, he remained tight-lipped, the same as before.

But then, a little over an hour into the drive, Nash launched a surprise attack.

He turned the volume down on the radio. That was her first clue something was up. Then he drew a couple of deep breaths, as if he was pulling in strength for things to come. She tensed as he turned to look at her.

"Skylar, we need to talk."

No, we don't. She kept her mouth shut and continued to stare through the windshield. Even though he'd been her rock throughout the funeral, had been his kind-hearted self once more, that didn't change things between them now.

"All right, how about I talk, and you listen?" he continued when she didn't answer.

She lifted her shoulder in a shrug. It was a free country; she couldn't stop him if he wanted to get something off his chest.

"I want to apologize for what I said the other night. I was out of line. You confided in me, and I used that information to hurt you, and I'm sorry." His gaze drifted from the road to look at her. "I mean it," he added. He left a space for her to fill, but she refused to answer, and so he continued, "I also want to give you my solemn promise, that I would never try and coerce you into speaking about Craig, or convince you to report him. It's your life, and it's ultimately your decision."

As apologies went, it was a pretty good one. He almost had Skylar believing him. She guessed she owed him something in return.

"Thank you, Nash," she said politely. "I appreciate that. But I'm not sure I completely believe you."

He opened his mouth to argue, but she held up a hand.

"You are a cop, first and foremost. It's your job to put right any wrongs. To put the bad guys away, where they belong. So, I don't expect you to understand my reasons for keeping this to myself. And for asking you to do the same."

"Yes, I'm a cop, but I'm not the straight-down-the line sort of guy you're making me out to be. I realize everything is not merely black-and-white. There are shades of gray to most stories."

She considered his words. Watching his hands resting easily on the steering wheel. He had long, graceful fingers. Skillful fingers. That knew exactly where to touch her. He'd taken his jacket off and rolled the sleeves of his dark shirt up to the elbow as soon as they left the chapel, and her gaze travelled up his exposed forearms, focusing on the tiny blond hairs covering his tanned skin. Then she merely looked at him, not knowing how to answer.

His grip tightened on the steering wheel. "You can trust me to keep your secret, Skylar. I know you've lost your confidence in most people. But you need to learn to find that trust again. I can help you."

She looked at him. He was possibly correct. She could feel the significance of his words shooting holes through the vulnerable walls around her heart. Over the past week, she'd been slowly coming to the conclusion that Nash was the most trustworthy man she'd ever met. But what if she had faith in his words and began to believe in him, and he let her down? That would be far worse than not letting him into her heart in the first place. Wouldn't it?

"Maybe you're right," she said finally. "Maybe I do keep myself shut off from people too much. But that's the way I've chosen to live my life. And it suits me. I'm happy to leave things the way they are."

But was she really? Nash was offering her something. An olive branch. A potential life outside of her self-imposed cocoon. If only she'd reach out and take it.

Nash sighed. "Even if you won't accept my apology, will you please consider staying on a little longer at my place? If you go home to Stormcloud, we can't keep you safe; I can't keep you safe."

"I know, but it's okay," she said softly. "It's not your job to keep me safe, It's mine. I'm going home, Nash."

They sat in silence for the rest of the trip home.

Just as they hit the outskirts of Dimbulah, the police radio Nash had installed in his console, so he could stay in touch with Schroeder on the drive, crackled to life.

"Constable Willow has requested our help. He picked up a drunk and disorderly this morning, and he's going crazy in his cell. Really ripping the place up. He thinks he means to do himself harm. Can you head toward the station? It should only take a few minutes."

Nash glanced at Skyler. "Skylar wants to swing past my house and pick up her things before we head out to Stormcloud. Why don't you come around there when you're finished?"

She'd already discussed this with him this morning. She had a bag of clothes to collect, as well as a box of food that Nash had insisted he'd never use, if she left it in his pantry.

"If you're sure, sir?" Schroeder said. Even Skylar could hear the distraction in the young constable's voice. It was clear she wanted to go and lend a hand to calm the unruly prisoner.

"Yes. I've got it covered."

"Thanks, sir." Skylar heard the relief in her voice. "We'll meet you at your house in ten, and follow you the rest of the way out to Stormcloud from there."

A few turns in the road later, Nash pulled his car into the driveway. Skylar studied the little white cottage. It really was quite cute, with its wooden windowsills, standing up on stilts.

She sat in the car and waited until Nash drew his gun and checked down both sides of the house. Then he came around to collect her from the passenger seat, and she swallowed her impatience as Nash led her up the stairs and opened the front door, keeping her tucked in behind him. He made her stand in the living room and wait, while he checked each room was clear. She tapped her foot agitatedly. The gunman was obviously tired of chasing them. He was probably too concerned with dodging the police net they'd put out to capture him, to worry about them anymore.

She watched Nash disappear into her bedroom, the last one at the end of the hall.

There was a small sound behind her. Before she could even swing around to see what it was, a large hand came up to cover her mouth and the cold metal of a gun barrel pressed against her temple.

CHAPTER TWENTY-TWO

For a split second, Nash didn't believe what he was seeing. He stood frozen in the hallway; weapon still pointed at the floor. His eyes must be playing tricks, because the gunman from the jungle had just appeared through the doorway and put a pistol to Skylar's head. It was his imagination replaying nightmarish scenarios.

Then the man spoke and shattered any illusion that this wasn't real.

"Drop your weapon," he demanded.

Nash stared at him, desperately hoping for divine intervention. But in the end, there was no other option. Slowly, he bent his knees and placed the Glock on the ground.

"Good boy," the man said mockingly. "Now, you're going to do exactly as I tell you, or your girlfriend's brains are going to end up all over your lovely, white walls."

Skylar let out a whimper from behind the man's hand, blue eyes dilated with fright.

How had he missed this guy? He must've been hiding outside, waiting to pounce. Nash had only done a superficial sweep because he was distracted. He was so stupid. But now wasn't the time to drown in self-flagellation. He could do plenty of that once he got Skylar away from this madman.

"We're getting outta here. You're going to drive, while me and Blondie sit in the back. Got it?"

Nash nodded, not trusting himself to speak.

"First of all, hand over your phone." The man pointed at the coffee table with his pistol, and Nash saw Skylar's phone already sitting there. "Well done," he said, when Nash did as he was told. "After you." The gunman tilted his chin toward the door and took a step back, dragging Skylar with him, so there was room for Nash to move past.

Even as he raised his hands and walked slowly through the door, he was assessing the man. It was definitely the same guy from the jungle. Same height. Same muscular build. Same menacing, gravelly voice. And he was dressed exactly the same, as well. Long, dark, cargo pants, a black T-shirt, combat boots, and utility belt loaded with ammo slung around his waist, along with the black backpack over his shoulders. Nash couldn't see a sign of where he'd struck the man with his knife. It seemed as if this guy had shrugged the injury off. Clearly a man not to be trifled with. The rifle he'd lost out in the jungle had been replaced by a handgun; a 9mm Beretta, if Nash was correct.

But there were signs that the man had perhaps been living rough. His clothes were dirty, as if they were the same ones he'd been wearing in the jungle. Dirt was ingrained in the lines on his face and the furrows on his forehead, as well as around his fingernails and creases of his palm. And he stank, as if he hadn't showered in a week.

Nash stepped down the stairs slowly, exaggerating his limp, hoping that if he took his time, Schroeder might appear around the corner in the police cruiser.

Nash rolled one scenario after another through his head as he hit the bottom step. Could he possibly defeat this guy? Or at least delay him until help arrived? Because once he got them both in the car, they were on their own. The man had

Skylar held in front of him, using her as a shield as he followed Nash down the stairs. So Nash couldn't lash out without hitting Skylar first. The gun was no longer pointed at her head, which meant he'd probably moved it to the small of her back, so it was less visible to any passers-by. But it was no less deadly.

In the end, Nash couldn't come up with any idea that wouldn't put Skylar in direct danger, so he had to step behind the wheel of his car and watch, powerless to do anything else, as the man shoved Skylar in the back seat and followed after her. Skylar struggled, turned, and kicked out with her long legs at the man, catching him in the stomach, and he grunted in pain and surprise.

Quickly, he raised his gun and pointed it directly at the side of Nash's head. "Go on, my lovely, try that again. I dare you."

Skylar sucked in a sharp breath, and turned to sit properly on the seat.

"Yeah, I thought as much," he sneered.

"Gimme that," the man said, pointing to Nash's police radio. When Nash gave him the handset, the guy ripped the cord out of the main receiver. And there went Nash's last chance at communication. "Head north, out of town," he directed.

That was the road to Gamboola. And it went straight past Stormcloud Station. Nash started the car and backed out of the driveway, praying the police car would turn down the road in front of them. But no such luck. Nash kept quiet, checking on Skylar in the rear-view mirror.

"How was the funeral?" The commando asked. "You both look lovely, by the way."

Nash stared at him in the rear mirror. Was this guy trying to make small talk now? Or was he merely gloating? Rubbing it in their faces that he'd caused the death of the pilot. It proved one thing, however. That the gunman had known their every move. He knew where they'd be today, and when they'd return. And he'd laid his trap. It was just sheer luck on the gunman's side that Schroeder had been diverted. Or was it? He couldn't possibly have engineered the scene down at the station. Could he?

Skylar turned a look of shocked disbelief on the man. "You utter bastard," she snarled. "Where are you taking us? You can't do this. You know the cops will be on you soon. You—"

Without warning, the man lashed out, striking Skylar in the temple with the butt of his gun. "Shut the fuck up," he growled, as Skylar slumped in the seat. "That's for the kick in the guts." He grinned.

"Hey!" Nash yelled, the car veering across the road as he turned to see what was going on in the back seat.

"Keep driving," the man yelled. "Or I won't have a problem killing her here and now." In the mirror, Nash saw him point the weapon at Skylar's prostrate body.

Fuck.

Nash returned his focus to the road ahead and steadied the car. It'd do no good if he crashed now. Although… The idea may have merit. While Nash had his seatbelt on, the commando wasn't wearing one. But then, neither was Skylar. Nope, he couldn't take the risk she might be flung from the car and killed if he intentionally crashed. He'd have to come up with another plan.

The road to Gamboola unfurled in front of him. No other cars were visible either ahead, or behind. They were on their own.

"Just keep going," the commando said.

Less than ten minutes up the road, the commando spoke again. "Slow down. There's a turnoff on the left in about two-hundred meters."

Nash slowed the car, but he almost missed the overgrown,

dirt track heading off at a tangent from the highway.

"Here. Here. Turn here," the gunman yelled, and Nash had to brake hard. There was a thump from the behind him as Skylar's unconscious body slid forward and hit the rear of his seat.

Shit, he needed to be more careful. Was Skylar even okay? She hadn't made a sound since the bastard had hit her. It wasn't a good sign to be unconscious for this long. He wanted to stop the car and jump out and check that she was okay. But he ground his teeth together and kept driving.

His sedan bumped and shuddered down the potholed track. This road hadn't been used in a long time. The open woodland of the floodplains encroached along the edges. He had to steer around a couple of clumps of mulga growing onto the track. The late afternoon sun slanted through the sparse trees, glowing orange in the dust raised from his tires. There was nothing but trees and sky as far as the eye could see. They were completely alone out here.

Five minutes later, the woodland opened, and a clearing appeared. A couple of ruined buildings lay sagging and abandoned around the edges. An old homestead, perhaps? Nash didn't know enough about the history of the area to figure out who this land might've once belonged to.

They must only be a couple of kilometers off the main highway, if that. And only around twenty kilometers out of town. Close, but yet so far.

"Over there." The commando pointed at a small building, a shed of some sort. It looked newer than the rest, made of corrugated sheet metal.

Nash parked his car beside the shed, where the man indicated.

There were tire tracks in the dust around the shack. Motorcycle tracks, by the looks of them. Nash had been wondering how the other man had travelled around the area, and now he thought he had his answer. There'd been no car parked in the street when they'd arrived at his house today. It didn't mean the commando hadn't parked it elsewhere and walked, but a motorcycle would be much easier to hide, and get rid of once it was no longer needed. And a motorcycle would be easy to ride around the bushland tracks out here. Which might solve the question of how the gunman had gotten into his back yard unseen.

"Carry her inside," the man instructed.

Nash slowly exited the car as the man stepped out and watched him from the other side. Skylar was sprawled on the rear seat, motionless. Her black dress was all crumpled up at her waist and her feet were bare where her shoes had fallen off. He opened the door and leant in. Turning her over so he could see her face, he called to her gently, "Skylar. Can you hear me?" A large purple bruise spread across the left side of her cheek and up her temple.

That fucking bastard. Nash almost stood up and went for the guy. He had no right to do this to her. But the only way either of them was going to survive was for him to keep his cool. Stay focused and wait for the right moment to get this guy. He felt for a pulse in her neck and was happy to find a strong beat beneath his fingertips.

It was awkward, gathering an unconscious Skylar into his arms, smoothing her dress down to maintain her dignity, but he managed somehow. The extra weight put a strain on his injured leg, and he stumbled a few times. But he was determined not to fall. The commando laughed, as if hoping Nash would drop her. Like this was some sort of entertainment for him.

The door to the shed was ajar, and Nash shoved it the rest of the way open and went inside. While small, it was relatively neat. And it became obvious with one glance that this was where the commando had been hiding out over the past few days. This guy must have a military background. Everything was squared away. The single bed by the wall had been made with razor-sharp corners. It was hot inside, with no way for the heat of the day to escape the tiny, metal shed. The only light came from a single window, up high on the far wall, and through the open door.

Nash wasn't sure why this hut was here. It was at least ten years old, by the looks of the rust forming on some of the outside walls. Had the commando stumbled across this place? Or did he have an accomplice? Or even a network of accomplices?

Robinson had told him only this morning, that the gunman's brother, Stan the Man, was still refusing to talk. But they were digging through Stan's life and beginning to close in on his friends and associates, finding out more about the social network he hung out with. Society's underbelly, if Robinson was correct. Some of Stan's acquaintances were well known for their connections to outlaw biker gangs. The gunman had divulged that Stan was his older brother. Nash hadn't told Skylar this, but Robinson thought he might've identified the gunman. It seemed Stan was the eldest of five brothers. The police were in the process of tracking the siblings down. It seemed they'd all done a stint in the army at some stage—following in their father's footsteps or some such bullshit—and they were now scattered all over the country. Only one had a fixed address, and he lived in Perth, so was probably out of the picture. Robinson's men had been compiling data on the other three brothers, trying to track them down. But this was a very reclusive family, that kept their identities and secrets close to their chests. And now the police might have an inkling as to why. At least two of them, and perhaps more, had been snipers in the army, with links to organized crime. A whole family of guns for hire, it seemed.

Someone was bound to talk, sooner or later. But that

wasn't going to help him now.

What would help him was finding out what the gunman had planned.

Carefully, he placed Skylar on the bed, untangling her limbs and rolling her onto her side. She groaned, which was a good sign, but didn't open her eyes, even when he stroked her hair away from her face.

The gunman was watching him from the doorway, eyes glittering in a beam of sunlight streaming through the open door.

He needed to engage this guy, to see if he could glean any information. He sat on the edge of the bed, hand placed protectively on Skylar's hip, and adopted what he hoped was an unthreatening tone.

"You're a pretty smart guy. Even with all that police protection, you got to us in the end." If this fellow's ego was half as big as his fat head, then stroking it with barely disguised flattery might work.

The gunman made a rude noise. "Please. Don't insult me. Police protection, my ass. I knew it'd only be a matter of time before you fucked up. All I had to do was bide my time. And slip that old drunk a few hundred to kick up a ruckus at the jail this morning." The gunman sneered.

Nash wasn't shocked to hear the diversion at the jail had been engineered. This guy was smart and determined. Pity he was on the wrong side of the law, he would've made a great cop.

"Did you know I was watching you?" the man continued in a thoughtful tone. "I think you might've felt it. I even followed you into town and saw you take your little woman, here, shopping. So attentive, you were."

He knew it. Knew that something had been wrong that day in Main Street. Why hadn't he listened to his gut?

"You didn't heed my other little omen, either, did you?"

the gunman asked with a smirk. "I left you a sign, but you ignored it. My pockets were full of those little rocks, after your girlfriend pushed me down the slope. I wondered if you'd see it, but once again you disappointed me."

He'd been right, the pebbles had been left there as a warning. Nash resisted the urge to stand and get up in this guy's face. He needed to let him think he had the upper hand. So, he remained sitting on the bed, Skylar's leg warm beneath his hand.

"Look…" Nash hesitated, and then added. "What should I call you?" If they were going to have a conversation, a name would be good.

The other man leered at him. "I ain't no fool. You don't get my true identity." The gunman took a step inside and then leaned against the wall, pistol casually held in his right hand. "Call me Jacko; that'll do for now."

Nash gritted his teeth. That name didn't match any of the three brothers; it wasn't even close. Nash wondered if it'd been a call sign from the army, or perhaps a childhood nickname.

"Right. Jacko, I'm Nash King and this is Skylar Williams." Personal details were always good. They made a victim seem more human if a perpetrator knew their name, knew their story, and how much they stood to lose. "And we both—"

"I know who you are," Jacko interrupted. "Do you think I'd accept a contract without knowing who my marks were? I know a lot more about both of you than you might think. I've done my research." There was a deeply menacing quality to Jacko's tone that sent a spike of fear down Nash's spine. "And don't try that psychobabble shit on me. When the time comes, I won't have any qualms about killing you."

Nash could no longer sit still. After a quick check to make sure Skylar was still breathing, he stood. "We know you're working for Sanders. It's only a matter of time before the noose closes around you. You should let us go. Why the hell are you keeping up this charade?" The shed seemed all the much smaller now he was standing, with Jacko looming in the doorway. Three steps would carry him over to the hateful man, and he could take him by the throat and push him up against the wall…

Nash took a deep breath and clenched his fists at his sides.

Jacko stood straighter and fixed Nash with a sinister gaze. "Because I've never, I repeat, never, left a contract unfulfilled. This is a matter of pride. You got away from me in the jungle. You won't get away from me now."

Nash took a step forward before he stopped himself and came to a halt in the middle of the room. He held his hands up, palms facing forward. "Look, if you agree to talk, to spill the beans on Sanders, we can make sure the judge goes easy on you. If you let us go free, they'll see that as a sign of goodwill." Would logic work on this guy? Probably not, but it was worth a try.

"Not going to happen," Jacko sneered. "Oh, by the way. This one is payback for the knife to the shoulder, you bastard." Before Nash could react, the commando spun around and landed a heavy kick in his guts. Nash double over, gasping in pain and shock.

Jacko landed another kick, this time to Nash's wounded thigh, and he dropped like a sack of potatoes to the floor with a howl of agony.

"I've had enough of this conversation." Jacko loomed over him.

Nash had no time to avoid the boot coming for his head. Pain exploded behind his eyes, and his world went dark.

CHAPTER TWENTY-THREE

Skylar stretched her arms and legs. What had happened to her bed? It wasn't nearly as comfortable as she remembered. Or maybe she was in Nash's bed. A secret smile stole over her lips. Was he lying next to her, asleep? She reached out a hand but found empty air. Where was he?

She rolled her head sideways on the pillow, and an agonizing pain shot through her temples. Her eyes flew open as she clutched at her head, but it was dark, and she couldn't fathom where she was.

"Good evening, sleepyhead," a voice came out of the darkness. Who was that? She thought she recognized that voice.

"Nash?" She dared not sit up, otherwise her head might split open. When no one answered, she said again, "Nash? Is that you?"

"Nah," came the laconic reply. "Your boyfriend's a little tied up at the moment."

Then everything came flooding back in a blast of reality.

The gunman.

He'd found them.

And he'd hit her with his gun. She must've been knocked out.

She did try and sit up then, but slowly, cradling her head in her hands. She needed to see what was going on. Where was she? And where was Nash?

Her head still throbbed, but as long as she kept her movements slow and smooth, it was bearable.

It was so dark; Skylar could hardly make anything out. All she could ascertain was she was in some kind of room, sitting on a bed. Who it belonged to, she had no idea. There was a small window up high to the left, but that only showed her a starlit sky. Night had fallen. She'd been unconscious for a while; a few hours at least.

Suddenly, a light flicked on, and Skylar cried out, covering her eyes. The light hurt her head. But she needed to see for herself. Forcing her hand away from her face, she squinted into the brightness.

The gunman sat on a chair over by a small table, near a partially open door. It looked like they were in a shed or small outbuilding.

Nash lay on the floor between her and the gunman, trussed up with ropes at his ankles and wrists, which had been pulled behind his back.

"Nash," she called helplessly. But he didn't answer, and that's when she saw the terrible bruising on his face and blood trickling from his nose. He'd been beaten, and now he was unconscious. Without any thought for herself, she launched off the bed and crawled to his side. She almost ended up in the fetal position as pain lanced through her brain. But she fought through it, and then sat still beside him until the pain subsided a little.

"You fucker," she said between clenched teeth, as she took Nash's face between the palms of her hands. He was breathing. That was good.

"Yeah, that's me," the gunman said with an evil grin. Then he watched with seeming delight as Skylar tried to gently wake Nash. His handsome face was pale and bloody, his hair caked in blood, as well. She wanted to lie down on the floor and cradle him in her arms and make this all go away.

"It's probably time he woke up, though. I need to get this finished. I've got better places to be right now." The gunman stood suddenly, and Skylar only had time to sit up and direct a scathing glare at him, before he dumped a whole jug full of water all over Nash's face.

Skylar wanted to reach up and scratch his eyes out, but then Nash groaned and spluttered. The water had worked, Nash was awake. Even if she despised the gunman's methods, Skylar was absurdly pleased to see Nash's blue eyes fix on her.

"Are you okay?" he croaked.

"I'm alive," she replied, stroking his cheek, wiping some of the water from his face.

"Thank God." Nash leaned his cheek into her palm and stared up at her. Emotions so strong she could hardly name them flooded through her.

"Enough chitchat," the gunman interceded. "It's dark now. We can start."

"Start what?" Skylar glared at him.

"You, go and sit on the bed," he commanded. She was slow to comply; she didn't want to leave Nash. But when the gunman nonchalantly touched his weapon, nestled in its shoulder holster, she did as she was told. He didn't have to draw the gun, she already knew what the barrel of his pistol felt like pushed against her skin.

The gunman strolled toward Skylar, and the rope dangling from his hand drew her gaze.

"Stand up," he commanded. She thought about disobeying him, but what other option did she have, really? "Hands behind your back."

She rolled her eyes, but did as he told her. It only took a

few seconds for him to tie her wrists together, then he spun her around and pushed her down to sit on the bed. The jolting movement caused her head to throb, and she cried out in pain.

"Look, Jacko, let's come to some sort of agreement," Nash croaked from the floor.

"I don't think you're in any position to talk, my friend." The gunman sounded almost convivial. Jacko, that was what Nash had called him. At least he had a name now. Skylar wondered what else she'd missed while she'd been unconscious. But even though his tone was easy, he was rough with the rope, yanking her ankles together painfully as he tied the first knot.

"Let her go," Nash pleaded. "Take me. You can do whatever you want to me. But leave her out of this."

Jacko turned to look at Nash. "Much as I'd like to negotiate with you, mate—because I will admit you have both been formidable opponents, I've never had to work so hard to complete a contract before—I'm afraid the contract calls for both your heads on a spike."

What the hell? Was this guy for real? Was he giving them a backhanded compliment with one breath and then threatening to kill them with the next? What sort of man was this Jacko? And what did Nash think he was doing? Trying to use himself as a bargaining chip to gain her freedom. Over her dead body. She wasn't about to let him sacrifice himself for her.

"Nash King," she said hotly. "You will not do anything of the sort. I—"

Jacko slapped a hand over her mouth and then followed it with a large piece of duct tape. "That's enough from you, woman." Jacko said. "Like I said, neither of you is in a position to bargain here. I'm running the show. Patty was a bloody walk in the park compared to you pair."

What had he said? Had he just admitted to killing Patty as well? One more reason to hate his guts, and Skylar's blood began to boil. With a quick flick of his wrist, Jacko tipped Skylar backward, and then lifted her legs to lay her straight on the bed and rested her head on the pillow. He manhandled her as if she weighed nothing, but he was also surprisingly gentle. That didn't stop Skylar's anger from spiraling, however. She tried to kick out, but with her legs tied together, it was a completely ineffective move; she was more like an irate caterpillar than anything else. A feeling of complete powerlessness washed over Skylar. Trussed up like a pig going to slaughter, with her mouth taped shut, she couldn't even plead for her own life.

This joker was going to kill them both. Skylar couldn't stand the idea of Nash being dead.

"What are you planning on doing with us?" Nash asked. Skylar heard the resignation in his voice. Surely, he wasn't giving in?

Jacko took one more look at Skylar before he straightened. He was so tall; his head nearly brushed the ceiling. Jacko stared reflectively out the small window. "Perhaps I might retire. Sanders paid me well. And it's gonna be harder to stay out of sight after this stuff-up. Now I'm on the fucking police radar. Thanks to you guys." He glared down at Nash.

"That's not what I asked," Nash growled.

"I know." Jacko knelt down, and it took a moment for Skylar to realize he was taping up Nash's mouth, too. Now they were both bound and gagged. Completely helpless. Then he patted Nash's pockets, and Skylar thought the guy had gone completely mad until she heard the sound of jingling car keys.

"Not the best getaway car," Jacko mused. "I'll have to ditch it soon. But it'll do the job, for now. You two wait here, while I go sort out a few things. I won't be long. Then I'll let you in on my little plan," he added gleefully.

Jacko disappeared out the door, and she and Nash were left alone in the shed.

Skylar rolled onto her side so she could look at Nash. He scooted around so he could tip his head up and stare back at her. This was what it had come down to. How long did they have before the gunman came back? His sky-blue eyes fixed on hers, and she poured all the words she couldn't say through her own gaze as she stared back at him.

She'd thought she'd felt powerless to stop Craig back when he'd been beating her every other day. But then she'd finally come to realize that she could escape him; that it wasn't her fault Craig was like he was. And day by day, she'd grown stronger, devised a plan to leave him. Then the day after she'd escaped, he'd found her and raped her, as a punishment for leaving him, and she'd retreated inside herself. Retreated from the world, from the unfairness of it all. Deciding that she would live a strong life on her own terms, not reliant on anyone else. That she never need truly trust another human being again; apart from her family.

But her time with Nash had changed all that. Changed her perception of herself. Had given her hope.

But when he'd pushed her too hard the other night, she'd acted on instinct, letting old habits dictate her decisions.

Now she wanted to take back all those hurtful words she'd uttered the other night. She hadn't meant them. She knew that Nash was only trying to help her. And perhaps she should let him. Logically, she understood that to move on from any trauma, you needed to release it first. To get closure, find justice, and then improve day by day. And she thought that's what she'd done. But now she realized an important part of the jigsaw was missing. Justice. If she were to truly move on, then she needed to confront Craig. And get justice for herself. Nash had been right.

As she stared down at Nash, another surge of that all-encompassing emotion threatened to overwhelm her. It took her a moment to comprehend what it was. It'd been so long since she'd felt something this pure and strong.

Love.

She was in love with Nash.

He was everything to her. If only they could get out of this alive, she'd tell him so. She'd been stupid and spineless, and it'd taken Nash to wake her up out of her small, safe little world.

Tears leaked from her eyes. She wanted to whisper the words in his ear, shout it out to the world.

Almost as if he was reading her mind, his own beautiful eyes filled with tears, as well.

They both lay there, unable to speak, unable to reach each other, crying.

Jacko strode back into the building. "Right. I've got everything sorted. Let's have a little fun." He rubbed his hands together. "So, Nash, me mate. You wanted to know what I have planned?" Jacko knelt down next to Nash. "Like I said, I make a point of researching my hits thoroughly. Call me a perfectionist." Jacko gave a shrug of delight. "And so, I know all about your little episode in that car crash, where your friend nearly burned alive. That was pretty scary stuff. But it's why you became a cop, right?"

Skylar's breath caught in her throat. What was this bastard saying? Nash's eyes had gone hard, and he was struggling on the floor.

"So, I figure the one thing you'd hate the most in this world is to watch someone you care about burn, while you lay helpless, unable to save them. What do you think? Am I on the mark there?"

Nash let out a roar of rage from behind his gag and tried unsuccessfully to lash out at Jacko. The gunman merely stood and stepped out of range. "Yeah, that's what I thought," he said ominously.

This time, her heart stopped beating. No. Surely, he wasn't going to burn her alive? While Nash watched? Surely, no one could be that cruel? That brutal?

Then Jacko glanced at her with cold, glittering eyes, and she knew he could.

CHAPTER TWENTY-FOUR

Nash bucked and thrashed and struggled until he could no longer breathe, and his wounded leg was red-hot with pain, but to no avail. No. No. His heart was breaking. He finally went limp, and as if Jacko had been waiting for the opportunity, like the moment a wild brumby irrevocably gives in to its fate, the gunman grabbed him under the shoulders and dragged him out of the shed.

Nash held Skylar's gaze as he was towed backward. Tears streaked her face. Those tears of love he'd seen in her eyes had been replaced by tears of terror. Then he lost sight of her, and he was outside. Jacko dropped him on the ground and went back to secure the door.

"I still need to figure out how I'm going to kill you," Jacko mused from beside him. "But perhaps after the trauma of watching your girl die in a fire, a bullet to the head might be a small mercy. What do you think?"

Nash grunted, sending the man daggers with his eyes. Jacko smiled and dragged Nash farther back until they were a good fifty meters from the building. He leaned Nash against the trunk of a large eucalyptus, where he'd get a good view of the shed as it burned. It was dark outside, the only light spilled from the small side window and escaped through cracks in the walls and around the roof, but otherwise they were in complete darkness. But the darkness was his friend.

Behind his back, Nash was furiously twisting his hands forward and back. Flexing, then releasing. The rope rubbed his skin raw, but Nash ignored it. Even back in the shed, when Jacko had been telling them his plan, Nash had felt a little give in the ropes around his wrists. Not a lot, but enough to give him hope. And now he worked those ropes like his life depended on it. Which it did. The evening air was warm, the heat of the day slow to leave the country. And Nash had worked up quite a sweat with all his thrashing and struggling; continued to work up a sweat as he fought against the ropes. His palms were slick with perspiration, as were his arms and wrists. And the moisture acted as a lubricant.

Even while he was working his bonds, Nash kept an eagle eye on everything going on around him. Jacko had moved Nash's car, he could see the shape of it farther down the driveway, ready for Jacko's getaway. He twisted his left arm up and sideways, as far as his screaming tendons would allow, while at the same time contorting his hand, pushing his thumb down until he thought it might dislocate. The ropes slipped a little. He held his breath. Now all he had to do was get his knuckles through and…

His left hand was free.

But there was no time to rest. Chest heaving with exertion, the tape over his mouth making it hard to breathe, he worked on his right hand, keeping as quiet as possible so as not to attract attention.

Jacko stood a few feet away, staring at the shed.

"I removed all the debris and shrubbery," Jacko said conversationally. "I don't want to start a bushfire and alert the authorities, now do I?" He gave a deep chuckle of satisfaction. "And I'll monitor the fire, make sure it doesn't break containment lines."

Nash watched him like a hawk. The other man's attention was almost completely on the building in front of them, which was good for Nash. The ropes didn't want to let go of his other hand, and he nearly gave a grunt of frustration. He had to get free. He had to.

Jacko turned to cast a quick glance back at Nash and he froze, pretending to be slumped against the tree, conceding defeat. Jacko turned back to continue studying the outbuilding. Darkness really was Nash's friend. Surreptitiously, he drew his knees into his chest and eased his right hand around to find the knots binding his ankles tight.

Jacko walked slowly toward the shed and picked up a small metal can hidden in the darkness by the corner of the door. He began to splash the petrol on the walls, on the door and on the roof.

An all-encompassing dread filled Nash as he watched the other man's careful deliberation. It was like the weight of the whole world was on his chest, forcing the air from his lungs. He fought the fear, taking two deep breaths through his nose and compelling his fingers to keep working on the knot. For a pro, the gunman had been sloppy with his knots. Perhaps he had so much confidence in his ability to cow them with his threats and his weapon, that he'd overlooked knot-tying 101.

Jacko flicked his wrist, and a match flared in the dark.

A low groan echoed in Nash's throat.

The match sailed through the air and the petrol erupted in sudden flames. The fire spread at breakneck speed, up the wall and onto the roof.

Skylar.

Oh. Jesus. Skylar. He had to get to her.

At the sight of the flames, his fingers became paralyzed, but the thought of Skylar immediately drove him on.

Jacko stood with his back to Nash. But then he turned and strode over to where Nash sat, propped against the tree. Nash tucked his hands behind his back, hoping that in the darkness, and crazy flicking shadows cast by the flames, the gunman wouldn't notice his bonds were loose.

"The flames are so beautiful," Jacko called out. "But I nearly forgot. I want to see your face as you watch your girlfriend die. Watch the hope fade in your eyes."

He was coming back to gloat, the bastard.

Jacko hunkered down next to Nash and brought his face in close. "How're you feeling so far, mate?" he asked with an evil edge to his voice.

He had to act quickly, so Jacko didn't have time to go for his weapon. In a rush, Nash brought both hands around in front and rammed them up into the gunman's chin. At the same time, he pushed up to standing and shook the last loop of rope from his ankles, as Jacko went sprawling backward into the dust.

He dived on top of Jacko, grabbing a handful of dirt and rubbing it in his eyes, hoping to blind the other man. Jacko bellowed like a wounded bull, but wrapped his arms around Nash's back, wrestling for control.

They fought like dogs, rolling and scuffling in the dust. Jacko managed to land his knee directly in Nash's wound and he gave a muffled scream of pain through the duct tape, but he didn't let go. This was going to be a dirty street fight. There were no gentleman's rules here, and Nash knew he had his work cut out for him. Jacko was taller and broader than him, and possibly had more brawling experience.

But Nash had a small advantage if he could manage to remain on top, so he locked his legs around Jacko's waist, grunting with the effort of holding the other man down while he bucked and twisted beneath him. Then he grappled for the weapon strapped to Jacko's side with his left hand, smashing his right fist repeatedly into the other man's face, raining down blow after blow.

Suddenly, as if by magic, Nash had the gun grip in his hand. He tugged with all his might and the weapon released from its holster. He checked the safety was off and pointed it at Jacko's head, expecting the man to stop fighting; to surrender like any normal human being in the same situation. Instead, Jacko snarled and lunged for the gun.

Nash had no choice.

The gun went off; the sound echoing around the clearing, and Jacko collapsed to the ground.

For a moment, Nash sat astride the man, too stunned to move. Had he really just defeated his enemy? Could it have been that easy? He checked for a pulse. Nothing.

The snapping sound of the fire devouring the shed brought him back to the present and to his true goal. To rescue Skylar.

He stood up and jogged toward the burning building, ripping the tape away from his mouth. There was no time to catch his breath. If he didn't act now, Skylar would die.

The door was completely engulfed. There was no way through it. Flames licked up over the roof, bright orange and almost merry as they consumed the petrol Jacko had poured over the building, working their way inside. The steel walls glowed red with the heat.

Flames rose high into the sky.

Flashbacks of the car crash assaulted his mind. Flames had ignited almost the instant they hit the tree. Nash was disorientated and dazed, not understanding what was happening, at first. Then the flames licked at his legs, and he screamed. But he somehow managed to release his seatbelt and stumble from the car, his trousers on fire, he'd rolled on the ground to put out the flames.

Then Mic's screams reached his ears, and he'd rushed around to the other side of the car. He froze, the terrible scene before him too dreadful to process. Precious seconds wasted as his friend burned.

Nash had tried. He'd reached in and undone Mic's seatbelt and then, when the flames had got too bad, he'd ripped off his T-shirt to protect his arms and tried again. But he hadn't been strong enough to rescue Mic. The only reason he'd survived was because the constable had pulled him out.

The heat from the flames devouring the shed were like a brand to his skin. The scars on his arms and legs throbbed in sympathy.

He couldn't do this. He hadn't been strong enough back then, and he'd failed his friend. And he wasn't strong enough now, either. He took a step backward, away from the flames.

But there was no one else. Nash was alone. If he didn't rescue Skylar, then no one would. He couldn't let her die. If she died, he wouldn't survive the aftermath. Part of him would die, too.

He forced his mind to think, forced his logical cop brain into action, pushing the frightened teenager to the back of his thoughts.

The door wasn't an option. There was a small window in the back. He ran around the building. The flames hadn't reached the back wall yet. The window was at head height, and possibly big enough for him to crawl through. But how would he get Skylar back through if she were unconscious? He kicked at the metal wall in frustration, but his foot hardly made a dent. That's when he noticed a seam, where two sheets of steel were joined, right below the window frame. A weakness. Could that be exploited?

He looked around for something he could use; the flames cast more than enough light for him to see by. There were pieces of old, rusted machinery scattered everywhere among the ruins. An old car sat amongst the acacia shrubs, slowly falling to pieces fifty meters away. He ran over to inspect it. The car was so old it even had a metal bumper, which was lying on the ground in front of the wreck. Nash scooped it up, and using it much like a battering ram, he ran at the back wall of the shed. His first hit shattered the glass in the window, and plumes of smoke billowed outward. His second hit caused the corrugated sheeting to crack and fold inward near the window frame. He continued to batter the same spot repeatedly, ignoring the rusty metal slicing into his skin until his palms became slippery with blood. The window frame cracked and collapsed inward, widening the opening.

"I'm coming, Skylar," he shouted. Could she hear him? The roar and crackle of the flames was becoming so loud he could hardly hear himself think.

With one final, almighty thrust, the bumper broke through the wall, with Nash crashing in after it. Nash expected the flames to light his way once he was inside the shed, but the air was filled with dark, choking smoke, making him cough raggedly. Roiling and black, so that he couldn't see his hand in front of his face. But he didn't need to see, he remembered exactly where the bed was; to his right against the side wall. He felt his way along in dark. It was like the pits of hell in here, so hot the sweat dried straight off his skin. *Please let her still be on the bed.* He was coughing uncontrollably.

His feet hit something on the floor, and he tumbled forward.

Skylar. She must've rolled off the bed. He felt around her body with his hands. She was still bound and gagged. But there was no time, he needed to get her out. Using the fireman's lift, he hoisted her limp body over his shoulder.

Up until now, he'd been ignoring the pain in his thigh, but Skylar's weight almost buckled his leg with the strain. With a roar of rage, he used every ounce of strength he had to take one step and then another, maneuvering out through the gap in the busted wall.

They were free. His breath was rasping in his throat, and he sucked in great lungfuls of clean air, still coughing.

Moving as far away from the burning shed as his leg would allow, he gently lay Skylar on the ground and sat back on his haunches.

"You're safe now," he rasped, carefully removing the tape from her mouth.

But Skylar didn't respond. Her eyes remained shut, her body limp.

She wasn't breathing.

No time to think. He fumbled with the rope around her hands, taking too long to undo the knots. Then he rolled her onto her back and tilted her head back and commenced CPR.

Thirty chest compressions. Two quick breaths. Repeat. The training had been drilled into him. He'd had to use CPR just the other day on an old man who'd collapsed in the middle of Dimbulah's main street from a heart attack. But this was different. This was the woman he loved.

"Come back to me, baby," he chanted between the pumping motion of his hands.

After five cycles, he stopped to check for signs of life. Resting his fingers on her neck, he felt for a pulse and listened for breathing over her mouth.

Nothing. A sob escaped his lips.

He started the cycles again. "Come back to me. I love you," he chanted over and over.

There was an infinitesimal movement of Skylar's eyelids.

He lifted his hand from her chest and watched for signs. Was her chest moving?

She coughed; a sound so slight he might've missed it if he hadn't been watching for it.

"That's right, baby," he encouraged.

She coughed again, and her eyelids fluttered. She was coming back to him.

He cradled her head in his hands and stared down at her face as her eyes slowly opened. "It's okay," he crooned. "I've got you. We're safe."

She stared up at him for many uncounted moments until a fit of coughing racked her body and she tried to sit up.

"Where's Jacko?" she asked, eyes still dazed and unfocussed. Her voice was so raspy with smoke, she could hardly form the words. "We have to—"

"He's dead," Nash said with finality. "You don't have to worry about him."

"How…?"

"Over there." Nash pointed to the inert form lying in the dust between the burning shed and the ruined farmhouse. "I killed him. He won't hurt us again."

Nash freed her ankles from the ropes, and then helped her shuffle backward until they were up against the trunk of an enormous tree. He cradled her in his arms, using the tree as a backrest, her head laid back on his shoulder. They were far enough away from the fire now so they could watch it consume the shed without fear. Both of them continued to cough. They needed oxygen. Skylar could have lung damage. He should call an ambulance.

"I'll be right back," he said, easing himself out from behind Skylar.

"Nash, where are…?"

He hobbled over to Jacko and felt around in his pockets until he found what he was looking for, and held it up with a wave of triumph. The man's cell phone.

Nash hobbled back to Skylar, sliding in behind her again and cradling her once more. The phone was locked, but he didn't need a password to dial 0-0-0. He made the call, stunning the woman in dispatch to silence for a few seconds as he relayed who he was and what his situation entailed.

"They're sending an ambulance and a couple of fire trucks," he told Skylar. Funnily enough, Jacko had been right when he said the fire wouldn't spread. The building collapsed in on itself, sending a shower of sparks skyward, but the bare earth around it was enough to keep it from catching hold of anything else.

They sat in silence, watching the shed burn. He'd never felt more at peace than in that single moment, with Skylar safe in his arms. He'd done it. He'd been strong enough, after all. And she was alive because of him. They both were.

"Did you say you loved me?" she asked suddenly, voice still husky.

"What?" Had he said that? He didn't remember, it was all a blur. Perhaps he'd thought something along those lines. But had he said it out loud?

"I'm sure I heard you say you loved me," she continued. She swiveled in his arms so her face was close to his. "So, do you?"

He studied her blue eyes by the firelight. "Yes," he replied simply. "I do."

Would his answer scare her away? Just this morning they'd been fighting about her lack of trust, how she liked to live her life shut off from her true feelings. She'd been prepared to move back to Stormcloud and end the good thing that'd been growing between them. Had something changed since then?

"Good." She turned and lay her head back against his shoulder, her breath rasping on another cough.

Good? That wasn't what he'd been expecting.

"Because I might be in love with you, too."

He didn't look at her, but his heart leapt skyward. It was so typical of Skylar to understate everything. But right now, he'd take whatever she was offering. Because he knew he couldn't live without her.

CHAPTER TWENTY-FIVE

Skylar stood and stretched, bringing the bunch of freshly picked basil to her nose to draw in the spicy scent. It was good to be back in her kitchen garden again. She'd missed the simplicity and peace that spending time with your hands in the dirt could bring. The sky was a soft peach color, the last vestiges of the sunset disappearing over the escarpment. The air was warm and buzzing with the noise of insects on the wing.

It was a week today that she'd been released from the hospital, after spending two days being monitored for smoke inhalation. Nash had spent another two days in hospital after she left; his leg needed more stitches put in after he split it open during the struggle with Jacko. Skylar had wanted to stay with Nash, to sleep curled up beside him in his hospital bed like a lost kitten, but everyone urged her to come home and convalesce; telling her that Nash was in good hands. Nash had been the loudest advocate of all, and so she'd done as they asked. But she missed him. This whole week, she'd missed him like crazy.

Her lungs still ached if she over-exerted herself, and she was prone to coughing fits occasionally. For the first few days, she recuperated in the family suite, spending long hours sleeping in her bed, or watching mindless TV in the lounge room. She stayed away from the hustle and bustle of the lodge and the guests, preferring to cloister herself away, letting her wounds—which were all superficial—and her lungs heal. But after three days in her cocoon, she finally became tired of being house-bound and began to putter around the lodge, renewing her connection with the workings of the station and spending time with the staff.

Wazza and Alek had treated her like she was made of spun glass, which made her laugh. If only they knew the full details of what she'd had to do to survive, they'd understand she was much stronger than they knew. Julie had been much more pragmatic, making sure Skylar ate all the food she put in front of her, and telling her funny jokes to lighten the mood. Bindi and Sasha had welcomed her back with hugs and tears. And Daniella had been more attentive than Skylar could ever remember. Steve had been Steve. Down-to-earth, but also gentle. It made her glad she had such a good man for a stepfather.

But it was Daisy who'd offered her the greatest comfort. Skylar was finally ready to stop keeping all of her emotions and yearnings bottled up, and Daisy was the perfect sounding board. They'd talked for hours late into one night about love and men, and Daisy helped Skylar sort out her feelings for Nash. Daisy had been ecstatic when Skylar finally admitted that she'd fallen for Nash, and she encouraged her to let love in and see where it took her. It reassured Skylar to see that Dale and Daisy had been able to make their complicated lives work. Love had found a way with those two. It gave her hope that perhaps she and Nash might also have a future together.

Skylar glanced at the raised garden bed. The weeds had almost taken over her herbs in her absence. She was going to have a word with Dale about that, he should've done a better job looking after it for her.

"Hey, sis, where are you?"

Speak of the devil.

"Over here," she called. "Down by the herbs." She let her gaze drift over her garden as she waited for her brother. Without conscious thought, her eyes landed on the cabin below her young orchard. The cabin where she'd confronted Dan Sanders. A spontaneous shudder ran through her. If she'd known exactly how evil a human being Sanders would turn out to be, would she still have entered that cabin?

Probably.

Because she couldn't walk away, knowing another woman was being abused without trying to help. Maybe she might've handled the situation differently. Not gone in alone and unprotected. And maybe if she had, Patty might still be alive.

But in some ways, the act of walking through that door to confront the monster had started the chain of events—terrible and frightening as they were—that eventually led her to break out of her own cycle of self-oppression. It helped her awaken from a life half-lived. It'd led her to Nash.

The sound of booted feet swishing through the grass alerted her to Dale's presence, and she turned to study her younger brother as he strode down the hill. He had on his ubiquitous Akubra hat, long jean-clad legs stretching out. He looked up and smiled, the dimple in his cheek lighting up, and Skylar felt her heart lift. It was so good to be home again, surrounded by family.

In a burst of spontaneous joy, she reached out and hugged him as he came near. For a second, Dale started at her surprising show of affection, but then he pulled her in for a bear hug. She was determined to break out of her self-imposed style of remote aloofness. From now on, she was going to demonstrate to her family how much she loved them every chance she got.

"You okay?" he asked, when he finally stepped back. There was a huskiness to his voice that told her he was holding back his emotions; she knew how much it meant to him to have her back, safe and in one piece.

"I'm okay," she replied with a nod. "I'm doing better each day."

"Good. You know we're all here for you. If you need someone to talk to, I'm your man." He thumped his chest like a male gorilla might, and Skylar laughed. Her brother, the joker. But she could see the truth of his words behind his attempt to lighten the mood.

He looked down at the basket in Skylar's hand and narrowed his eyes. "You're not allowed back in the kitchen until tomorrow. You need to take the doctor's advice seriously, sis." Dale frowned at her. "Julie and Bindi have this under control, so stop fussing."

"I'm not fussing," she replied lightly.

"Don't get pedantic on me. I know you've been in the kitchen today because Julie snitched on you."

"I have been in the kitchen," she admitted. "But I promise I'm not interfering in the prep for the guests' meals. You're right, Julie has it all under control."

"Then why are you down here collecting herbs?" he accused.

"Because I'm cooking for Nash tonight." She smiled at him sweetly.

"Oh."

That took the wind out of his sails for a second.

"Well, that's different," he said, returning her smile with a dimpled one.

"Is it?"

"Yes. I like Nash. He's good for you."

"Yes, well, I don't need you getting involved with my love

life," she said, a little more haughtily than perhaps she should've.

"Love life? I like the sound of that. It's been so long since I've seen you with a man." He raised his gaze to the sky for a second. "I don't think I've seen you with anyone since you split with Craig."

Skylar's grip on the wicker basket tightened. She still hadn't told her family about her treatment at Craig's hands. She would tell them, soon. When she worked up the courage. They deserved to know. And she needed to tell them so she could move on. But not tonight. Tonight was about her and Nash.

"I think you might be right," she said, keeping her tone light and conversational. Picking up the hem of her long skirt, she began to walk up the hill, back toward the lodge. Reaching out a hand, she took her brother's, and they ambled along in companionable silence.

When they reached the back door, Dale tugged her around, so she had to look at him. "I'm glad you're here with us. And I'm glad you're giving Nash a chance. He's a good guy. He'd make a great brother-in-law."

"Now, don't go jumping the gun." Skylar slapped Dale on the shoulder. "It's very early days yet."

"Yeah, I know," he drawled, and opened the door to let her inside.

"Would you do me a favor?" she asked, giving him a saccharine smile.

"Whatever my sister wants, my sister gets." He parodied a low, sweeping bow.

"Would you set up the small fire pit down by the billabong for me?"

"Oooh, a picnic, how romantic," he cooed, and then stepped out of reach before she could slap him again.

"Just do it, bro, and stop the childish comments." Skylar

hid her smile as she slipped into the kitchen, where Julie and Bindi were in the middle of last-minute preparations to begin service. All the guests would be seated, sipping on a specially chosen white wine to accompany the entrée of crisp wontons filled with guacamole and topped with Cajun grilled prawns.

Skylar felt a spark of adrenaline, but she damped it down. Tonight was her last night of freedom before taking control of her kitchen once more. She'd let Julie and Bindi do their thing and take the accolades. They'd done an admirable job of keeping the guests happy while she'd been indisposed. Their meals hadn't been the gourmet wonders that Skylar produced, but they were solid, healthy, and tasted great, that was the main thing.

"Hey, Sky," Julie said, acknowledging her stepsister with a tilt of her chin. It was hot in here, with both large gas burners going as Julie fried up the prawns. She swiped an arm across her forehead, pushing her short, caramel hair back from her eyes.

"Hey, Jules," Skylar replied. "Looks delicious." Skylar slipped into the large cool room to retrieve her picnic basket filled with all the goodies she'd baked during the day. There were cold cuts of meat, cheeses, mini salmon tarts, tomato and caramelized onion pickle, some of her famous chocolate brownies, and a bottle of champagne. She tucked two long-stemmed glasses, along with the fresh basil in the basket, and put a picnic rug on top, then waved at Julie and Bindi and headed outside.

"Have a great night," Julie called after her.

Oh, she was planning on it. Butterflies jumbled in her belly as she walked toward the parking lot. She and Nash had talked every night on the phone, but that wasn't the same as seeing him in the flesh. She smoothed down her long skirt and brushed her hair over her shoulder. She'd gone for the boho look tonight, a more relaxed, feminine look than normal. Would Nash like it?

Right on time, Nash's car appeared on the other side of the billabong, coming slowly up the long drive, raising a plume of dust as it went. He pulled up in the parking lot and she could already see the smile playing over his lips, and all her qualms evaporated.

"Hi, gorgeous," he said, stepping out of his car.

"Hi, handsome," she replied, and then almost laughed at her faux pas. Because Nash's face was still battered and bruised. But the gorgeous man she'd fallen for was there, right beneath the surface, and she rushed around the car to embrace him. Strong arms wrapped around her shoulders, and she felt like this was the only moment in time that mattered. Just him and her. He lowered his head and without thinking, she put hungry lips to his. He kissed her back with such fervor that she thought her clothes might melt right off her.

Suddenly, she remembered his wounded face and drew back with a gasp. "Oh, I'm sorry. Did I hurt you?" She ran gentle fingers down his temple, tracing the unbruised side of his jaw. There was a large cut above his eye, which was healing nicely, and a few new abrasions over his left cheek— reminders of Jacko's boot as it landed in his face—to go with the older gash he'd gained from the crash. Two things that remained undamaged, however, were Nash's brilliant blue eyes, which fixed on her with hungry abandon, and his spectacular smile that turned her insides to melted goo.

"No. And even if you did, nothing's going to stop me kissing you right now," he growled and leaned down to devour her mouth once more.

She kissed him until he understood how much she'd missed him. Until she could no longer breathe, and she didn't care if she was making a spectacle for all the guests to see.

It was Nash who finally drew back when Wazza, who was

walking between the staff quarters and the lodge, gave a loud wolf whistle. "Get a room," he called, and Nash looked up and grinned.

"Come on." Skylar took him by the hand and led him through the growing dusk toward the billabong. He took the basket from her, and they walked hand in hand along the grassy edge of water. Nash walked with a slight limp, and she kept her pace to just above ambling, more to take in their beautiful surroundings, than to cater to Nash's wounded leg.

Steve kept the grass neatly trimmed in areas around the billabong, while the rest was allowed to grow wild with native greenery. Right in front of the lodge, where the ground sloped gently toward the small lake, was the largest grassy area, and this was used for big gatherings, guest picnics, as well as a space to pull up the canoes and paddle boards. Farther around to the left was a more secluded spot, hidden behind a stand of ironbarks, which could be used for more intimate gatherings. As they strolled toward the clearing, Skylar saw the flicker of flames through the trees. Dale had done as she asked and lit the fire pit for her. He was a good man.

"This is…stunning," Nash said, his hand tightening on hers when he saw the fire and the picnic rug with a scattering of cushions set up on the gentle slope with the billabong in the foreground. Dale had set up the rug without her even having to ask, and it looked all the more romantic for his subtle touches. Dusk had settled around the shoulders of the escarpment, the first evening star visible as a brilliant point of light high up in the darkening sky.

"I thought you'd like it," she said, leading him to the checkered blanket. She handed him a bottle of bubbly and held out the two glasses for him to fill. The loud pop of the cork sent the birds in the nearby trees into a sudden flurry of wings, and Skylar giggled as she watched the indignant birds circle the billabong a few times before settling back down on their perches for the night.

"Cheers." Nash held up his glass, which sparkled in the light of the flames. "To us. And to survival," he said.

"To the future," Skylar added. "Would you like to eat first? Or enjoy the view?" she asked after they'd both taken a satisfying gulp of the golden liquid.

By way of an answer, Nash set aside his glass and lay down on the picnic rug, putting one hand behind his head and laying the other out in an invitation for her to come and snuggle up beside him. And she willingly obliged.

They lay together, staring up at the heavens, listening to the sounds of the birds settling in for the night, and the insect orchestra winding up to their nighttime crescendo. She nestled in closer to Nash's warm body, listening to his heartbeat beneath her ear. This might be the closest thing to pure bliss that she'd ever experienced.

"This is nice, Skylar," Nash said, breaking their silent interlude. "I've been dreaming about doing this with you all week." His voice was deep and honeyed.

"Me, too," she agreed.

"And with all that time to think, I've also been wondering where do we go from here? I want to spend more time with you, but we both lead complicated lives…"

"Do we need to have a plan?" Skylar jumped in, then immediately regretted her words. That was her old self talking, she needed to find a better vocabulary, a better way of expressing herself.

"No, we can play it day by day, if that's what you'd like." He kept his eyes directed toward the stars, his thumb drawing lazy circles on the top of her arm, as if completely unfazed by her answer—had indeed been expecting it—and she relaxed beneath his touch.

"Sorry, I didn't mean to sound flippant. But this is all new to me, and a lot of it's not going to be easy."

"I realize that. Baby steps. That's all we need right now. As long as they're steps in the right direction."

"Yes, baby steps, that's it," she agreed, with a heartfelt sigh.

"But while we're on the subject of steps, I heard through the grapevine the other day, that the Patterson place might be coming up for sale."

"The Patterson place?" Skylar wracked her memory banks. "Oh, you mean the old, converted miner's shack this side of town?" Skylar had never been to the property, but had heard about it through the local gossip mill. The house had been built back when the gold-mining rush had brought people in their droves to the area in the early nineteen-hundreds. The original building had been constructed from local sandstone, and was solid, with a period charm to it, but the place had been abandoned and lain empty for nearly twenty years. When the Pattersons bought it, they'd fixed it up and added on more rooms and outbuildings, so by all accounts it was a charming country home. The property had never been big enough to run cattle; it was more of a hobby farm. But Merv and Beryl had been happy to potter around and grow veggies and run a herd of goats on it.

"Yep, that's the one. Old Merv had a fall a few weeks ago and they've decided to move to the city, where they can be closer to their daughter."

"Oh, that's a shame." Old age could be a bitch sometimes.

"Yes, the community will miss them. But I figured that now I'm extending my contract for another three years, I may as well stop renting and buy a place. What do you think?"

"Wait. What?" Skylar sat up. "You're extending your contract?"

"Yes." He smiled wickedly up at her, eyes glinting in the firelight. "I told Robinson the other day that I wanted to stay on."

"That's great, Nash." Skylar leaned in and tasted his lips. She remembered him talking about it the night they'd had dinner together in Cairns. Back then, he'd been tossing around a lot of reasons to stay. So, she knew it wasn't merely her he was staying for. But she also knew she was probably a major factor in his decision. The old Skylar might've been a little freaked out by that news. Because the old Skylar didn't do commitment. Or trust. But the new Skylar allowed herself to be a tad pleased that he'd be staying. It'd give them a chance to see if this could work. And she wanted it to work.

"When I heard about The Patterson place yesterday, it was almost like fate."

"Fate?" she repeated, confused.

"Yes. Merv built a huge mechanic shed out the back; he was a bit of a vintage-car buff. It's got room for up to four cars, and it's all set up with benches and equipment."

Skylar thought about how Nash had admired his father, and how they'd bonded over tinkering with cars when he was a teenager, before he'd lost him and then gone off the rails.

"I was even thinking of perhaps running a youth outreach program on the weekend, teaching kids' basic mechanics, how to repair their own cars, that sort of thing."

"That's an amazing idea," she answered slowly. Country kids often felt isolated and left out, not able to access the same support as city kids could. A place for them to gather and do something constructive would help.

"And there's room for me to start a veggie garden. And of course, I'd love your input in renovating the kitchen, if you'd like to lend a hand."

"Are you asking me to move in with you?" What happened to the baby steps he'd mentioned? He was asking her to change her whole life.

"No, babe, I'm not."

"Oh." She wasn't sure if she was happy or insulted by his answer.

"I know how important your role as chef at the lodge is to you. And even if they do eventually send me a constable to help with the work, my job is a demanding one, taking up a lot of my time," he added. "But the house is close enough that you could come and stay the night sometimes. If you want to."

Wow, he was good. She made a mental note never to underestimate Nash King. He was a negotiator extraordinaire. He seemed to know what she needed better than she knew herself. And was only offering as much as she was prepared to give.

"I do want to," she agreed, lying her head back on his shoulder. "And it's close enough that you could come and stay with me sometimes, too."

"It is."

"So, we could spend some nights together and the rest of the time…"

"Lead our complicated lives. Doing what's important to us," he finished for her.

"Interesting concept," she agreed. "I'll think about it."

She slithered out from beneath his arm and in one easy move straddled him, so she could look down into his face. "But right at this moment, I have other concepts that need exploring. Like this…" She dipped her head, and he came up to meet her lips. Kissing Nash until he was mere putty in her hands was what she had in mind right now. Until both of them were so out of breath, they lay panting in each other's arms. She just wanted to stare into his gorgeous face and get lost in his eyes. Forget about time, forget about everything. Just be with Nash.

"I love you," she murmured.

"I love you too, Skylar."
They were possibly the sweetest words she'd ever heard.

EPILOGUE

"It's way more spectacular than I imagined," Nash said, leaning over the edge of the rock face to watch the waterfall disappear beneath him. Davies Creek Falls was everything Skylar had told him it would be. It was magnificent. The meandering stream filled a natural pool, right on the edge of the cliff, where you could lie in the water and stare out over the unfolding hills below. The water escaped through a narrow point in the granite dam wall, where it cascaded over the huge boulders down the vertical bluff underneath.

"I know, right?" Skylar replied. "Pity I was about fifty miles out on my estimation of where we crash landed." She laughed, tilting her head to the sky and closing her eyes. He took the chance to drink in all her curves and long legs, sheathed in black leggings, with a crop-top showing off her midriff. Then she opened her eyes and sobered. "But it wouldn't have mattered if we found this waterfall, or the other one. You were in no fit state to appreciate anything by that stage."

"Oh, I don't know. I appreciated you lying next to me all night. I remember that much." He jumped across the small stream onto the flat platform, away from the edge, and gathered Skylar up into his arms. "It was kinda hot, with you all sexy and assertive, telling me what to do and then lying beside me to keep me safe."

"Yeah, it was hot, all right. Because you were burning up with a fever." Skylar sounded peeved, but the pink tinge at the top of her ears was a dead giveaway that she secretly liked the fact he thought it was sexy.

"I'm glad you were there to save me," he said, knocking her cap off her head so he could angle his head just right to reach her mouth and kiss her, stopping any more arguments she might've been forming in that beautiful mouth of hers.

This was day two of their journey of discovery into Lamb Range. Yesterday they'd visited the waterfall where they'd spent the night, after Nash collapsed from his wound; where he'd very nearly succumbed to blood poisoning. It was almost three months to the day they'd lain next to that waterfall. That'd been toward the end of the dry season, and the water had been merely a trickle. Now they were well into the wet, and the streams were gushing.

Skylar hadn't been sure she wanted to go back and revisit that place; she thought it might bring all the bad stuff back to the surface. But after Nash told her he wanted to do it, because his police psych had said it'd help with his recovery, Skylar had reluctantly agreed to join him. It was police protocol, after encountering a life and death situation—two life and death situations, really—to see an appointed psych for ten sessions. At first, Nash had only agreed to it because he wanted Skylar to do the same, to talk to a professional about her trauma, both the early stuff with Craig, as well as the part where she'd nearly been burned alive in a shed.

The early sessions had tried his patience, the counsellor getting on his nerves with all his probing questions. But after session three, something the counsellor said resonated within him. Something about how, until he truly processed the way the crash when he was a teenager had affected every choice he made after that, even well into his adulthood, then he'd never be able to move on. It resonated because he could see the same thing happening with Skylar. Denial might be a method of coping in the short term, but he was beginning to see that long term, it caused more damage than anything else.

The sound of voices brought Nash back to reality, and he released Skylar. She bent down to retrieve her hat just as another couple emerged from the trail leading up to the waterfall.

"Let's find a spot to eat lunch," Skylar suggested, but Nash knew she meant a quiet spot away from the other tourists. She led the way to the rear of the large pool, and they clambered over some boulders and up an embankment, emerging through the scrubby bushes higher up the cliff face. They found a flat rock close to the edge, and she dropped her backpack on the rock.

"We should do this more often," she enthused, doing a little twirl to take in the impressive views of the surrounding jungle wilderness.

"Yes, we should," he agreed, bending down to undo his pack and retrieve two bottles of water. "I'm glad you took two nights off. It gives us more time to…explore. Spend some quality time together." He handed her a bottle and took a swig from his, and swiped the sweat off his brow beneath the brim of his hat. Boy, it was hot today.

"Me too," Skylar replied, putting the bottle to her lips and drinking deeply before staring out over the green hills below.

Nash was proud of how far Skylar had come in regard to easing off her obsession with her job at the lodge. She now took the whole of Sunday off every week, letting Julie and Bindi take over for that one day, giving her and Nash twenty-four hours of magical bliss to spend together. It'd been her idea, which at first surprised him. But Skylar Williams was a determined woman. And she was determined to change her life for the better. Which included a better work-life balance. Although he knew she often found it hard to let go, and he'd caught her on the phone to Julie a few times during their supposed Sunday off.

Nash had bought the Patterson place two months prior and had been making it his own ever since. Old Merv had been pretty pedantic about maintenance around the place, so there wasn't a lot to do in that regard. But Nash's sparse furniture from his little cottage in town hardly occupied half of the bigger house. So, with Skylar's help he was slowly filling in the spaces with furnishings bought online. He never thought he'd enjoy the feeling of owning his own house as much as he did. It gave him a freedom, and a peace to do with the place as he wished, that he'd never even contemplated before. And of course, the best part was when Skylar came to stay. They spent every Sunday together, and sometimes she'd sneak over on other nights, after she'd finished her shift. Even if it was late, Nash always welcomed her into his bed. And she was helping him plant up his vegetable garden, and he was already reaping some of the rewards, by adding fresh veggies to his meals. Skylar was also playing a big part in redesigning the new kitchen. Work on that part of the house wasn't due to start for a few months, but the look on Skylar's face every time they talked about it was more than worth the cost of ripping out walls and buying the best appliances money could buy.

Originally, this trip was only meant to be one night, during Skylar's rostered day off on Sunday. But she'd surprised him a week ago by suggesting they go for longer. Nash knew it was a big step forward for Skylar. She'd always be dedicated to her work, cooking was her life, it helped define who she was. And it'd kept her sane during that horrible time after she left Craig. But she was slowly letting go, so that it didn't control her whole life anymore. He didn't like to brag, but he knew he had a lot to do with her softer attitude. Because she told him every day how much she loved him, and how much she missed him when she couldn't be with him.

Nash also had more freedom when it came to taking a well-earned break, with Constable Willow now a permanent fixture at the station. He enjoyed having the young constable around, he was smart and keen, and kept Nash on his toes.

"You want something to eat?" he asked.

Skylar nodded. "I'm starving."

He dug in his bag again and produced two packets of cheese and pickle—homemade with love by Skylar, or course —sandwiches. They chose a spot near the edge and sat down, shoulder to shoulder, to look at the view while they devoured their lunch.

Yesterday, they'd pitched a tent in the little regional park campground on the edge of the national park and had driven up to the parking lot, then hiked up the trial to the fateful waterfall, which they now knew was called Emerald Creek Falls. Nash wasn't sure what to expect when he arrived. But all he felt was ambivalence. Like he'd told Skylar, the only thing he really remembered was her snuggled up beside him, the rest was a blur.

Afterward, they'd driven back to the campground and cooked sausages in a slice of bread for dinner in the common kitchen area. Then they'd snuggled in their little tent all night, enjoying the novelty of trying to stay completely silent as they explored having sex while not waking their neighbors through the ultra-thin walls of nylon fabric. Nash didn't think he could remember a time when he'd ever felt happier.

"I'm glad we came," Nash said quietly. He thought about his next comment for a while before he spoke. "It's not so much closure that I got from this trip. More like perspective."

"I know what you mean." Skylar lay her head on his shoulder. "I don't see this place as where you nearly died or where Jacko led us on that terrifying chase through the jungle. I see this place as where we first fell in love."

"That's exactly it," he replied.

* * *

Yes, that was it. Perspective, not closure that was what this trip had allowed her to find. She pretty much had closure when she'd seen Jacko's dead body on the night of the fire. He was never coming after them again, and the spectre of his presence was washed from her mind, if not forever, then at least from taking precedence over her thoughts.

Dan Sanders, however, was a whole other matter.

"Any more news on the Sanders case?" she asked, managing to keep her voice light. It irked her that her throat closed up every time she thought about him. He was still a thorn in their side, perhaps always would be.

"Not really," Nash replied evenly. "He's due for sentencing next week. Now he's been found guilty of Patty's murder, on top of the other assault charges and our attempted murders, he'll go away for a long, long time. Twenty years, or more."

"Good," she said. But he must've caught the barely-there flicker of unease in her reply.

"You know he can't get to us now, babe? The courts have frozen all his assets. He couldn't raise enough money to pay for a coffee, let alone hire another hitman. That was a one-off contract, Robinson has done his homework. We're safe now."

"I know," Skylar replied. And she did know. But she also didn't trust that man. His hatred and narcissism ran deep. She wouldn't put it past him to find a way to get to them, even if that might be five years in the future. Thinking about Sanders brought another contemptible human being to mind.

"What about Craig? Will he be sentenced soon, too?" Her hand fluttered up to touch her wrist, but she stopped herself just in time. The counsellor had picked up on that habit of hers the very first time she'd seen him. It was a habit she was trying to break. And pressing charges against her rapist was going a long way to helping her do that.

"Yes. Probably next week, as well." Nash leaned his shoulder against hers. "Not too long to wait now."

She nodded. It'd been the hardest thing she'd ever had to do, stand up and testify against Craig in that courtroom. The way he'd glared at her had brought back all the old memories and she'd nearly sat down again without uttering a word, falling back into old weaknesses where she bowed to Craig's control. But one glance at Nash sitting in the front row had given her the courage she needed. Her whole family had been there, backing her up, as well. Daniella and Steve, Dale, Daisy, and Julie, all gave her the thumbs-up from their seats. And afterwards, as she exited the courthouse, before Craig had even been found guilty, she'd felt like a bird taking flight. Oh, the liberty of that weight lifting from her shoulders.

"I know I've said it before, but I'm incredibly proud of you, for standing up to him," Nash said.

"Thank you. And I know I've said this before, but if it wasn't for you, I may never have done it."

Nash made a disparaging noise. "Not true." Then when she glared at him, he added, "But I'll take the compliment, anyway."

Time for a change in subject, she didn't want to bring the mood down on this delicious summer day. "It'll be Christmas in a few weeks."

"Don't remind me," Nash groaned. "My mum wants me to fly down to Brisbane to spend time with her and my sisters."

Skylar patted his knee. Nash had already mentioned his dilemma, and she knew he still hadn't made up his mind about going to see them. But she'd been forming a plan over the past few weeks.

"There might be an alternative," she said with a mischievous grin.

He narrowed his sky-blue eyes, and she nearly got so lost in them she almost forgot what she'd been going to say.

"We always have a celebration at Stormcloud. All of our family, any of the staff who want to stay, and we make a whole day of it. Dale and Daisy will be there, and Daisy's inviting her brother and parents to join us. We have croissants and champagne for brunch, then a swim in the billabong. Then we play board games and open presents, or we might even drive up to the escarpment, before we finish the day off with a huge meal. I spend days in the kitchen preparing beforehand."

"I bet you do. And I bet it's bloody delicious," he said, leaning in to kiss her neck.

"It is. But that's not the point. There's plenty of room for you, and your whole family, if you want to invite them. They can all stay at the lodge, if they like." Skylar had met Nash's sister, Ashley, when she'd flown up to see him the first time he'd been in hospital after they'd been rescued from the jungle. Ashley had been delightful, and Skylar thought she'd probably get along well with her. But she was yet to meet Nash's mother, and the idea made her insides tremble. What would his mother think of her? And more to the point, how would Daniella get on with the other woman? Now, *that* made her insides tremble even more. But she was a grown woman; she could deal with a mother-in-law, if she had to.

"Really?" Nash's face lit up at the idea.

"Only if you want to," she added hurriedly. Too late to change her mind now.

"Thank you. That's not a bad idea. It means I get to spend Christmas with you," he said, taking her hand and rubbing his thumb over her knuckles.

"Our first Christmas together," she mumbled. It was a big step for her, inviting him into her life like this. Sometimes she still caught herself worrying that she was doing the right thing. He'd start a conversation about doing something together in the future, and her stomach would clench involuntarily. But he was worth it. He was worth giving up her self-imposed independence for. It was nice letting a man take care of her again. Look after her and pander to her needs. Especially her needs in the bedroom. Because she couldn't get enough of Nash. Enough of that hardened male body wrapped around her; inside her.

A familiar heat settled between her legs at the mere thought of him. If that other couple weren't still below them at the waterfall, Skylar may well think about pushing him down onto the rocks and having her way with him right here. There'd be enough time for that later tonight, cocooned in their little tent. All night long, if she wanted it.

But she had more she wanted to say to him.

"Stormcloud Lodge closes for six weeks over January and February. That's the wettest part of the year and guest numbers are low. Plus, it gives us a chance to rest and recuperate, get some of the maintenance on the station done."

"I think I knew that," Nash responded. "It's a good idea, the roads are almost impassable at that time. Makes my job harder, too."

Skylar pursed her lips. The whole of the top end of North Queensland often looked more like an inland lake than anything else during the wet. Not a lot got done during that time, and some homesteads became completely cut off for weeks or even months. Sometimes the only way to get around was to fly, which was why the helicopters were a godsend for Stormcloud. But that was what made her next idea all the more appealing.

"Maybe we could take a longer holiday, then. Take a week and fly down to the Whitsunday Islands. I hear they have a great resort we could check out. It's very private, with amazing food. What do you think?"

"You'd take a whole week off?" He covered his mouth in a mock imitation of shock.

"Don't be a fool," she slapped him lightly on the shoulder. "My family can manage without me for a week."

"Well, in that case, let me get onto Robinson and see if I can book some holidays," he said, brow wrinkling delightfully as he mused. "I'll probably only get a day or two over Christmas, that's when all the crazy stuff happens. You'd think people would stay at home and enjoy Christmas with their families, but it's actually one of our busiest times. But I think Robinson owes me at least a week in February, after all we've been through."

"I should think so," Skylar agreed. Time to drop the third bombshell of the day. Good things always came in threes, didn't they? Skylar gave a secret smile.

"I was thinking, that might also be the perfect time for me to move in."

Nash's head shot up so fast, Skylar nearly laughed, but caught herself just in time. "What? Move in? With me?"

"Yes. Although, I have noticed Constable Willow giving me a few sideways glances. I'm sure he'd have me, if you won't."

"Not a chance. He's not getting anywhere near you," Nash said, his voice deep and commanding.

She loved it when he got all growly and protective. But even when he was at his most possessive, she knew he'd never carry it too far. He always let her make her own decisions and never tried to physically or mentally control her. His love was unconditional. Which gave her the room she needed to breathe. And to be able to love him unequivocally in return.

Which was why it was time for her to make the big commitment and move in. Daisy had helped to convince her it was the right thing to do. She already spent a few nights a week with him. It might take a bit of juggling to get her schedule under control. Which meant no more late nights pottering around in the kitchen after everyone else was asleep. Now she had a reason to finish work and take the twenty-minute drive home.

Because Nash was her home.

She turned to see his blue gaze fixed on her. "I love you," he said. "And I'm going to prove that to you each and every day for as long as you'll let me."

"How about I let you do that forever?"

"That would be perfect." He took her chin between his thumb and forefinger and tipped her cap off for the second time today. A shiver of heat spiked through her as she anticipated his lips landing on hers, returning his passionate kiss with a craving of her own. This beautiful, golden man, with the surfer curls and electric-blue eyes, was hers for the keeping. He'd earned her trust the hard way, and then his compassionate soul had won her whole heart. She was his for eternity; she would treasure the rest of her life with him.

**Want to know more about Stormcloud Station?
Get your FREE and EXCLUSIVE Prequel Novella
MISTY SKIES**
Read Steve and Daniella's story.

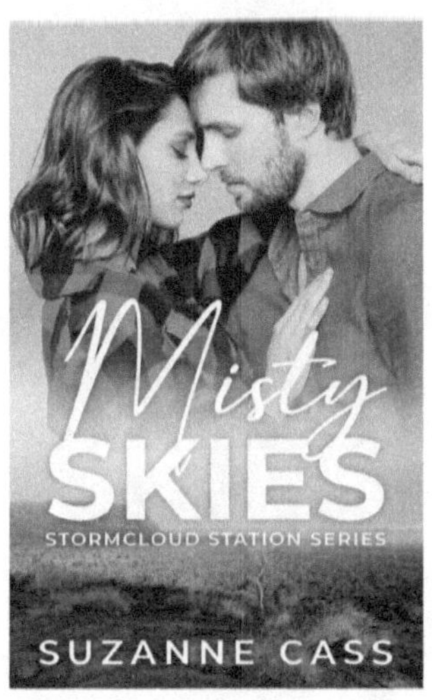

GO TO THIS LINK FOR YOUR FREE BOOK

https://dl.bookfunnel.com/xyuua14lyp

Stay in touch via my website
www.suzannecass.com

Facebook: www.facebook.com/suzannecassauthor/
Instagram: www.instagram.com/suzanne.cass/
Pintrest: www.pinterest.com.au/suzanne_cass/

If you liked Starlit Skies, you'll love;

Clear Skies

Fate and flooding rains brought them together. Secrets may tear them apart. Book 1.

Crystal Skies

Her heart was shattered the night he disappeared…now he's back. Book 3.

Also by Suzanne Cass
NEW
Stormcloud Station Series
(A Stargazer Spinoff Series)
Small Town Romantic Suspense
Clear Skies
Starlit Skies
Crystal Skies

Stargazer Ranch Romance Series
Small Town Romantic Suspense
Combustion: Prequel Novella
Wildfire
Firelight
Snowbound: A Christmas Novella
Snowfall
Cloudburst

Island Bound Series
Mystery Romance (on an Island)
Books can be read as stand-alone
Bound by Truth
Bound by Silence
Bound by the Stars

Colors of the Earth Series
Small Town Romantic Suspense
Books can be read as stand-alone
Shadows in the Dust
Shadows in Deep Blue
Shadows of Red Earth

Romantic Suspense
Single Title
Island Redemption

Glass Clouds
Chasing Bullets

Love in the Mountains Novella Series
Small Town Short Romance
Novellas can be read as stand-alone
Rain on a Tin Roof
Lost and Found
Rescue his Heart

Please Leave a Review

The greatest gift you could ever give an author is to leave a review. You will be helping other people to discover this book and making a difference to me as an Independently Published Author. If you liked this book and want other people to read it too, please leave a review.

About the Author

Suzanne Cass is an Australian author who writes rural romance and romantic suspense abounding with passion and danger.

Her debut novel, Island Redemption, won the Romance Writers of Australia Emerald Award in 2016. Suzanne was also a finalist in the 2019 Romance Writers of Australia RUBY award.

She had always had a fascination with the tough resilience of people who live in our amazing red-dirt outback country. When not writing about the characters that inhabit her head, Suzanne can be found roaming the Perth beaches with her border collie, or encouraging from the sidelines as her two sons play sport.

Stay in touch via my website

www.suzannecass.com

Acknowledgements

Starlit Skies is the second book in the Stormcloud Station Series. It's a spin-off from my latest series, set in Montana, USA, Stargazer Ranch. I wanted to do something similar, but with a deliciously Aussie flavor, situated on a luxury eco-resort and cattle station. I think Nash and Skylar's journey was both the hardest story to write, but also the most gratifying. They really had to fight hard for their HEA, and I learned a lot about the insidiousness of domestic abuse during my research for this book. I'm glad Skylar could move on from her trauma, because not all women are so lucky.

To my beta readers and my ARC team, who are essential to an Indie Author like me, I'm sending you all big (virtual) hugs across the globe. Big thanks to my editor, Tanya Saari for putting up with my total inability to learn where the comma's go. Thanks also to the other authors out there (my tribe) who offer me support, advice and a sounding board when it all gets to be too much. Isn't it great that all of these people can live scattered all over the world, but still belong to one big family, with one steadfast goal; producing and reading the next great book.

My hubby, Gary needs a special mention, as do my two beautiful sons, who are now gorgeous young men. Thank you for your unconditional love. I'm so very grateful to all the readers who have bought and enjoyed my books and who send me emails to let me know how much you love them. Writing for you is what keeps me focussed and motivated.

www.ingramcontent.com/pod-product-compliance
Lightning Source LLC
Chambersburg PA
CBHW032001130726
47903CB00012B/438